SPIES DON'T RETIRE

The Seaview Series

Barbara Angermeier Malcolm

Barbara Writes

Barbara Writes
Barbara Angermeier Malcolm

Cover design by GetCovers.

eBook: ISBN 978-1-970552-13-3
Paperback: ISBN 978-1-970552-14-0

Publisher: Barbara Writes

Published in the United States of America

This book is dedicated to my late husband, Don.
You were there when this story was born but left before it was
finished.
I'll think of you every time I read it.

CONTENTS

CHAPTER 1

Rose

I was uncomfortable in the enormous ballroom. There were too many people milling around and talking all at once. Not a fan of crowds, I'd have been happier at home in Seaview with Iggy in the sitting room reading a book or talking.

"I'm one of the few islanders here who isn't a server or a musician," Iggy whispered to me.

We were in the ballroom of Billie Holland-Smythe's ridiculously large house on the highest hill in Anguilla

I knew Billie liked to stir things up. That October evening, she was hosting a birthday party for the newly crowned King Charles III far away in England. It signaled the beginning of the social season for the expats on the island. Billie had invited all of them, even if they weren't British. I didn't know Billie well—she and I moved in different circles—but quite a few of the other expats' families and friends had stayed at Seaview when they visited the island. I assumed that was how we'd gotten invited. A rumor was going around that there were a couple of retired spies on the island and Billie planned to introduce them to each other that night.

We were standing in the crowd watching people greeting each other, laughing, and talking with friends around us when a gray-haired woman handed Iggy her empty glass, "Get me another champagne, will you please?"

Both of us just stared, Iggy with the empty glass in his right hand and his own drink in his left. He didn't glance at me.

He didn't have to.

I cleared my throat and said, "I'm sorry, my husband doesn't work here."

A blush rose from her chest to her cheeks. "Oh my gosh, I'm so sorry. I thought he was..."

I let her flounder for a minute, then offered her my hand. "Rose Solomon. I own Seaview Bed & Breakfast in Sandy Ground. And this is my husband, Iggy Solomon. You thought he was a server." No need to tell her I met him when I bought the bed-and-breakfast almost two years ago. I needed someone to replace the wiring—and he was the electrician I hired.

She snatched the glass from Iggy's hand and walked into the crowd.

Iggy wasn't the only Islander at the party, but he was the only man wearing a white shirt like the servers. It was still too hot to dress up in formal attire. Not that everyone had gowns and tuxedos handy, but we were all in our best tropical evening wear—which was what passed for formal on a Caribbean island.

"I guess I could get a part-time job," he said. He let his shoulders slump as he tried to blend in with the guests.

"Don't be silly. She was just a thoughtless woman. Pay no attention."

He looked at me as if I didn't understand, then he walked us over to talk with Susan and George Clemment.

George's brown hair was gray at the temples, giving him a distinguished, sexy look. He usually wore khaki shorts and loose button-down shirts, but that night he was in dark slacks and a white guayabera shirt. Susan blended in with all the resort-clothes-wearing women on the island with her graying blond hair and wardrobe of colorful print blouses and linen pants. It was her sharp green eyes that set her apart.

Billie and Susan Clemment had become fast friends and for weeks the two of them had scoured the island shops looking for ingredients for pseudo-British fare and decorations fit for a distant king's birthday.

"I was here for hours helping Billie decorate," Susan said to me.

Fabric festooned every doorway and window. "Where did you find all of this bunting and flags?"

"Billie had most of it on hand," she said. "The rest we ordered from Amazon."

"Amazon had this stuff?"

"You can get just about anything on Amazon." She lifted the hair from her neck. "I thought I'd die climbing the ladder to swag the windows and doors. Air conditioning is only good if you're sitting still, especially in a room like this."

A room. That was one way of describing it. "I never thought there was a house—well, a mansion—on Anguilla with a ballroom. Seems like an awful lot of house for one person."

Billie's ultra-British voice came from over Susan's shoulder, startling me. "That's why I bought the place. I knew I'd want to have big parties and none of the other houses I looked at had a room big enough." She slid an arm around Susan and pressed the younger woman to her side. "I don't know what I would have done without Susan this year. She had a lot of great ideas for the party and helped design the invitations. She even suggested we order them online, which saved me hundreds, even with overseas shipping costs."

Billie was reliving her hippie days with her long, nearly white hair worn parted in the middle and tapering down her back to fade into a point just above her still-firm behind. Her misty blue eyes didn't miss a thing as she scanned the room to make sure that everything was going the way she wanted it to. She had an extensive wardrobe of kente cloth dashikis and gauze wrap skirts she wore over ancient Birkenstocks. Her jewelry was made from petrified wood and oddly shaped pieces of various semi-precious stones, changing it to suit the state of her chakras or to enhance her aura. She reminded me of the rich little hippie girls I went to college with. Despite her appearance as the antithesis of a royalty lover, Billie took her British-ness very seriously. Like many expats, she thought that living so far from her native land made the celebration of any special holidays even more important to her cultural identity.

I wondered which local printer on Anguilla or Sint Maarten had planned their year around Billie's usual order and was now out of luck. I made it a practice to use local businesses whenever I could, even if it cost a little more. With all the rumors going around about my character, I needed allies wherever I could find them.

The room was filling up and the noise level rose as people greeted friends and visited the hors d'oeuvres table. There was the usual complement of expat couples, a mix of Americans and Brits with a few Eastern Europeans thrown in for good measure.

The party was well underway when Dimitri and Irina Roskova made their entrance. They'd been on the island for six months, though I hadn't gotten to know them very well. They had stayed at Seaview when they were scoping out Anguilla as a possible retirement spot, but I hadn't seen them since. None of their friends or family had stayed at Seaview. They paused in the ballroom's doorway and surveyed the inhabitants as if they might change their minds if the mix wasn't right.

Irina posed like an Art Deco statue, her back arched, her head cocked, hands cupped together as if holding a butterfly near her cheek. Dimitri complemented her languid grace, but rather than gazing dreamily off into space like his wife, his cold gray gaze raked the room. When he spotted George and their eyes locked, I could almost hear a click.

George stiffened and glanced at Susan to see if she'd noticed. She must have. A mask of steely determination replaced her usual soft expression, and her green eyes hardened like malachite. When her eyes met George's, an almost imperceptible message passed between them. But I saw it.

Both Dimitri and Irina straightened.

"Darlings, I have been waiting to introduce you." Billie caught hold of Susan's hand and dragged her toward the Russians. Susan passed her champagne to me and grabbed George's arm, making them look like a comet's tail trailing behind their hostess.

Nice. I loved being ditched for more interesting guests.

For their part, Dimitri and Irina had drawn together, his arm tight around her waist.

The hum of conversation in the room faded as people noticed the drama unfolding before them. All I could hear was the soft music of the orchestra in the corner and Billie's chirping voice.

"Dimitri and Irina Roskova, I'd like you to meet Major George and Susan Clemment."

The couples stood staring at each other. Susan's green eyes shot sparks across the small gap between them; Irina's black eyes were as cold as a Siberian winter. The men reached out to each other and barely touched fingers before dropping their hands to their sides.

"We've met," George said.

Billie's eyes glittered, and it was obvious that she knew exactly what she was doing. "I'll leave you to get reacquainted." When she turned back to the room, the stunned gazes of the rest of her guests momentarily stopped her. She flicked a finger, and the waitstaff moved among the crowd offering champagne and canapes. Conversations resumed, and the orchestra continued to play.

The initial tension faded or was masked within a few seconds. Their bodies relaxed a bit from the ramrod straight attitudes of their meeting. The British couple looked comfortable, like they were holding a normal conversation with new friends. The Russians looked like startled deer caught in the headlight of a runaway train.

An ugly snarl lifted the corner of Dimitri's mouth as I overheard George say, "I never expected to find you on this desert island again, old chap. I had you pegged for something more tropical, like Fiji, where the native girls are more, um, accommodating." He aimed a small bow at Irina. "Not, of course, that your husband would ever..." His voice trailed off at a not so gentle pat from Susan.

"I'm sorry, Irina, is it?" Susan said. A curt nod answered

in the affirmative. "Irina, I'm sure George was just joking about Dimitri being interested in other women. You know how men get when they retire from the chase of business, a bit dotty."

Irina's knuckles whitened as she took an even firmer grip on her husband's arm. "I am not familiar with that expression," she said in a gravelly voice, quite unlike her normal dreamy tones. "But if that means your husband is imagining he is familiar with mine, he cannot be. Before tonight, I'm sure Dimitri has never seen your George."

A server carrying a tray of glasses approached the quartet and offered them drinks. The ladies each reached for a flute and handed it to their respective husbands; the men's eyes did not break their glare into the other's. Once all four of them held glasses, George raised his in salute to the opposite couple. "To your health." He and Susan drank. Dimitri and Irina did not. George turned to his wife. "Come, dear, we should circulate."

She gave a nod, linked arms, and drew her husband away from the couple in the doorway.

As the British pair walked away, George turned back to the Russians, still frozen in place. "I'm sure we'll see each other again soon enough. We can discuss old times."

The Roskovas didn't stay long at the party.

Iggy and I watched the spectacle that Billie made of introducing the new arrivals to the island. "But they've already met, months ago, at Seaview," I said. "The men even took a long walk together that day. I remember it clearly because it was the first time George and I went diving together."

Iggy shook his head. "I wonder what Mrs. Holland-Smythe is playing at. She had a motive for bringing the two couples together so publicly."

"I agree. Something's going on." I set Susan's champagne flute on the tray of a passing server and took a fresh one. I sipped the bubbly drink and wrinkled my nose. "This stuff always makes me want to sneeze. You know, Susan said that George and Dimitri worked for competitors. I wonder if they worked for their governments. That would explain the tension between them."

The partygoers resumed their chatter, and the hum of voices played in counterpoint to the background music of the orchestra.

"I wonder where Mrs. Holland-Smythe found an orchestra with tuxedos. They have got to be suffering in this heat," Iggy said.

Both of us turned to survey the quintet of formal musicians playing at the end of the large room.

"I would loosen my tie if I was trapped in one of those suits." I tugged at the neck of my blouse. "It's too hot in here with all of these people. Even with the ceiling fans on the air is hardly moving."

**

I lay curled in Iggy's embrace but couldn't sleep. Why had Billie made such a spectacle of introducing George and Dimitri? Susan said that they worked for competitors, but did that fact earn them the sly look on Billie's face when she dragged George and Susan across the floor? The Roskovas hadn't stayed at the party for long after that. Rumors had flown in whispers around the room that George was a spy and tried to turn Dimitri or vice versa. That Susan and Irina were the spies and their husbands' work was the cover for their actions. Was Billie hoping that one of them would pull out a pistol and shoot the other? How would they ever coexist on this little island? I was afraid that one of them wouldn't be alive for long.

I looked at the clock. After midnight. I needed to get to sleep. Seven o'clock would come soon enough when I needed to be up to start the coffee and make breakfast for my guests. Iggy's arm tightened around me as I wriggled into a more comfortable position and finally drifted off.

CHAPTER 2

George and Dimitri

"What did that foolish Holland-Smythe woman think would happen when she introduced us?" George fumed on the drive across the island to their home in Sandy Hill. "Did she hope that one of us would pull out a gun and shoot the other?"

Susan reached across and patted his thigh. "I don't know, George. I don't know what she expected to happen. It was a rotten thing to pull, and I plan to let her know at the first opportunity."

George shifted the Rover to slow down, barely avoiding a wild goat standing in the middle of the road. "Get out of the way, you mangy thing." He stuck his arm out of the window and waved at it.

"Don't yell at the goat. It can't help being wild. And if you hit it and kill it, I'll have to learn how to cook curried goat. I don't want to do that."

By the time they got to their two-story home on a small stretch of beach, George had cooled off a bit. He parked the car, locked it, and escorted Susan into the house.

"I'm going to call Roskova," he said, picking up the thin Anguilla phone book that had just been delivered. He found the number and made to tear out the page.

Susan laid her hand on his and said, "Leave it. We may want to call someone else on that page."

George looked at the number long enough to memorize it, closed the book, and laid it down on the desk. He looked at the time.

"After midnight," he said. "Too late to call now. I'll wait until morning."

Susan ran her finger over his hand and looked at him from under her lashes. "What will you do until then?" She turned and walked up the stairs to their bedroom, where she undressed, put on her robe, and went into the bathroom to clean her face. George stopped in the doorway as she sat at her vanity, brushing her hair. Her robe hung open, and he could see her breasts reflected in the mirror.

"God, you're beautiful."

She smiled. "You say that every night only because I allow you to ogle my breasts."

"True. Well, partly true, but even bundled up in a parka, you are the most ravishing woman I've ever seen."

The ivory back of her hairbrush clicked against the glass surface as she lay it down. She held out her arms. "Then come ravish me."

Not needing to be invited twice, George hurried into the bathroom to brush his teeth and run a quick razor over his face. He undressed on the trip from the bathroom to the bedroom, leaving a trail of clothing behind him.

Susan was already in bed when he lifted the sheet and slid in beside her. Her hands cupped his cheeks. "You shaved. I thought only young men shaved at night."

He kissed her on the lips and then nuzzled between her breasts. "Don't want to scratch your silken skin, my dear."

After their lovemaking, he stroked her until she fell asleep and turned away from him. He lay on his back with his hands behind his head, pondering what he would say to Dimitri Roskova in the morning. Hours passed, and he didn't sleep. He finally slid out of bed, pulled on some cotton pajama pants, and went downstairs to pace. Soon the house was too confining, so he eased open the door, put on a pair of sandals, and went outside to pace on the badly paved road in front of the house. Out there his pacing took on the vigor of a forced march, his arms swinging, his knees lifting, and his breath coming out in grunts.

***

Dimitri and Irina barely spoke on the drive home from Billie Holland-Smythe's party.

Irina said, "That is a foolish woman. What did she think would happen?"

"I do not know, dushka, I just do not know."

In their bedroom, Irina unpinned her hair and let it drape in a black waterfall across her shoulders. Dimitri walked up behind her and pressed his face into the fragrant hair. Irina shrugged. "Not tonight, Dimi, not tonight."

His hand fell away, and he turned to undress on the other side of the room. In a very few minutes, they were in bed and Irina's breathing evened out. Dimitri knew she slept. He was wide awake. Months ago, when he had seen George Clemment in the kitchen of Seaview when they were looking over the island with an eye to moving there, he never imagined that the two couples would decide to retire here. He thought their talk that day had discouraged George from moving to Anguilla, but evidently not. They should have chosen a more economical island to retire to themselves, but Irina had learned that there was a Literary Roundtable group among the expats, so she could share her poetry with them and an Art League where she could discuss art with people who might know something about it.

"I need stimulation, Dimitri. I need to live in a place where people use their minds."

"But our pension will not stretch as far on this island. We will have to be very careful."

She shook her head. "We have had to be careful before. We can do it again."

The matter was settled.

They found a small two-bedroom duplex in a lower-class neighborhood away from the beach that they could afford. Dimitri bought a rattletrap brown car that had too many miles on it. He had fresh retread tires put on it and got the local mechanic to give it a once over.

The mechanic stood looking at the heap and wondered what Dimitri was thinking of buying such a car, but he went over the engine and found that it wasn't in too poor a condition. He changed the oil, put in a new fan belt and a new set of spark plugs. "That is as good as it is going to get, Mr. Roskova," he said, handing over his bill.

Dimitri gulped at the total and paid with cash.

**

Equal parts disappointment and anger mixed in Dimitri's heart. Dimitri felt disappointed because he and Irina were the target of jokes by people they considered their friends, and he was angry that Billie Holland-Smythe could be so stupid. How could she be certain that neither he nor Major Clemment wouldn't pull out a pistol and dispatch the other? It took all his self-control earlier not to slap the smug self-satisfied smile off Billie's face as she dragged the Clemments to meet him and Irina. His next impulse was to turn and flee, but that would have just added fuel to the fire that stupid woman had ignited. It would have been bad enough for them to meet by accident in the market or on the beach, but to be made a spectacle of by that meddling woman was the worst.

Dimitri lay awake staring at the gecko pacing the borders of the bedroom ceiling, stalking the unlucky moths that blundered in. He played over and over the brightly lit ballroom; the orchestra playing a jazzy tune, a few couples dancing but most standing in small groups sipping champagne and chatting. Entering, Irina looked like an Art Deco statue, and he did his best to preserve his standard icy demeanor after Major Clemment's brown eyes began boring into his. Dimitri's blood ran cold when he realized Billie planned to make the four of them the entertainment, the gossip of the evening, by forcing them to acknowledge each other so publicly.

He tossed and turned until Irina murmured in her sleep. He got up, put on an undershirt over his pajama bottoms, and went out to smoke the island's harsh Nevada cigarettes on the patio and think about what he would say to Major Clemment the next time they saw each other. Dimitri stood staring out over the roofs toward the inky western sky, smoking one cigarette after the other, and thinking about how his comfortable retirement was about to change when the phone rang.

He hurried into the house to answer it before it disturbed Irina. "Hello?" he said, too many cigarettes making his voice raspy.

"Colonel Roskova, we need to meet."

It was Major Clemment, sounding like he had been up for hours, too.

"Meet? I, uh, I am not feeling well."

There was a pause. "And yet we will meet," came the reply. "I propose we meet at the Rose Inn in Island Harbour in an hour. It's out of the way and won't be busy this time of day."

"Da, I will meet you there."

George heard the click as Dimitri hung up, then he waited thirty seconds more to listen for anyone else on the line or the telltale hum of a recording device.

"You're meeting him." Susan's voice came out of the dim doorway behind him.

George put the phone down softly and said, "Yes. We have to figure out how we're going to handle being together on this small island. He could have picked any other Caribbean island. Why did he choose this one?"

"Maybe because you two met last winter at Seaview and he wants something from you." She sat at the table. George got a cup and saucer from the cupboard, poured coffee, and set it in front of her. "Thank you, darling." She caught his hand and pressed it to her cheek. "I thought we had finished with all of this."

"So did I." George sat down across from her, his mug of coffee in his hand. "What can he want from me? I retired over five years ago. Everything I know is way out of date. The same with him. What could I get out of him that would be worth anything?" He sipped the rich Sumatran brew. "I thought I was through with all of this, too. But here he is, a fact I can't ignore."

Susan hummed as she sipped her coffee, her pinkie elevated as if she were at an elegant tea party.

George went on. "We met a few times over the years. I always thought he was as tough as steel. The man last night and the one I just spoke with on the phone sounded like he wouldn't have made a decent courier, much less an agent."

"Maybe he's afraid of that harpy of a wife. She is the most snobbish and unpleasant woman I think I've ever had the displeasure to meet. Anyway, I'm sure we can just avoid the Roskovas. Why do you have to stir the pot by meeting him?"

"Because I don't want to spend my retirement dodging around an island this small, trying to stay out of their way. Plus, after last night's spectacle, everyone will be talking. We need to get our stories straight. I'd better get ready. We're meeting at seven-thirty." He dropped a kiss on the top of her head and went upstairs.

Before she had finished her coffee, George was back showered, shaved and dressed.

"Won't you be early?" Susan said. "Didn't you always say that the first one to a meeting gave up power?"

"I did, and one does." His smile reminded his wife of a shark. "I want to do a bit of recon first." He jingled the keys in her direction. "Wish me luck."

"I wish we had picked any other island to retire on."

But George was already out the door.

CHAPTER 3

Rose

I slapped at the alarm when it rang at seven o'clock. We hadn't gotten home from Billie Holland-Smythe's party until almost midnight, and it had taken me some time to fall asleep. I snuggled back into my pillow but knew that I couldn't lie in bed. There were guests asleep upstairs who expected coffee and breakfast, and I was the only one to make it. Iggy's arms tightened around me as I moved to get up.

I turned to kiss him and said, "You have to let me up. It's time for me to turn back into an innkeeper and get the breakfast started."

"Mm, stay here for just another minute," he said, nuzzling my neck.

I cupped his face in my hands. "If I stay here for a minute, I'll be here an hour. I don't want to look around to see four angry guests ranged around our bed demanding coffee and egg casserole. Let me up."

He laughed and then made a pouty face. "I could shoo them away to have you to myself, but I will let you go for now." His arms tightened once more and then released me, patting my rump as I turned away.

I slipped out of bed, warm with the thought that my husband wanted me by his side, and went into the bathroom to shower and get ready for the day. In the kitchen, I lit the oven to preheat and got busy cutting up fruit to serve alongside the egg casserole I prepared the night before. It was after eight o'clock when I heard the first stirrings from the guest rooms overhead. That was my signal to put on the coffee so the aroma would let the guests know that breakfast was on the way.

Janet Fielding, my first guest last year, was back for the second time. She said she'd had so much luck writing in the yellow room that she had to come back for another month. I was thrilled Janet was back and couldn't wait to invite her to be my special guest at a Literary Roundtable meeting.

I asked Janet to bring extra copies of her books along so that if members of the Literary Roundtable wanted to buy one, they would be available. I was especially excited that Janet had brought copies of *Three Cheers for Murder,* the book that she worked on during her first visit. Janet had even dedicated the book to me, *To Rose Lambert, for her hospitality and grit weathering Hurricane Alphonso during the writing process.*

Today I brewed a special coffee as a welcome to the new guests. I had a few pounds of Mt. Meru coffee from Tanzania that were a thank you gift from one of my satisfied guests. It produced a rich brew that had a slight citrus aroma and taste. I loved it and hoped that my guests would like it too.

Janet was the first one downstairs. "I smelled the coffee, and I had to hurry down. Is this that coffee from Africa you told me about?"

"Yes, it's from Tanzania. One of my guests is involved in supporting the coffee growers in that part of the continent and sent me some as a gift."

"I'm surprised you're willing to share it with us." She poured herself a mug of coffee and tipped in a little creamer. She held the mug up to her nose and sniffed. "Oh, this smells terrific." She took a sip. "And it tastes good too, kind of citrus-y. Thanks for sharing, Rose."

"You're welcome. I won't be serving it every morning, but I thought it'd be a good welcome drink." While we talked, I laid out placemats and napkins on the three small tables scattered around the open lobby. I wasn't sure how the guests would arrange themselves, so I laid every table to give them a choice. I went back into the kitchen to silence the ringing timer and take the egg casserole out of the oven.

Janet followed me and leaned on the door between the lobby and the kitchen. "So, how's married life? It's been a few months since your wedding. Are you still glad that you took the plunge?"

"Absolutely. Iggy is a dream of a husband, and he's so handy. He can fix just about anything that goes wrong around here. Saves me a fortune in service charges. He's worth it just for that."

"I heard that." Iggy's voice rumbled from the doorway into the owner's apartment. "So, you only keep me around to fix things?" He walked over to the kitchen island and gave me a peck on the cheek. "Good morning, Janet. It is good to see you again. Are you starting on a new book this visit?"

"Good morning, Iggy. Yes, I've got a first draft to finish and have good luck when I write in the yellow room." She lifted her empty coffee mug. "Headed for a refill." And she walked back into the lobby where the other three guests were getting their first mugs of coffee.

I carried a tray with four bowls of fruit and four sets of silverware out into the lobby. Janet sat at one table, but the other three were standing around the coffee pot. "Where would you like to sit?" I asked.

Two of the guests were friends and sat together at an empty table. Janet turned to the third guest and invited her to join her. After everyone was seated, I distributed silverware and fruit bowls to the women. "You can get started on the fruit. I'll bring out plates of egg casserole in a jiffy." I picked up the tray and left the room.

When I came back from delivering the egg dishes, Iggy slid his hand up and down my arm. "Did you mean it when you said that I am only good as a handyman?"

"Good heavens, no, but I'm not about to detail our married life to a guest. She doesn't need to know what a treasure you are in so many ways. You keep me connected to the Anguillan community, tell me all the news, plus you're great to snuggle with." I nuzzled his neck and rubbed his back. "Go grab a mug of coffee before it's gone. I made the Mt. Meru coffee that Aleta sent while I serve us breakfast. I know how you love it. Would you like toast?"

***

Iggy came home from doing an electrical job in Island Harbour on the north end of the island with a tale to tell. "I stopped at the Rose Inn to see my Auntie Bonita and who should I see there, but George Clemment and Dimitri Roskova having a cozy breakfast in the corner."

"Did you talk to them?"

"No. I suspect they were hiding out from their wives, trying to figure out how they will live on this island together and stay apart."

"Didn't they see you?"

Iggy shook his head. "I stayed in the kitchen drinking coffee with Auntie Bonita and Claudius the cook. She sent her granddaughter Noreen out to wait on them so we could visit."

From what I saw at Billie's party last night, those men were natural enemies. Maybe they were dividing up the island at their breakfast meeting so that they didn't have to interact. I wondered what the Art League and Literary Roundtable meetings would be like if Susan Clemment and Irina Roskova joined both groups. Irina was a published poet, so I assumed that she'd be active in the Roundtable. I knew Susan was a knitter since she had come to my knitting group last year when they were here looking for a retirement home. She also manipulated digital photos on the computer to make Impressionist-looking art prints she sold out of a gallery downtown, so I knew that she'd join the Art League. From the looks the men gave each other at the party last night, I didn't think they would get along. Maybe the wives would stay far apart too.

CHAPTER 4

George and Dimitri

George drove his too big Range Rover up the narrow island roads, pulling over when he met a bigger vehicle. The early morning trucks were unwilling to yield the right of way to such an ostentatious SUV. George knew he didn't need something that flashy, but he'd spent his working years driving nondescript agency cars and the size and style of the Rover pleased him. He parked in the full sun when he got to the Rose Inn. He wanted to intimidate Dimitri by showing him his ride. There were no other cars in the gravel lot, so George did a little reconnoitering. He paced slowly down the narrow gap between the Rose Inn and the neighboring building. It had discarded cigarette butts and drink containers. It smelled of smoke and beer and showed signs of being a thoroughfare. Standing shielded in the shadow, he looked up and down the street that fronted the Inn, watched an old man shamble into the convenience mart across the street, and a herd of goats straggle toward him on the unkempt verge. Confident that he didn't detect a trap, he emerged and slipped quietly into the street entrance of the Rose Inn, startling an old lady who was crossing the lobby.

"I'm meeting a friend for breakfast," he said.

She flapped her hand toward the hallway. "Back there."

He followed the direction of her gesture and found himself in an empty room with tables scattered around in it. A swinging door on the right wall obviously led to the kitchen, since he could hear voices and the clatter of crockery. He checked his watch to see that Dimitri was five minutes late. "Clever. At least he hasn't forgotten everything." Not wanting to lose face and appear to be the first to arrive, he continued down the hallway until he came to the men's room. He ducked in there, catching the ripe scent of urine as he did.

Dimitri pulled into the parking lot and saw the glittering Range Rover parked where no one could miss it. He drove past the Rover and parked his brown sedan in the shade. Dimitri walked from his car through the open door of the Rose Inn. He saw no reason to go around to the front; he went in the back like everyone else did. The short hall wasn't quite long enough to give his eyes time to adjust from the glaring sunlight bouncing off the white gravel parking area, so he paused in the doorway to the small dining room. His eyes probed the corners of the room, looking for Major Clemment. "Damn," he cursed under his breath, knowing he would convey his nervousness and relative weakness by being first to arrive. He heard the scuff of a shoe on the tiles behind him and turned to see a silhouette of a man framed in the doorway.

"We could spend all morning dodging around, both of us trying to be the last to arrive." It was Major Clement. George walked toward him and stood beside him like a genial host.

"I am letting my eyes adjust to the darkness," Dimitri said.

George chuckled. "Right. Just like I was in the men's room." George extended his arm. "Let's go in together so neither one of us loses face."

By unspoken agreement, they chose the table in the darkest corner of the room, and each sat with their backs to the wall.

George looked at the man seated beside him and smiled. "Did you ever think we'd get this old?"

The humor and friendliness of the question disarmed Dimitri. "No, I never did."

George waited for him to say something else. When he didn't, he tried again. "Thirty years ago, it would have been unthinkable that we meet, not for coffee, not for anything."

A small smile flitted across Dimitri's lips, loosening his expression. "No, if we had met, one of us would have surely shot the other, I think."

"I think so too."

A teenage girl in flip-flops wearing a floral apron over torn jeans and a skin-tight pink tee shirt came out of the kitchen and stopped next to their table.

"What can I get you?"

"Coffee." Dimitri said and George nodded in agreement.

She tucked her pencil behind her ear and stuffed the order pad in her apron pocket. In a few minutes she came out of the kitchen balancing a tray holding two mugs of coffee in one hand. Her face bore a look of concentration as she swiveled the tray and set it down on the table. She put a mug in front of each of them.

Careful not to let it show, George nearly laughed at the serious look she wore. He was also careful not to offer to help or to grab his mug. He had a hunch the old woman he'd met in the lobby was the grandmother of this girl and was watching from the kitchen to make sure she performed her tasks correctly.

"Are you ready to order?"

George shook his head. "We haven't looked at the menu. We're old friends meeting after not seeing each other for years. Give us some time to talk."

She nodded, picked up the tray, and scuffed back to the kitchen.

George and Dimitri's hands collided over the menus.

"We had better figure out what we want before she comes back too soon," Dimitri said.

"My thoughts exactly."

They spent a quiet minute perusing the menus before closing them and putting them back into the holder.

After they had drunk about half their coffee, each of them staring around at the empty tables, George cleared his throat and set his mug on the scarred table. "How did you and Irina end up here?"

Dimitri carefully placed his mug on the paper coaster in front of him. "When the Soviet Union collapsed, there weren't many jobs left for people like me. I wasn't so active anymore. Mostly I had finally become my cover, a university literature professor. A year after the dissolution, they offered me a pension. I knew they had in mind that a younger person would need the job more than me, so I took it."

George picked up his coffee and drank a bit. "What made you come here?"

Dimitri fiddled with his mug. "Irina and I talked. We decided we were tired of freezing our asses off in the Moscow winters. We looked for someplace warm all year round."

"Sounds a bit like us," George said with a chuckle. "But why this particular island?"

"When we visited six months ago, we discovered that there was an active art and literary community on the island. Those were the people we wanted to associate with, so we found our little duplex and moved. It has not been easy to adjust to the heat, but it is better than what we left behind. It is a good place for Irina to write her poetry." Dimitri returned the question. "Why did you come here?"

"I got edged out of my job too, five years ago when the government changed, and more liberals held the reins. One of them decided that there were too many old spooks sitting behind desks gathering useless information, so they looked us over and pensioned off the oldest of us." He looked up, hoping to see their young waitress coming to refill their mugs. George could hear a conversation in the kitchen, but no footsteps coming their way. He put his mug down in disappointment. "Susan and I had what I imagine was a very similar conversation to yours with Irina. Neither of us wanted to spend our dotage shivering in jolly old England, so we cast about for a place in the sun, clichéd though that is. I love to scuba dive, and we'd been here on holiday a few times and thought we could afford to live here fairly well. We came down about six months ago, found a place to buy in Sandy Hill, went home to clear things up and sell the house, and three months later, here we are."

The girl came back with the coffee pot just as they had drained their mugs. George held his mug out to be filled, but she shook her head.

"I am not so good at pouring. I do not want to burn you."

He set the mug down. "I don't want that either."

She filled their mugs with fresh coffee, set the pot down on the table, and pulled out her order pad. "Are you ready to order?"

George leaned over to Dimitri. "We had better order, or her grandmother will come out here and start smacking us around."

The girl's face lit up with the thought that someone else could be afraid of her grandmother's wrath.

Dimitri went first. "I will have two eggs, over medium, sausage... you have sausage?" the girl nodded. "And white toast with real butter, not margarine." He grinned sheepishly at George. "What Irina doesn't know can't hurt me."

"I'll never tell, old boy." He smiled at the girl and said, "I will have the banana pancakes with real butter and bacon. And make sure the bacon is crispy. I can't abide flabby bacon. It reminds me of field training, all that raw meat. I'd like a large glass of orange juice first." He caught himself admiring the sway of a too young behind as the waitress went to put in their order.

"I can't eat bacon," Dimitri said. "All that fat reminds me of the old days when you couldn't get decent meat." He sipped his refreshed coffee. "George, how are we going to do this?"

"Do what?"

Dimitri pleated his napkin, caught himself in the nervous gesture, and stopped. "Both of us live on this tiny island now, when we spent so much of our lives on opposite sides?"

George looked at his old enemy with a steady gaze. "I don't see that it will be much of a problem. Who, besides Susan and Irina, knows the truth?"

"I think anyone at that party last night is talking about nothing else. I think Billie Holland-Smythe knows more than we think."

"What makes you say that?"

Dimitri half-turned toward George and draped his elbow over the chair back. "You could not see her face when she was dragging you and your wife toward us. There was an unholy glee in her eyes, a nasty mischievous knowledge that she knew exactly what she was up to."

"Hmm, you might be right. I seem to recall that Billie's brother Bertie worked in Intelligence for years. I wonder if he inadvertently let a few things slip."

"Or maybe not so accidentally," Dimitri said.

George nodded at him. "Too right. I'll have to have a few words with Susan when I get home. She and Billie have become fast friends in the last few months. God forbid she's been doing a bit of her own blabbing in the wrong ears."

Soon, the waitress brought their meals. She carefully set the platters down in front of the men. "More coffee?"

"After." They said together.

The food was good, and conversation was at a minimum as they addressed themselves to their plates.

George laid down his fork and knife. "That was good. I won't be telling Susan what I had for breakfast."

"Me too. Irina would not approve of all of this butter," Dimitri said, slathering another piece of toast with butter and jam.

George looked at Dimitri. "So, what are we going to do about living so close to one another? Billie Holland-Smythe will not let it go. We can't eliminate her. We can't buy her off. She thinks it's funny that we were political adversaries." He picked up his mug, saw it was empty, and set it back down with a clunk. "Damn that Bertie. I always knew that he was a blabbermouth, but I never thought that he would tell his sister secrets better kept unsaid."

"Can you eliminate him?" Dimitri said with a wry smile.

"No, he's dead. Killed in a car crash in Istanbul a few months ago. But the damage is done."

The grandmother appeared at their table with the

coffeepot. Both men pushed their mugs forward for refills.

George said, "Thank you. The food was good."

She nodded. "Good. I will send Noreen out for your plates."

"It makes little sense for us to be enemies when our countries have made peace with each other," he continued.

"No, it does not. We both spent our working lives living a lie. Now that we are retired, it will be a relief to be friends," Dimitri said.

George looked at his mug ruefully. "I'll pay for all of this caffeine later."

Dimitri sighed. "Da. I am not used to all this rich food either. I can see I will have antacids for lunch. But it will be worth it. That was an excellent meal."

"Can we be friends?"

"We can try."

They talked about their hobbies. Dimitri was an avid birdwatcher and knew how to snorkel. George loved to scuba dive and snorkel.

"Maybe we can do things together. Learn about each other's interests. What could it hurt?"

They ended their meeting on a cheerful note, each of them feeling that they had ironed things out, made strides toward their own personal détente.

George reached for the check that Noreen had put in the middle of the table, suspecting that the Russian's pension wasn't as generous as his. "I'll get this one. You can get the next one."

Dimitri reached for his wallet. "Let me leave the tip."

CHAPTER 5

George and Dimitri

Both couples lived in the same general area of the island: the Clemments in a two-story house by the sea with views of the sunset and a narrow beach just steps from the patio, the Roskovas lived a few blocks inland where the rents were much lower, and they had a view of the surrounding houses. Dimitri was working with their landlord to make a garden around their tiny porch to attract the birds he loved to watch and give them a little privacy from their neighbors.

George drove home humming to himself. He stopped at a liquor store and bought a bottle of champagne to show Susan that all was well.

Dimitri puttered along toward home chewing his lip and wondering what Irina would say when she found out that he had met the enemy and planned to make friends with him. Irina wasn't a forgiving type of woman. She would have a firm opinion and wouldn't hesitate to share it. Dimitri stopped at the flower stall under the gigantic tree on the edge of town and bought a bouquet for Irina. Then he drove down into Sandy Ground to see if the fisherman Billy had any of his catch left to sell. Maybe he would be lucky and there would be a lobster. He was in luck. No lobsters, but Billy had a nice piece of mahi mahi left to sell. Dimitri was happy to take such a rare and tasty treat home to Irina.

Each man arrived home at about the same time, each ready to brag to his respective wife about how masterfully he had managed a sensitive meeting and to reassure "the little woman" she had nothing more to fret about. How wrong they both were. Each entered his home bearing his returning hero's gifts, but neither fish and flowers nor champagne had the desired effect on the waiting women.

***

"Fish. You bring me wilting flowers and fish and expect me to pat you on the head and say good boy?" Irina was incensed. "This man represents all that you fought against for all those years and you're willing to throw it all over for what? For nothing." She strode around their small duplex kitchen and living room, waving her hands in the air.

Dimitri tried to melt into the background. When Irina got angry like this, she was impossible to talk to. Better to let her fling words and gestures until she ran out of steam.

"Did you just open your mouth and spill out all the state secrets you have been keeping all these years? Did you give the British major everything, or did you keep a shred of your dignity?" She turned and pinned him to the wall with her angry eyes. "Six months ago, I knew you would fold up like a house of cards when you said that you met him in Seaview and went for a walk with him. Where is your backbone, Dimitri? Where is the strong iron-willed man that I married?

"How can you be such an idiot? I send you off with strong words and you come home like a whipped puppy talking about new friends and swapping retirement stories. I can't believe how gullible you have become. The sun has addled your brain. How foolish must that British major think we are to be lulled into incautious speech by a smiling face and a slap on the back? And you come in carrying a packet of fish, fish for God's sake, like you have gotten the Lenin Medal and a handful of drooping flowers and think it makes it all better.

"I saw the look in their eyes as Billie led them toward us. He was like a graying lion and her an ice fury. I saw the whiteness of her knuckles as she clutched his arm. Does she think her silly woman act ever fooled me? I knew all the time how scheming and false she was. She flits around with her new best friend, Billie, pretending to be an artist and then, when she discovers I am a poet, she shares she is a poet too. When I ask her what books she has published, she has the gall to blush and say she's only had a few verses published in women's magazines. Women's magazines! As if the printing of a few lines of doggerel or some simpering rhyme about love or trees or, God help us, grandchildren count as real poetry.

"I have nearly given up sharing my poems with anyone who asks. Real connoisseurs of poetry don't have to ask. They have read my work and understand it. The few times I allowed flattery to get the better of me and shared my work with women who asked, they would read it and get that confused look on their faces like it is my fault they are too obtuse to understand, hand it back to me and say, very nice. One or two would pretend to understand the depth of my words and pressing their lips together, hand it back in silence as if they were too moved to speak. Please. Good poetry should birth discussion. I would rather they had told me I was full of shit and flung my words back to me. At least then I would know that I had touched their emotions.

"Now, you sit there at our rented table looking more like an old man than I have ever seen you look and tell me you are ready to make friends with the English couple. Have you forgotten the years that you gave to the Soviet Union? The times that the British stole our secrets, subverted our agents, sent whores to seduce our people into selling the heart of our country for a few rubles? It is disgraceful to think that just because new lines were drawn on a map that we will all forget what came before and lie down like beaten dogs. I will not allow my husband to become a lapdog for that conniving Major Clemment.

"What could he want from us after all these years? What secret could you still be carrying that would earn the attention of a man like Clemment? I will be vigilant to make certain that you are never alone again. I will make sure that the fiend cannot pry from your lips whatever it is he seeks."

Irina's narrow chest was heaving when she finished her rant. Dimitri stayed still throughout the whole tirade, happy that their neighbors had already left for work. She took a deep breath and looked at the things she had flung onto the table and picked them up.

"Dushka, thank you so much for the lovely fish and the bouquet." She kissed him. "Why don't you see if we have any mail while I put the flowers in a vase? Maybe we can have a walk before lunch."

Dimitri had sat and watched the emotions play across Irina's face. It seemed like a long walk to the mailbox.

***

Things were no better at the Clemment house. Susan pushed the bottle of champagne aside when George held it out to her. "What do you have to celebrate, George? Did you and Roskova exchange secrets at your little rendezvous? I can't believe that you would be so gullible as to think that you could be friends with a Russian spy." Susan stood with her arms folded across her chest and her lips pressed tightly together. "This goes against everything you stood for all these years. What are you thinking?"

George put the champagne into the refrigerator. "I think that of all the people I have met in my retirement, Dimitri Roskova is the only one who would understand me. I kept up a charade all those years that I was supposedly working in the British Fisheries Department. All those years when our friends and relatives plagued me for cut price fish for their family celebrations, no one, not one person, could understand the stress of living a lie for your entire career. Not even you, Susan." George started pacing up and down in the kitchen. "Dimitri knows. He was supposedly a professor at a university but in reality, he was ferreting around for a disgruntled secretary or an overstretched middle manager who might spill their secrets for a little money, a lot of liquor, or a good time, just like I was." He stopped his pacing and leaned on his fists on the table in front of his wife. "That's right, we each prostituted ourselves for queen and country and we have no one to talk about it with but each other."

Susan put up her hands as if to fend him off. "All right, George, all right. You go on being friends with the enemy, but don't come crying to me when he worms some long-held secret from you."

"Retired, Susan. We are both retired. We don't deal in secrets anymore."

Susan stood up and fixed him with a steely glare. "You've said it before, George. Spies don't retire."

CHAPTER 6

Rose

After the party, rumors flew, and my phone didn't stop ringing.

"I heard Dimitri had been an agent with the KGB posted in England and had tried to 'turn' George, or vice versa."

"Someone said that George had had an illicit affair with Irina, or Susan had, and it had ended badly."

"Susan and Irina? I don't see it."

"Someone told me that George was a double agent, and Dimitri knew it and was blackmailing him."

"I heard Susan is a spy in deep cover. She doesn't really love George and is in love with Dimitri." Most of those who thought that were women who had the hots for George.

To my eye, Susan and George were one of the happiest couples on the island. George was popular among the male expats. Mason James, the gallery owner, said that George was a fair golfer, a terrible fisherman, and a genial loser at poker.

The Roskovas were a tougher nut to crack. Dimitri was an active and enthusiastic member of the birdwatcher's group on the island, but he didn't mix with the men outside of their outings. Irina was a different story. She held herself aloof from the other expatriates and never listened to stories of people's children or grandchildren. "I do not have time or interest in such goings on," she said to one woman holding out her smartphone with the photo gallery cued up. Once was enough for the rest of the women to be reluctant to share any of their thoughts with her.

***

In the last few years Billie Holland-Smythe's first queen's and now king's Birthday Party had become the de facto start of the island social season among the small expatriate community. Introducing Major George Clemment and Colonel Dimitri Roskova was the shocking pinnacle of that year's party. For at least a week, not much else was talked about over fences and in the shops when friends met.

"You should have seen their faces. I thought Roskova was going to murder George or vice versa."

Those who had witnessed it enjoyed a measure of celebrity among those who could not attend or were uninvited.

"You were there? What did everyone do when they were face to face?"

"We all just stood there staring at the four of them, looking daggers at each other."

Everyone knew that Billie carefully chose her guest list. Being on it conferred a sort of cachet and being passed over spurred many a woman to examine her social skills and rethink friendships, hoping her name would be included the following year. Billie's soiree launched a months-long series of parties and barbecues that defined the cooler, winter months' social whirl on the island.

Those who had lived on the island the longest eagerly anticipated certain of these parties. Miriam Wilson and Jane Carey, retired teachers from Boston, hosted a beach party that was legendary. They had an entire pig shipped to the island that they roasted in a specially built pit on their property bordering a rocky beach on the south end of the island. From some secret place, they got sweet corn on the cob that was roasted over open coals. They also hired a steel drum band to play long into the night while their guests drank endlessly flowing rum drinks. Miriam and Jane always danced the limbo after midnight, to everyone's delight. They were amazingly flexible for a couple of old broads.

Mason James was the traditional host of the winter exhibition opening gala at his Cinnamon Gallery. He was a patron of the arts who specialized in works by primitive and local artists. His parties started with wine and hors d'oeuvres in the gallery, and then moved to his home for a traditional Caribbean feast with curried goat, yams, and platters of grilled lobster and other fresh-caught seafood delicacies.

At each of these parties, and many more throughout the months of that winter, a sort of division grew in the expatriate community, supporters and friends of Irina on one side, those loyal to Susan on the other.

***

Susan sat beside me on the next knit night at Seaview. "I'm so glad that none of Irina's friends knit. It's so refreshing to come here and be calm." She spent a few minutes knitting on a new pink sweater for her granddaughter. "Did you know George met Roskova the morning after Billie's party?"

Iggy had seen them together and told me about it, but I shook my head. "No, I didn't. Did he tell you what they talked about?"

"He brought home a bottle of champagne and told me he and Dimitri had decided to be friends and that Irina and I would be friends, too." She snorted. "I ask you. Me being friends with that Russian woman will never happen. Not in a million years."

"No, I can see that." I kept knitting on the dishcloth on my needles. "What did you tell him?"

"I said that Roskova was obviously after something that he knows or knew, and he should guard his tongue. Then George said that he'd had a lifetime of practice keeping his mouth shut and I need to have a little faith."

"It will be difficult to avoid them on an island this small and with the two of you wives in the same art and literary groups."

"Difficult," she nodded her agreement. She knitted a few stitches on the sweater. "But not impossible."

CHAPTER 7

Rose

If the first meeting of the Literary Roundtable after Billie's party showed how the rest of them would go, I wondered if I'd made a mistake in joining.

Irina looked around in horror that there were no officers, no minutes, no proper organization to the group. "What do you do? How do you keep track of the meetings?"

Jane Carey said, "We just talk about the books we're reading and then have snacks."

I could see by the look on Irina's face that wasn't good enough. By the end of the meeting, we had a board of officers with Irina as President, and a Secretary to take minutes. There was even a Treasurer although there was no treasury or membership dues. I was certain that Irina was planning to change that, too.

"I will bring copies of *Laid to Rest*, my first book of published poems, and share them with you at the next meeting. Then we will have something worthwhile to talk about." Her tone of voice invited no argument.

Miriam, who sat next to me, leaned over and said, "I'm glad I'm not a writer. I think anyone who isn't up to Irina's standards will be in for a rough time."

"Agreed," I said, looking around at the stunned faces of the surrounding women.

I knew that a few of the women, Susan included, were amateur poets, and Naomi Minten wrote short stories that were printed in literary journals. The shift in climate of the meetings made me think twice about inviting Janet Fielding or one of my other writer guests to come speak at the Literary Roundtable meeting. But I decided to cut off any hurtful remarks Irina or anyone else might make. I could be assertive too.

Billie Holland-Smythe had been suspiciously quiet throughout the evening. Was she hoping for fireworks between Irina and Susan? If she was, I prayed she continued to be disappointed.

***

Turned out that my hope Susan and Irina would avoid each other was a forlorn one. They both joined the Art League where Susan displayed her computer enhanced reef and floral photos that looked more like Impressionist art than photography and Irina compared it to "cheap motel art." I could see Susan turn pale when she heard that, and she slid down in her seat to hide behind the person next to her.

Things weren't better at the Literary Roundtable. What had been an ordinary book discussion group and gossip session turned into a bi-weekly poetry slam with Irina reading her poetry and Susan slamming it as "unintelligible."

By the third meeting, the members of each organization separated themselves into a group of Susan supporters and another of Irina supporters. They rearranged the chairs so that instead of a circle, they were in two clumps on either side of the room. I was in the unenviable position of trying to stay neutral. I wanted to stay that way because I really only belonged to the groups to make sure that the members remembered Seaview when family or friends were coming to visit. Many people didn't have room for guests and Seaview was an economical option for visitors.

Suddenly, the air at both the Art League and Literary Roundtable meetings on the island pulsed with more than just artistic fervor or literary passion. Neither Susan nor Irina was willing to give up their memberships in either group. Everyone knew that to miss one of the meetings was to miss being knowledgeable about island goings on and, even more important, whoever was not at a meeting automatically became the chief topic of conversation.

***

At most of the meetings, I sat in the middle of the room away from each group so that I could remain friends with Susan and cordial with Irina. I felt lonely and out of place but refused to choose sides. It was a relief when Miriam and Jane sat with me. I felt more sympathy for Susan but wanted to stay in Irina's good graces. Irina was a hard woman to get to know. She had an elevated view of herself and wielded her power in the Literary Roundtable like a club. I was afraid to say anything to her about being a little more sympathetic to the other women whose writing might not be up to her high standards. After all, they were a small group of amateurs living together on a small island with limited opportunities.

I was excited that Janet Fielding was on the island and had agreed to be a speaker at the next Literary Roundtable meeting. I had hoped that one of my writer guests would consent to come to a meeting and speak about her writing process and success, and now Janet had. Hopefully Irina Roskova would hold her tongue and not try to overpower Janet with her literary superiority.

Irina, in her position as President of the Literary Roundtable, could keep a tight rein on the discussions and had considerable influence over who was invited to introduce either a favorite passage or poem for discussion at meetings. Susan sat with her sycophants in the back row of the meeting, sharing, just a bit too loudly, her opinion that Irina was a famous poet only in her own mind. A mixture of shocked gasps and embarrassed giggles followed that opinion.

The Literary Roundtable meetings took on the aspect of a junior high cafeteria with half the women in the room on Susan's side and the other half on Irina's. As a woman entered, she would gravitate to either side depending on her loyalties, darting poisonous looks at her perceived enemies.

The entire war started in earnest after Susan got the chance to read a few of her poems one evening when Irina begrudgingly called on her. She prefaced her reading by saying, "these probably aren't very good," in the way people, especially women, do when they are looking for reassurance.

Unfortunately, Irina took the opportunity after Susan had read her admittedly amateur poetic efforts to say loudly, "You are right, Susan. Your poems aren't very good." The collective gasp that the statement generated nearly caused the curtains of the meeting room to flutter.

Normally, the women were very supportive of each other's efforts. The group, until Irina's arrival, had consisted of poet wannabes. Irina was the first member who had published extensively and who had a reputation outside her family as a poet. I was sure Irina felt she raised the tone and level of the group by freely sharing her vast experience and knowledge. Naomi stayed quiet about her publishing credentials.

Irina led the Literary Roundtable meeting, so she could let fly with her down-her-nose views of Susan's poems. Irina said, "Not up to even our lowered standards, is it, my dear?"

Susan had deflated like a popped balloon and sat down without speaking the rest of the evening.

"Tripe," Irina said, scanning the group as if daring anyone to contradict her. "Ladies, see how a modicum of approbation gives license to such superficial tripe? In my book, *Laid to Rest*, in the eponymous poem which we have read, I used words like bullets as a weapon against tyranny, not as Susan has, as a feather duster to tickle a reader saying, in essence, look how clever I can be."

With every word lobbed in her direction, Susan sank lower in her seat and her cheeks burned redder. The women seated around Susan looked away in embarrassment as she sniffed, plunging her hands in her purse and pockets looking for a tissue. Finally, Susan jerked the napkin out from under her teacup to carefully wipe unshed tears from her lower lashes.

Irina kept up her destruction of Susan's poems the rest

of the evening, earning her a few allies who also considered themselves above the rest, at least in literary terms. Most of the attendees felt sorry for Susan and squashed any thought they had ever entertained about daring to read their own secret scribblings to the group, at least while Irina was in charge.

Susan held her head up as she left that night in the center of a fluttering circle of consolation.

***

I was happy when Iggy and I were invited to the expat's parties. I enjoyed meeting the variety of people who attended them and my ability to network my bed-and-breakfast among them. Iggy's freelance business grew too when people discovered he was a licensed electrician and an accomplished and conscientious worker.

One night when Susan sat next to me at a cookout she said, "You know, I can't wait for the next knitting night. None of Irina's groupies knits, so I can have one evening without having to wear armor and fend off sniping comments."

I kept my mouth shut and just nodded. Better to appear agreeable but not say anything to offend someone. I felt like I was walking a tightrope in those gatherings.

Iggy spent most of the time at the parties by my side. Often, I would thread my arm through his and include him in my conversations. I tried to encourage him to join the men's discussions, but he just shook his head and said he'd rather spend the time with me.

"I know nothing about birdwatching or diving or American sports, so I have nothing to contribute to the conversations. I am happy being your arm candy."

I burst out laughing. "Arm candy? Where did you hear that?"

Iggy smiled down at me. "I read it on a tee shirt a tourist was wearing. It said, 'I am my wife's arm candy' and I thought it sounded like a good thing to be."

"Well, I'm happy to have you on my arm." I squeezed his arm to my side.

CHAPTER 8

Rose

Miriam and Jane were active members of both the divers and snorkelers group and the birdwatchers. They were also involved with, but much less active in, the Art League and Literary Roundtable. It was through them that George and Dimitri heard of their wives' running verbal battles.

At the next snorkeling group event after Billie's party, I stood near where George and Dimitri were getting their gear organized when Miriam put her bag down next to them and elbowed George. "You know that your missus has started up a war with his wife?" She nodded at Dimitri standing next to George.

"I thought something like that was happening. Tell me about it. When I ask, Susan just cries."

"Well, they've been ripping each other up at the Art League and Literary Roundtable meetings. Susan read one of her poems and Irina spent the rest of the evening bashing her with every breath. Now Susan is not a great poet, but no one deserves to be hit over the head with it all the time. Irina has a lot to say about Susan's artwork, too. Says it should hang in a cheap motel. It's a wonder Susan comes to the meetings when she gets treated like that."

George fumbled while attaching his snorkel to his mask strap. "Susan didn't tell me that. I wonder why she goes if she gets treated that way."

Jane leaned around Miriam to add. "I wouldn't put up with

it if I was the target of that Russian's sharp tongue."

"Doesn't Susan retaliate?"

"She tries, calling Irina's poetry unintelligible, but mostly she just sinks lower and lower in her seat. I think she even cries but tries to hide it."

George turned to Dimitri. "Did you hear that? Susan came home crying from the meeting because Irina was loudly critical of her poetry. Is there any way you could call off your wife? She's making Susan's life hell."

Dimitri shook his head. "No, I know what she is doing, and it's more than my life is worth to try to change her mind. Irina is convinced that you are trying to pry secrets from me and will not hear that we are just friends."

"Susan too. She is certain that you only talk to me to get me to loosen my tongue. I tell her that everything I know is out of date, but that doesn't make any difference. She's talked herself into it, and I can't convince her otherwise."

We picked up our fins, and I followed them into the water to put our fins on while standing in the shallows. "I blame Billie Holland-Smythe for this mess," George said. "If she hadn't made such a spectacle of introducing us at her king's birthday party, none of this would have happened."

That first snorkel over a shallow reef a few yards from shore blew Dimitri's mind. George lent him a plastic fish I.D. card on a lanyard to attach to his snorkel vest and he spent the entire time finning over to George, pointing at something on the card and then pointing down at the reef. When we left the water, Dimitri was transformed. No longer was he the silent and brooding man everyone but George was familiar with. He chattered to anyone who would listen about the wonders he had seen. He pointed to the Parrotfish on the card, saying, "I saw them in every color all over the reef." Dimitri waved his arms around with enthusiasm. "There was fire coral with a baby eel twined around it. Don't they get stung?" Mike Angerer just shrugged and kept lighting the charcoal grill. Dimitri quizzed each of us about how often the group met and if there were any other places where he might see even more of the fascinating sea creatures.

I hurried to towel off before the salt water could dry on my skin, making it feel sticky, and tried discreetly to get the sand out of my swimsuit bottom. I watched with amusement as Dimitri's countenance changed from his usual dour look to one of incredible fascination.

One of the other men had Paul Humann's Reef Set books that identified not only reef fish but also critters like shrimp and sponges and a separate volume about corals and plants. Dimitri sat happily while Mike and Mason tended the grill and slapped the burgers on for the group's lunch, talking to himself, repeating the Latin and common names and chortling with glee when he came across the list in the back of the fish book that allows a person to note where and when he has seen a particular fish. "Just like a birder's life list," he exclaimed. "I must get one of these books and begin immediately."

During lunch, he circulated among the dozen participants that day, asking questions about which masks were best, which fins were the most comfortable, and where he could get himself a set of those fish I.D. books. Mason and George had to chuckle to see the change in Dimitri.

Mason leaned over and said, "George, I believe you have created a monster today."

George smiled. "I'm just returning the favor. They paired me up with him at the birders' outing last week and he whetted my appetite for that with his knowledge and spotting skills. I've already bought new boots and a better pair of binocs. Dug out a pocket notebook to start my bird sighting life list, too. Susan is thrilled that I have another excuse to get out of her hair so she can futz with that computer of hers in peace."

I remembered when the books were first published. In fact, I bought *Reef Fish* from the previous owner Ian at Tamarind the year Jim and I were certified to dive. At lunch I sat with Miriam and Jane and said, "We aren't going to tell Irina how cozy Dimitri and George were today, are we?"

Jane shook her head. "No, we are not. Why make Dimitri's life a living hell when that wife of his cracks down on his activities on the island?"

"I figure if they were clever enough to avoid one another throughout their working lives, they're clever enough to figure out how to coexist in retirement without giving away the farm," Miriam said. She and Jane got up in search of something to drink.

George sat down in the empty chair next to me. "Do you think my old enemy had a good time today?"

"Yes, I do. I remember how I felt after my first reef dive. I was sure that no one else on earth had ever seen the wonders I saw that day. That bubbling enthusiasm still surprises me every once in a while, when I'm finning along and see something new. There's nothing like it." I took a bite of my burger. The burger was cooked perfectly for me, medium rare, with cheese. I chewed and swallowed, licking off the catsup that threatened to drip on my shirt. "How did the birdwatching go?"

"Oh, you know about that, do you?"

I nodded. "I suspected that the two of you would acquire each other's favorite hobby so that you'd have a reasonable excuse for being seen together."

George touched my arm. "You won't say anything to Susan, will you? I'd never hear the end of it if she thought I was getting together with Dimitri often."

"No, I won't tell. I guess the two of you are smart enough to figure out how to spend time together. And I need to stay neutral if I want women on both sides of this situation to recommend a stay at Seaview for their visiting family and friends. I can't risk my business by choosing sides."

Dimitri walked over to us, clutching the *Reef Fish* book to his chest. "I think I have found all the fish I saw on the reef today. I need to get one of these books so I can start my life list. Do you know where I can find one?" he asked.

"I bought mine at Tamarind years ago when they were first published," I said. "I'll bet Thomas still carries them in the shop. Otherwise, there's always Amazon."

Dimitri frowned and looked down at the now damp pages he held. "I do not think I can afford overseas shipping costs. I will check at the dive shop tomorrow." He turned to go back to his towel draped over a rock. "Or maybe I will stop on my way home today."

CHAPTER 9

Rose

My employee and helper, Geneva, and I were working on the laundry when her sister Minerva stopped over. "I am sorry to disturb you, Mrs. Rose. I thought Geneva would be finished working by now."

"That's no problem, Minerva," I said. "This is the last load of towels that need folding. Geneva, you go on and visit with your sister. I can finish this little bit myself."

"Are you sure, Mrs. Rose?"

"Yes, I'm sure. You go on and enjoy your visit."

"Come into the kitchen," Geneva said. "I will get my things, and we can go down to Johnno's for a cool drink."

"I do not want to go to Johnno's. Silas will come over to sit with you, and I want to talk to you alone."

Geneva nodded. "All right. Let me ask Mrs. Rose if we can sit out at the table here on the patio." She walked over to where I was folding towels on top of the dryer and asked me.

"Of course you can. Why don't you pour yourselves some iced tea and have a pleasant visit in the shade? I'm on my way inside to finish tidying up the kitchen once I get these towels put away in the back room. Then I think I'll sit down and read for a while." I piled the folded towels into the laundry basket and carried it into the back room.

It didn't take me long to finish my chores. I stretched out on the loveseat in our little sitting room and picked up the book I'd been reading. It was one of Janet Fielding's cozy mysteries and it was hard to put down. After a time, I realized I could hear the two young women chatting. I tried to ignore them, but it was difficult. I knew Minerva was Billie Holland-Smythe's housekeeper, so I listened.

Minerva was saying, "Mrs. Holland-Smythe keeps calling me Minnie. I tell her I prefer to be called Minerva so that I can keep my place. She does not understand that I would lose authority over the rest of the staff if she was so familiar with me."

"She calls you Minnie? You do not look like a Minnie to me, no mouse ears."

"Oh, be serious. How would you like it if Mrs. Rose called you Gennie?"

"Mrs. Rose would not do that. She respects me. Every once in a while, she invites me to have lunch with her and I do, but I feel awkward, like she is trying to be friends. I want to keep my place too, but I do not want to lose my job either."

"Exactly. I tell Mrs. Holland-Smythe that if we were too familiar, her house would not run as smoothly. I do not think that she has had very much staff in the past, at least no staff from the islands."

"Do you think she will give up trying?" Geneva asked.

"No, I do not. She is not the type of woman to give up once she has her mind set on something."

Overhearing that exchange gave me something to think about. It seemed like island women had a lot of self-respect and dignity and they intended to preserve it. Maybe I needed to be more formal with Geneva. I'd ask Iggy what he thought.

***

I volunteered to host the next Literary Roundtable meeting at Seaview. Geneva and I worked hard to polish the wood floor in the lobby until it gleamed and made sure that there were extra chairs to accommodate the crowd.

Iggy built a small bookcase out of some of the leftover scrap wood from last year's construction for Janet to use to display copies of her books. The little bookcase sat on top of one of the tables and the muted colors of the old paint enhanced the colorful covers of the books.

Geneva helped me make a platter of small sandwiches. I pulled out my favorite sandwich filling recipes and made pimento cheese and olive and nut spread. I was surprised when I found a single bag of pecan pieces at the IGA, which was just what I needed for the spread. It was lucky that I had bought a giant pack of dessert size paper plates and four packages of cocktail napkins the last time I was at the Eastern Store because I didn't have enough small plates for a crowd.

And what to drink? Lemonade and iced tea would do just fine with a pitcher of water for those who preferred that. I was relieved that wine wasn't a regular beverage at the meetings. I couldn't afford to buy enough wine for the whole membership. I thought about sangria, which I've always found refreshing, but after looking up the recipe that my daughter Marie used, realized that would cost even more. We'd just stick to the non-alcoholic drinks.

Members of the Literary Roundtable began arriving, and it was soon clear that Seaview's lobby wasn't big enough for the Susan and Irina camps to be separated by much real estate. I hid a smile when the groups had to mingle. Irina swept in wearing her signature dark gray wide-leg pants and a tunic with bell sleeves in dove gray. She stopped short when she realized that the only place left to sit was next to Susan. Susan didn't look pleased either when her archenemy sat beside her.

I raised my voice. "I think we can get started." The talk in the room petered out. "Tonight, I'm happy to have Janet Fielding, novel writer and author of several cozy mysteries, as our guest. Janet was my first guest at Seaview, weathered Hurricane Alphonso with us, and still finished the first draft of her novel, *Three Cheers for Murder,* while the storm raged. Janet, welcome to the Literary Roundtable. We're happy to have you with us tonight." There was scattered applause from the members as I sat down in the folding chair I had wedged into the corner behind Janet.

"Thank you, Rose," Janet said. "I'm glad to be back at Seaview, glad to be back in Anguilla, and glad to be here with you all this evening. I started writing popular fiction when I was in college. I was writing all kinds of dark, emotional stuff and my grandmother challenged me to write something that she and her friends would like to read."

That got a chuckle from the crowd. "It took me a while, but I managed, with the help of one of my creative writing professors, to crank out a manuscript for a cozy mystery in a semester. My prof dared me to look for an agent to get the book published. I attended a writing conference in Milwaukee, had a couple of meetings with agents, and was signed by one of them. My agent found me a publisher who wanted more of the same and soon, so I just about chained myself to my desk and got busy writing."

Janet picked up one of the paperbacks off the table beside her and opened it to a marked page. "Let me read you a little of the book I wrote right upstairs in this very building."

By the time she had finished reading three pages of *Three Cheers for Murder,* I could see that most of the audience was on the edge of their seats. There was a brief silence and then applause.

Irina turned to the woman on her left and said, "Well, that was interesting, but it is not up to the great Russian novelists."

A few of the women in the group shushed her, but the damage was done. Janet's face turned pale, and she stopped smiling.

I stood and stepped up to Janet. "Why don't we let people come up to look at your books? I'm sure that some of them will be interested in purchasing a signed copy."

Janet shook her head, but I took her arm and eased her into the chair I had been sitting on. "It'll be all right," I said into Janet's ear. "You had them in the palm of your hand until Irina spoke. Smile. I'll get them moving."

I picked out a few of the women I had noticed were rapt as Janet read and encouraged them to go up and talk to the author.

Once they were on their feet, more people clustered around the table where Janet sat. Wallets were opened and books were sold.

Irina held herself aloof from the crowd and a couple of her supporters stood with her, but the rest of the women helped themselves to refreshments and talked among themselves. Those who bought books were eagerly showing each other the signature on the title page and reading the blurb on the backs of the books.

"Oh, I can't wait to get home and start reading," one of them said to her friend.

The other woman nodded. "When we're done, we can swap. You can read mine and I'll read yours."

With every sale, Janet's hurt expression faded. By the time she had run out of copies of her books to sell, her smile was wide and unforced.

***

Susan was the newly elected Vice-President of the Art League because of her computer-enhanced digital photographs' popularity in the local galleries. I overheard Irina say that manipulating a mediocre photo with a computer and calling it art was shameful, but she agreed Susan was good at cutting mats and selecting frames.

Susan used George's reef pictures and took her own digital photos of flowers, plants, and scenery and manipulated them on her computer until they looked like impressionist art. She had taken her works around to the galleries on the island, and Mason James at Cinnamon Gallery had agreed to hang a few of them. They were an instant hit with the tourists. Susan could barely keep up with the demand. A few of the other expats were painters, and they had a lot to say, good and bad, about Susan's computer-generated art. She kept the prices of her pieces low, which made them very competitive with the hand-painted art that hung alongside them. Of course I bought one for Seaview.

Irina wasn't shy about voicing her opinion of Susan's art. "I think a chimpanzee could do as well," she said at one meeting.

After I got home, I looked at the photograph that I'd

bought from Susan. I could tell it was an underwater photo, but couldn't really tell what it was. Sponges, surely, and probably parrotfish if that smear of aqua was any hint, but the rest of it was just blurs of colors.

Iggy walked up to my shoulder and peered down at the photograph. "What is it?"

"I'm not really sure. Underwater on a reef somewhere, I think, but it's hard to tell anything in the blur."

"Why did you buy it?"

I turned to look Iggy in the eye. "To support Susan and to spite Irina. Oh, Iggy, I just can't warm up to that Russian woman. She's so negative and superior acting. There isn't a soft bone in her body."

Iggy shook his head. "I cannot warm up to any of your new friends. They look down on me."

"They don't."

"They do. They think of me as one of the servants, like the servers, housekeepers, and musicians. It is like I am one of their pets. They are happy to have me around when something goes wrong with their electricity, but they do not have time for me as a man."

"But they're nice to you, aren't they?"

"Polite. They are polite, but they do not want to be friends with me. They are not interested in my thoughts on things, they are only interested in telling me about how wonderful they are."

I put my arms around him. "I'm sorry, sweetheart, I didn't realize that was happening. I suppose the opposite is happening to me with your friends, but I thought it was a cultural thing, not a racial thing."

He leaned his forehead touching mine. "I suspect it is both on both sides. My friends are cautious with you because you are white and American, and your friends are cautious with me because I'm not white and Anguillan."

"Cautious. That's a nice word for what seems to happen on both sides." I slid my arms around his waist and pulled him close. "You aren't sorry that you married me?"

"Oh no, not for one minute. I just have to figure out how to navigate my way through." He held me tight. "This is not a new storm. It is just one that you are not used to having to weather."

CHAPTER 10

Rose

It was Saturday, and I hurried to finish serving breakfast so that my guests had plenty of time to eat and pack before checkout time. For once, the egg casserole hadn't set in the middle in the usual time. Instead, it took ten minutes longer. I worried that something was wrong with the oven, or maybe just I hadn't set the temperature correctly.

Iggy left early. He had an electrical job to finish up at a rental duplex in Sandy Hill. I sent him off with a scrambled egg, toast, coffee, and a kiss.

Geneva poked her head in to say good morning before she put her purse on the shelf in the backroom and put on her apron. "What can I do, Mrs. Rose?" she said, coming into the kitchen and tying the apron strings behind her back.

"You can peek out to see if the guests are finished eating so we can get started washing the dishes. The egg casserole took more time than usual and I'm feeling rushed." As she walked toward the doorway into the lobby, I heard chairs scraping on the wood floor as people got up to leave.

Geneva came back carrying the tray laden with plates, silverware, and coffee mugs. "I can get these dishes started. You sit down, have some coffee, and catch your breath," she said.

I stood and looked at her for a few seconds, nodded, and did what she said. At the first sip of coffee, I felt my shoulders relax and let out a sigh. "Thanks, Geneva. I needed a breather. I don't know why I let a minor problem with the baking set me on edge." I could hear people walking around upstairs in every room. I hoped they were checking every corner, so they left nothing behind. I'd had to ship back phone chargers, favorite swimming suits, and one time even a wedding ring.

Once Geneva and I finished cleaning up the breakfast dishes, I went out into the lobby to make sure that I had everyone's bill ready when they came to check out. Once that was accomplished, the guests started trickling down to the reception desk.

"Thank you for choosing Seaview. I hope you enjoyed your stay," I said.

Hack and Anna Louise raved about a local restaurant they found called Tasty's. "It was dim inside and furnished with mismatched tables and chairs, but the food was wonderful. We had goat roti with peas and rice and ate every bite."

"That's one of my favorite lunch spots when I'm out doing errands." I handed them a few brochures after they paid their bill. "Share these with your friends or leave them in a café for someone else to pick up. I'd really appreciate it."

Anna Louise said, "I don't know if I want to share Seaview with everyone. It's such a great place to stay. I'm afraid you'll get too popular, then there won't be room for me when I come back. And I will be back. You can be sure of that."

"Thank you. I'm glad you feel that way. Would you mind leaving a review to that effect?"

"I'd be happy to. I'll also recommend a visit to the Sandy Hill Bay Petroglyphs. We loved trying to interpret the images on the rocks. I can't get enough of that kind of history."

"I've never heard of those," I said. "Might be worth a Sunday drive to see them."

My daughter Marie had warned me not to have too many brochures printed because they're costly and most people do their vacation research online. But I had gotten some reservations from people who had picked up a brochure in a coffee shop or at the gym, so I considered it money well spent.

Geneva and I spent the rest of the day cleaning and

preparing all the rooms for the new guests and cleaning the bathrooms. Over the last few months, we had settled into a routine, so we were more efficient juggling cleaning and laundry every Saturday to be ready when the next week's guests arrived late in the afternoon.

Two couples and two singles checked in, one right after the other. They had all arrived on the same flight and once they got their rental cars, came right to Seaview.

The first couple introduced themselves as Ed and Betty Whealan. "We're from Cincinnati, Ohio," Betty said. "I'm sure you don't know where that is."

"On the contrary. My daughter lives in Lexington, Kentucky, and when I used to drive down from Wisconsin, I'd drive across Indiana to Cincinnati to go over the Ohio River there and get into Lexington from the north."

Betty shook her head. "It's a small world, isn't it?"

"It sure is. Let's get you checked in and into your room."

It didn't take long to put them into the registration program, scan their credit card, and escort them to the yellow room on the sea side. As soon as I came downstairs, the rest of the new guests were clustered in the lobby. I smiled at them all and said, "Welcome to Seaview. Who arrived first? It won't take long to get you checked in so you can get started vacationing."

After a little polite maneuvering,

"You were here first."

"No, I think you were."

they sorted themselves out, and we got down to business.

Warren and Amelia Burns were a Black couple from suburban Atlanta. "We're looking to do some scuba diving while we're here," Warren said. "I read that the dive shop is next door. Is that right?"

"Yes, it is. Once you've gotten settled in your room, you can head over to Tamarind, look over their dive operation, rent gear if you need it, and get signed up for some boat dives."

"What about shore diving?"

"There are a few bays around the island with small coral

reefs that are adequate for shore diving. The big draw for divers in Anguilla are the wrecks that you can visit with Tamarind. A couple of them have been down long enough that they look like fairy castles with all the sponges and sea fans on them. I love diving on them."

Amelia said, "Oh, you're a diver? You should come with us one day while we're here."

"I'd love to. Thanks. I'll see how the week goes and let you know." I asked Geneva to lead them up to the turquoise room on the garden side of the bed-and-breakfast and turned to check in the last two guests.

Lucy Ralston had reserved a seaside room and was eager to sit at the window and watch the ocean. "I get sunburned easily, so I'm usually out on the beach in the early morning and in the evening. I never miss a sunset." Geneva escorted her to the salmon room.

Nancy Hernandez waited patiently while I got the others checked in.

"Finally," I said. "Sorry to make you wait."

"That's okay. I'm not at work and I'm not at home. I read the framed article about Ernest Hemingway. Was he really a guest here?"

"He was, years and years ago, but I found this picture and autographed fishing lure when I renovated, so I framed it." While we talked, I entered her info into the registration program, scanned her credit card, and told her a little about the island. "Let's get you up to the lilac room, and you can get into shorts and get relaxing." I motioned to the waiting Geneva to escort Nancy to her room.

As they left for their rooms, I offered each new guest a fruit and cheese plate along with a split of wine (their choice, red or white) or iced tea if they preferred and told them about being able to store a bit of food in baskets in the fridge and use the microwave to reheat the leftovers from their doggie bags. As they got to their room, Geneva told them that the decorations on their towels matched the color of their room so that they could tell them apart if they left them in the bathroom. We were getting pretty practiced at giving our canned welcome speeches.

I heard footsteps and looked up to see Warren and Amelia Burns come down the stairs. I was tidying the registration desk and making sure that all the new guests were on the books.

"All settled in?"

"We're off to the dive shop," Warren said.

"Have fun. I'll try to join you one day during your stay."

Lately I had had no diving guests and George had a bad head cold and wasn't diving until it cleared up, so he didn't need a buddy. I missed diving but had been so busy I hadn't made time to go. Part of me wished Amelia wasn't a diver, so I'd feel obligated to accompany Warren on a few dives, but she was, so I didn't. I couldn't go tomorrow because Sunday was Geneva's day off, so there was no one to clean up after breakfast in my absence. Of course, there was Iggy, but I couldn't expect him to do the dishes when I was gone diving, and Sunday was his day off too. I enjoyed spending the day with my new husband. We had plans to take a picnic to Limestone Bay and spend the afternoon swimming and lazing in the sand.

After Geneva had left for the day, I started the oven to preheat it while I made shepherd's pie for supper. It had become one of Iggy's favorite suppers and I was lucky to find ground beef, carrots, and potatoes at the grocery that week. I boiled and mashed the potatoes, cooked and mashed the carrots, browned the onions and ground beef, and added the other ingredients. Then I assembled the casserole and went to put it in the oven, but the oven wasn't hot. "I really don't need this," I said. I turned the oven off and turned it on again. That time the gas ignited but the oven must have been full of gas, because it blew the oven door open and knocked me on my behind.

Ed Whealan rushed in from the lobby. "Oh my god, are you all right?" He reached down to help me to my feet. "Were you hurt? What happened?"

I let him help me up. "Thanks." I gingerly closed the oven door and made sure the oven was turned off. "I think there's something wrong with the igniter. The oven didn't light, but the gas must have filled the oven because when it did light, it blew the door open and knocked me down." I laughed a little. "This is a fine welcome to Seaview, a gas explosion that almost blew up the owner."

"You need to get that fixed before you really blow yourself up."

"I'll have my husband look at it as soon as he gets home." I put my hand over my chest to try to still my racing heart. "You're Ed, right?"

"Yeah. I'm also a retired firefighter. Don't let your husband fool around with gas. Leave it to a professional."

"My husband is an electrician but, you're right, I'll call someone right away. Thanks again."

Iggy came in the back door a few minutes later and said, "Why does it smell like cooking gas in here?"

"Help me open the windows to air the place out." We spent a few minutes opening windows and doors. I turned on the ceiling fans to get the air moving too. I explained about the minor explosion I'd just had and how I needed to call an appliance repairman.

"Are you all right? Were you hurt when you fell?" He swept me into a hug. "I can fix the oven."

"Are you sure? Do you know about gas ovens? I don't want you to get hurt or blow up the kitchen."

"I have done it before at home. All I need is a new igniter, a screwdriver or two, and a circuit tester."

Smiling at him, I said, "I have a replacement igniter. I ordered it when I ordered the stove because I didn't know if I could get one on the island if I needed it. I have other parts, too."

"I am so happy to have such a smart wife."

I heated the shepherd's pie in the microwave, not willing to take a chance on the oven again.

Iggy said, "I am glad that you made shepherd's pie even if it almost made the oven explode. I will get the new igniter installed after supper so that you will not have a problem again."

"Thank you, dear. It terrified me when that oven door blew open and I fell backwards. I thought that the whole place would go up next." I took a bite of supper and had a drink of water to chase it down. "How was your electrical job? Did you get it done?"

Iggy nodded. "It was at the duplex where the Roskovas live. They needed another outlet in their second bedroom for some computer equipment. I thought he was retired, but maybe not. Dimitri seemed a little nervous when I asked what he needed and where he wanted it. You would think he had a secret." He looked at me with one eyebrow raised.

"Well, if the gossip is true, he was a spy, so maybe he's spying on someone in Anguilla now." I got up and carried our plates to the sink.

"I will do the dishes tonight, Rose. You have a seat and keep me company. So, you say that Dimitri was a spy?"

I gave him a hug from behind. "Thanks for doing the dishes." I refilled my water glass from the pitcher in the refrigerator. "Yes, that's what all the gossip says, that he was a Soviet spy during the Cold War. I don't know who he'd find to spy on here, though. Everyone seems pretty harmless."

"What about George?"

"Oh, you're right. The first time George and I went diving we were having lunch here with Susan, and Dimitri walked in to fill his water bottle. He and George were stunned to see each other and ended up taking a long walk together. Wouldn't it be funny if they were spying on each other?"

"Funny and awkward." He set the last pot in the dish drainer and dried his hands. "Let me get my tools and I will install the new igniter. Can you get it for me?"

"I'd be happy to."

It wasn't long before he had the old igniter out and the new one installed. He tested it and it worked just fine. "I am surprised that it failed so quickly. Maybe it was defective. The newer appliances are not as durable as the old ones."

"The next time I place an order, I'll get another one so that we always have one on hand."

CHAPTER 11

Rose

On Tuesday, I went diving with Warren and Amelia Burns, two of my guests. I talked to Geneva on Monday, and she said she'd come in a little early so that I'd have time to get to the dive shop without being rushed. That worked well. I got breakfast made and served and then she cleared the tables and cleaned up the kitchen. The Burns and I walked over to Tamarind Dive Shop together and I signed up for the morning dive. Warren and Amelia had already filled out the Medical Release forms and mine was on file since I had a "locals" dive package. The three of us got weights and headed out to the catamaran. As usual, I slung my dive bag onto the boat and waded around to climb the boarding ladder at the stern.

"I see you coming, and I lowered the ladder," Freddie the boat driver said.

"Thanks, I really appreciate it. I'm too darned short and too old to hoist myself up on the bow from the sand." We shared a laugh. I retrieved my dive bag and sat down next to Amelia. I was glad to see that Warren and Amelia's dive gear wasn't showroom new. It was faded and a bit worn in places. "It looks like you two are active divers."

Amelia smiled. "We go on at least one dive vacation a year and we dive lakes around home, so our gear gets used."

Warren leaned across his wife. "Living near Atlanta makes it easy to hop a flight to somewhere in the Caribbean for a long weekend of diving."

"With all the choices out there, how'd you end up here, and for the entire week?"

Amelia said, "It took us two airplanes and most of a day to get here, so we decided to stay the week. Besides, it'll give us the chance to dive on most of the shipwrecks and do some shore diving, too. Warren read about all the wrecks around Anguilla on a scuba website. He liked the sound of the peaceful island and the opportunities for shore dives, too. It's hard to keep him out of the water."

"That sounds like my late husband, Jim. When we were on Bonaire, he'd want to do the two morning boat dives, an afternoon shore dive, and a night dive every day if I'd agree."

"Oh, we love Bonaire. The shore diving there is so easy and varied. It's hard enough to get there that we stayed for two weeks."

"I hear you. The last time we went there, we stayed for a month. That was amazing. We did lots of dives and I think even Jim was almost dived out."

As we'd been talking, the boat got pushed away from shore and Dougie started his dive briefing. We stopped talking to listen.

"Today we are going to be diving on the *M.V. Commerce*. She lies at depths of forty-five and eighty feet. The bow is shallower, is intact, and lies on a coral slope. The stern is down the slope at eighty feet. The ship is cut in half behind the helm and the deck is damaged. Sometimes people see stingrays in the sand around the wreck and the top of the wreck has a lot of healthy growth. The reef around the ship has barrel sponges and a lively population of fish like Bar Jacks, Barracuda, and Yellowtail Jacks. Keep your hands off the huge lobsters that hide under the side of the hull. You need a special permit to take them. We do not have one."

It wasn't a long boat ride out to the wreck site, so soon the boat slowed, and everyone got ready to dive. The three of us talked about how we liked to dive and made a plan before getting into the water. As we were lining up to giant stride off the boat, Dougie checked that there wasn't a current and made the announcement.

"It looks like all we have is a mild surge today, so pay attention to your position in the water and everything will be fine."

I loved that first plunge into the ocean, although the flurry of bubbles and the seep of the water in my wetsuit was a little disorienting. The water, while warm, was always cooler than I was in my wetsuit, so I shivered as it trickled down my spine. I rolled over face down and adjusted my mask and BCD buckles as I snorkeled to the mooring buoy where I'd meet up with my dive buddies. Warren and Amelia were waiting for me at the buoy. We went over our dive plan one more time, checked to make sure we were ready, and started our descent.

What started as a dark shadow resolved itself into the bow of the ship as we neared it. Sticking to our plan, we swam past it and descended to the stern where the propeller lay dug into the bottom. I saw an old car perched on the deck sitting a little drunkenly on four flat tires. There was a broken cargo crane pointing off the side that was covered with sponges and stinging hydroids that made the crane look like it belonged in a child's picture book. Around the shipwreck, schools of fish swam in and around the sponges, gorgonians, and sea fans that nearly covered the deck. It looked to me like a teeming cityscape. The rest of the divers from the boat swam nearby looking in the car windows and peering under things hoping to see big lobsters or tiny shrimp.

I started to follow my dive buddies along the stern section of the ship, but after a kick or two, I wasn't moving forward. I kicked again and went nowhere. I was caught on something, and my buddies were swimming away. "Hey, help," I called through my regulator, but my words went nowhere in the water. I turned upside down to try to see what I was caught on, but nothing was visible. Must be fishing line, I thought. How to get untangled. I tried to reach down to remove my fin, but it was difficult to contort my body with the bulky BCD on. I kept trying, knowing that I was using up air at a fast rate. I let the air out of my BCD so that it was flatter, and I could reach my foot easier, but that made me sink and pull whatever I was caught on taut. Just as I was feeling the icy fingers of panic dance up my spine, I felt a hand on my arm. Warren and Amelia had missed me and come back to see what the problem was. I put a squirt of air back into my buoyancy vest so that I was neutrally buoyant and pointed at my left fin. Warren went to check. Amelia stayed with me, her hand on my arm. I saw him pull his knife out of the sheath on his calf and cut whatever it was I was tangled in. I felt my foot release and let out a long, relieved breath.

I checked my air gauge and saw that I'd used up about 500 psi in my struggle, so I'd have to keep a careful eye on it for the rest of the dive. I didn't want to have to cut the dive short.

We worked our way up to the bow section of the *M.V. Commerce* where a Banded Coral Shrimp, looking like an animated candy cane, had set up a cleaning station on the helm. It waved its long white antennae to attract fish needing to have irritating parasites removed and algae cleaned off. It made me giggle to see fish of various types lined up like at a Saturday car wash waiting their turn to get cleaned.

Warren and Amelia were good dive buddies. Whenever I looked around, they were within a few feet of each other and me. Amelia held out her air gauge to me with a question in her eyes. I showed her mine and mimed how much air I had left. She nodded and did the same. We traded okay signals and kept swimming around and across the deck of the shipwreck. All too soon, Dougie signaled it was time to go back to the dive boat. That was okay with me. I was getting close to the last 500 psi in my tank. We swam slowly over to the mooring line and ascended to fifteen feet to perform a three-minute safety stop. Once we were back on the dive boat, we stripped off the tops of our wetsuits and dried ourselves so that we didn't get chilled. Then we changed our gear onto fresh tanks to prepare for the second dive.

I picked up my fin and saw that the monofilament fishing

line had wound itself around the buckle. I had to remove the buckle to unwind it so I could throw it away. "Thanks for coming back to save me."

Amelia patted my hand. "You're welcome. That's what dive buddies are for."

"That was an excellent dive," Warren said. "I enjoyed being able to see inside the ship a little. Too bad we couldn't penetrate the wreck, but it looked way too unstable."

I said, "I wouldn't have gone in even if it had been wide open with a welcome mat at the edge. I'm not comfortable with overhead environments."

"I don't mind it," Amelia said. "It's kind of fun to swim along the passageways where people used to walk, but if it's not your thing, it's no big deal."

I shook my head. "I couldn't even swim under the Town Pier in Bonaire, and I knew I could go to the surface under the pier and be in the air, but still it was too confining for me. It was kind of embarrassing and disappointing since I'd been so excited to dive there."

It was a short boat ride to our second dive site, Sandy Shallow, on the east side of Sandy Island. The most notable feature of the site was the forest of sea fans that proliferate over the area. The three of us swam out along the reef and back, sticking to about thirty-five feet and shallower, just enjoying the sea life and the feeling of flying that diving gives.

When we got back to shore, we dunked our gear in the rinse tank at the dive shop and Warren and Amelia hung their equipment in the gear locker at Tamarind. I took my dripping gear back to Seaview and hung it to dry on the pegs on the back porch. I invited them to join me for lunch since I was always ravenous after doing two dives. We had a pleasant chat, filled out our logbooks, and chowed down on some killer grilled cheese sandwiches I fixed for us.

As soon as lunch was over, I got busy helping Geneva with the laundry. She had already cleaned the bathrooms and replaced the towels in the guest rooms, so all I had to do was keep the loads moving and fold the dry towels and sheets before putting them in the back room. I felt guilty for leaving Geneva to deal with the work while I went diving, so I suggested she leave early to make up for having to work alone all morning. She didn't balk. In fact, she left so quickly I thought maybe she intended to ask for the afternoon off. Maybe she and Silas had plans together.

CHAPTER 12

Rose

I wished I could send Iggy to the grocery.

In Vista Market, if I met one of Irina's supporters in the produce aisle picking out veggies for a salad, she would say, "You agree Susan is a terrible poet and artist, don't you? When you read Irina's poetry, it transports you to another plane."

I wasn't much of a poetry reader, preferring to read a mystery or a menopausal chick novel, so I would hum and nod and excuse myself.

The reverse happened in the IGA.

A woman on Susan's side of the situation would say, "That Russian woman is just unbearable. How could she be so cruel to Susan at the meeting? And in front of everyone. I think that her poetry is too deep to understand. Maybe it's better in Russian. It must lose a lot in translation."

In my heart, I agreed that Irina's poetry was beyond me. I thought she had been mean to call out Susan like that in front of the group, but there was no way I was going to say that to anyone but Iggy.

I couldn't avoid one store over the other. I depended on finding the foods on my shopping list and always went to both stores and made a stop at the produce market under the tree at the edge of town, too.

"I need to find something to say to those women to get them to leave me alone," I said to Iggy after my last shopping trip had been extended by a half hour as I sought to extricate myself from the on-island Cold War.

"Can you just say that you like one of them over the other and leave it at that?"

"Oh no, I can't choose sides. My business isn't established enough that I can alienate one or the other of them. I depend on all of them sending their visiting friends my way." I started emptying the shopping bags and putting the food away in the refrigerator and the cupboards. "I'm just glad that Irina doesn't knit, or I'd have another battlefield to tiptoe through on knitting nights."

Iggy said nothing, just helped put things away.

***

When I met her at the produce market under the tree, Susan told me she was not looking forward to the next Literary Roundtable meeting. It was bad enough on regular nights to be stuck in a room with a bunch of other women trying to be polite to Irina Roskova. But at the next Roundtable meeting Irina was planning to read more of her poetry. Susan said, "If I didn't know better, I would have pegged Irina as the spy in that couple.

"Our former neighbors, Max and Harriet Fitzpatrick, are coming to visit next week. I'm really looking forward to having my old familiar neighbor around for a month. They're not staying with us or at Seaview, I'm sorry to say. According to Harriet, she would be more comfortable if they stayed in their own place where she could cook some of their meals. That couldn't have happened if they'd stayed at Seaview. I found a nice little bungalow for them to rent at a small resort near our home called Happy Holiday Homes. A Dutch woman and her Indonesian husband own it."

"I've heard of it," I said. "I'm hoping to meet her and compare notes about running a small hotel on Anguilla."

The bungalows had full kitchens, a roomy dining area that opened into the living room with a cable television, a spacious bathroom, and a pair of bedrooms with air conditioning. Each bungalow had its own covered front porch with a patio table on it. In addition, each one had a spigot and rinse bucket with pegs mounted on the end wall of the large porch for rinsing and hanging wet dive gear.

***

I wasn't looking forward to another evening of sarcasm and backbiting either, but I went anyway. I saw Susan pull into the lot of the restaurant where the Literary Roundtable was meeting. She sat in her car for a couple minutes, hoping, I presumed, for a group to walk in and maybe sit with, unless of course it was a pack of Irina's groupies. I wished Irina wasn't scheduled to read her dreary and incomprehensible poetry. I sat in my car enjoying the air conditioning and delaying going into the battleground the meetings had become.

Susan stood in the parking lot under the blazing sun, looking woozy from the heat.

I got out of my car planning to go make sure she was all right.

When I saw Irina pull into the lot in her rattletrap of a Toyota and, beyond all reason, pull into the parking place right next to Susan's, I figured Susan felt trapped. Irina's eyes bored into Susan's as she gathered up her purse and pile of books and got out of her car. The two women, natural adversaries, stared at each other over the top of Susan's little yellow Morris Mini Cooper, the only one on the island.

"Are you coming in?" Irina asked with a smirk.

"I haven't decided," Susan said. "Are you planning to read many of your poems?"

"As many as time will allow. You look pale. Do you not feel up to the intellectual challenge today?"

That little verbal jab seemed to make up Susan's mind for her. No matter if she fainted from the heat, I could see that she'd be damned if she would let that Russian harpy think she had chased her away. "I wouldn't want to miss the opportunity to hear your lovely poems, Irina. They are so thought-provoking and insightful. Too bad they are so out of style."

The women bared their teeth at each other in grimaces that passed for smiles, turned, and, to the amazement of the assembled women, walked into the Literary Roundtable meeting together. I followed them at a safe distance.

The two women peeled off and went to sit with their respective group of supporters. I felt conspicuous finding a seat between the two groups, waiting for Miriam and Jane to arrive. I knew uncomfortably that I sided more with Susan than with the difficult-to-like Irina, but I was determined to stay neutral.

Jane was smiling when she sat down next to me. "Did you see Susan and the Czarina walk in together?"

"You call her that too?" I had to smother a laugh. "I was right behind them."

"When I pulled in and saw them walk in side by side, you could have knocked me over with a feather."

"You and me both. You should have heard the gasp when they came in. I had to equalize my ears from the vacuum the indrawn breaths caused."

***

"I'm Switzerland," I had told Iggy. "I have to stay out of the fight if I want them to consider steering their arriving friends to Seaview."

"That must be a hard thing to accomplish. Are there any other women who are trying to stay in the middle?"

"Yes, Miriam and Jane sit with me. Aside from the three of us, the expat community has pretty thoroughly divided itself into two camps. You're either on Susan's side or on Irina's. I'm having a hard time staying neutral. I wonder how the husbands are doing. I know that they've each taken up the other's hobby, which has to make for some interesting outings. They're friendly to each other when I've been at the snorkeling group events."

***

I stood next to Susan at the next dive and snorkel club sponsored burger fry. She puffed up like an angry blowfish when she saw George flipping ready-to-be-eaten burgers from the grill to buns on a tray held by Dimitri.

George came over to bring her a plate and soothe her

anger. "My dear, I'm not the one who controls things. It was accidental that he carried the buns when I called that the meat was done."

"I suppose," Susan said with a frown. She made sure that we sat as far from the Russians as possible.

CHAPTER 13

George and Dimitri

George felt as if the Cold War was re-engaged, and the Iron Curtain re-hung on their little desert island once the grapevine hummed. Battle lines were drawn when he and Susan went to the Vista Market a week after Billie's party. Small groups of women huddled at the meat counter and in front of the produce, whispering as they passed. Susan didn't speak to the women in the produce department. He questioned her with his eyes.

"They're Irina's friends," she said as they rounded the corner and stopped in front of the cheese display.

When they reached the meat counter, a pair of women, who looked to George remarkably like the ones that they had passed earlier, crowded around Susan cooing their sympathy and giving George appraising looks. She sent him off to pick out some cans of soup so the women could cluck and simper without the bother of George in the area.

Dimitri and Irina had much the same experience in IGA. Little clots of Susan-supporters looked daggers as they passed, and Irina's sympathizers shot her meaningful looks and squeezed her hands.

Dimitri didn't understand how the fact that their husbands had been professional adversaries years before made Irina and Susan enemies.

The almost instant choosing of sides that the women did puzzled George. Why did it matter to them what he and Dimitri had done? And why, if the governments of superpowers were willing to become friends, couldn't their wives?

***

Through all the whispering and gossiping, sniping and backbiting that went on among the women, neither George nor Dimitri let it get in their way. They met to share stories over coffee, made dates to go fishing or snorkeling, Dimitri introduced George to the joys of tramping through the countryside wearing hiking boots, a sturdy hat and carrying binoculars looking for birds that stopped on the island on their long migration.

Susan was slightly suspicious when George asked for a Caribbean bird identification guide and stronger binoculars as a gift for his sixty-seventh birthday that March. "I understand that Dimitri Roskova is an enthusiastic birder, George. He's the president of the local chapter of the Audubon Society. You're not spending too much time with him, are you? I'm sure there are many things he'd like to weasel out of you and pass on to his masters, even after all these years."

"No, dear, I'm not," he lied. "There's not so much for us retired old duffers to do on this island. That American chap, Jeremy Minten, is a big birder. He and I and a few other men have decided to see if we can't put together a new edition of that old bird guide they sell on the island. It was published in 1993 and is hopelessly out of date."

"Well, just steer clear of Roskova."

"Yes, dear."

***

Irina glared at Dimitri at the beginning of April when he expressed a need for a better mask and more comprehensive fish identification book when his seventy-second birthday was imminent. When she questioned him about his burgeoning interest in snorkeling, he answered that Mike Angerer and a few of the other husbands had a bet on who could identify the most fish before June first. They were planning to donate the pot to the Marine Preservation Society. "So much more fun than writing a check, don't you think?" he said to his suspicious wife.

"You're not getting too close to that Major George, are you?"

He put an arm around his frowning wife. "Of course not, dushka, I know you think he is an evil man." But that was a lie.

***

Soon after their first breakfast together, George and Dimitri realized their wives were, if anything, more vehemently opposed to détente than any two warring governments could ever be. They had agreed to keep their meetings secret; after all, they both had a lifetime's experience of keeping secrets. They were careful not to be seen alone in each other's company too often and then only in accidental meetings in the market or on the street.

There were long-standing groups of snorkelers and birders on Anguilla, so each man developed an interest in the other's favorite hobby. That way, they could say truthfully that while they saw each other at the outings, it was just casual contact. It was easy to keep up the charade during the winter months when the flood of tourists was heavy. The meeting dates and times of the snorkelers' club and birdwatchers group were published not only in the local newspaper but in the free paper distributed to each resort and shop on the island. Just as Rotary Clubs, Alcoholics Anonymous, and the various churches encouraged visitors who attended at home to attend on holiday, so did the bridge clubs, the avid tennis players, and other groups.

CHAPTER 14

Rose

Iggy and I arrived at Bachelor's Beach for the expats Thursday cookout and stood surveying the scene. We didn't attend every week, but Iggy had no jobs that afternoon, so we went.

Dimitri and Irina walked past us and set up their chairs and umbrella near the grove of scrubby trees on the north end of the beach.

I said to Iggy, "You see how they are? Irina and her supporters will be on one end of the beach. You watch. Susan and her supporters will be on the other."

"Where will we sit?"

"In the middle with Miriam and Jane." I pointed at them. "We're the only sane ones trying to stay out of the fight."

We carried our chairs, umbrella, and cooler to the sunny center of the beach by the two women and got set up.

Susan and George came next. I was amused, and a little exasperated, when Susan hooked a hand on George's elbow and dragged him off to the clump of trees near the southern end of the strip of sand.

George stumbled after his wife; his arms filled with beach paraphernalia. With her back rigid and her head held high, Susan marched down the beach with as much dignity as she could muster in the soft sand. "But, dear, shouldn't we sit closer to the group?" George said. "We're pretty far away from everyone here." He looked longingly down the beach at his new friend, sitting like a cowed dog next to his imperious wife.

A steady stream of cars and vans were pulling up and parking. One by one, couples crossed the parking area carrying coolers and beach chairs. The women would look up and down the beach. Then they'd steer their hapless husbands either right or left depending on how her sentiments lay, Susan to the right, Irina to the left.

At both ends of the beach there was a tight group of umbrellas, chairs, and frowning women. A few paces from each encampment (that's the only word to describe them) was a confused-looking group of husbands. The men edged toward each other across the barren, unshaded gap between the groups. They looked like boys trying to escape a too strict nanny. One by one they were called by their wives and one by one they turned and picked their way through the mild surf to dive into the sparkling blue ocean. A few of the women stood and hollered at their escaping husbands, but then realized how exposed they were to their archenemies, so they sat rather abruptly to preserve a bit of their dignity.

One by one, a woman from Susan's side would bring up her contribution to the cookout, then a woman from Irina's side would come forward. I felt sorry for them that their loyalty to one or the other prevented them from joining in one group. If it wasn't so sad, it would have been funny.

I took my bowl of fruit salad to the table by the grill and greeted the women I passed. Jane came with me, carrying the dish of her signature corn salad.

"Where did you get fresh corn?"

"At the produce market under the tree."

"Oh good, Harmony must be back from visiting her daughter. She's been away from the produce market for the last couple of weeks. I missed her good fresh produce. I'll have to stop and pick up some corn. Iggy loves it."

Jane turned to me as we walked back to our chairs. "Have you ever seen something this crazy go on so long?"

"No, I never have. It's too bad George and Dimitri can't

convince their wives that the other one is basically harmless and just bury the hatchet. Preferably not in each other's back."

***

Through all the whispering and gossiping that went on among the women, neither George nor Dimitri seemed to let it get in their way. I heard from Iggy's Auntie Bonita that they met regularly to share stories over coffee at the Rose Inn. When we all went snorkeling, Dimitri and George always buddied up. Dimitri introduced George to the joys of looking for birds that stopped on the island on their long migration to and from their winter grounds.

One evening at knitting, Susan said she was suspicious when George asked for a Caribbean bird identification guide and stronger binoculars as a gift for his sixty-seventh birthday that March. "I know that Roskova's a big deal in the birding group. He's the president of the local chapter of the Audubon Society. I told George I hoped he wasn't spending too much time with him."

"What did he say to that?" I asked.

"He told me that there isn't much for retired men to do in Anguilla. That American chap, Jeremy Minten, is a big birder. He and George and a few other men have decided to see if they can't put together a new edition of that old bird guide sold on the island. It was published in 1993 and is hopelessly out of date, at least according to George. The same birds must come back year after year." Susan looked down at the sweater sleeve she was knitting. "I just hope he's avoiding that Russian. He assured me he was."

"I'm sure he is." But I knew he wasn't since I saw them snorkeling together at every meeting.

We both went back to our knitting.

CHAPTER 15

Rose

I ran into Susan and George outside the secure area in Lloyd International Airport awaiting their old neighbors, Harriet and Max. I was waiting for a guest who hadn't rented a car and needed to be picked up.

One thing you have to understand about island airports is that security is either so tight no one and nothing escapes unscathed or so lax that you wonder if the guy in the uniform is some bigwig's unemployable nephew. On Anguilla, it varied but usually fell on the lax side. People passed in and out of the swinging security doors with barely a challenge. Some headed off to the line of rental car kiosks at the edge of the parking lot, others sought friends to enlist their help in carrying the pile of too much luggage they got on the plane. Nothing, especially anything official, moves swiftly on an island. It takes forever for the Immigration people to work through the line of incoming passengers. We could see them straggle across the tarmac and line up in the tropical sun to wait their turn. One couple argued the entire way to the terminal. I hoped that wasn't Max and Harriet.

Then the passengers have to stand around by the single baggage carousel waiting for about half an hour while two scrawny guys haul all the baggage and cargo out of the plane. By the time arriving passengers get to that point, they've been trotting around the globe for at least that entire day. They'd been dragging themselves and their increasingly heavy carry-on bags through increasingly smaller airports with increasingly more Machiavellian customs agents impressed with the gravity of their importance on the front lines of world security.

Susan and George had been at the airport early and watched the plane land. They were accustomed to the long wait for Immigration and the luggage to arrive. Since my guest was on the same flight, they invited me to sit in the airport bar and have a drink with them while George enthused about all the dive sites he and Max would visit and how he hoped to interest him in bird watching. Knowing that Dimitri was one leader of that group made Susan frown, but I was relieved that she held her tongue to avoid starting an argument just as their friends arrived.

Once arriving passengers started trickling out of the baggage area, the three of us walked out of the bar. I had a sheet on a clipboard with "Parker" written on it in big letters so that my guest could find me. A young-ish woman with a brunette ponytail and a stuffed backpack came up to me and said, "Hi, I'm Trisha Parker. You must be Rose."

"Yes, I'm Rose. Is that all your luggage?"

She nodded and hitched the heavy pack higher on her shoulders. "Everything I need is in here."

"Then let's go." I turned and waved goodbye to Susan and George and led my guest out to my car parked at the arrivals area.

***

The morning after Harriet and Max arrived, I saw George and Max next door at Tamarind and went over to say hi. They were loading gear into the back of the Rover.

"Good, you've got two tanks each," Max said. "I was afraid we were only doing a single tank. Do you have weights for me too?"

"I do," George said. "Ten pounds, just like you said."

Max unfolded a map of Anguilla's dive sites on the hood of the vehicle. "Where to first?"

I had to smile. Trust a Navy man to latch onto the first map he finds and want to plan an assault.

"We're going to start at Mead's Bay." George pointed. "It's got an easy sand entry and good parking. Plus, once you get your weights set in the shallows, we can drop over the lip of the reef and hit one hundred plus feet if you're of a mind to."

Max broke into a big grin. "Oh, I've a mind to all right. I've been searching out this island on the Internet and I have a long list of sites I'd like to dive. Good thing we'll be here a month."

George laughed too, happy to have an old friend by his side. "Good thing. I'm glad you're here to dive with, not that there is anything wrong with the chaps around here, but I know I don't have to worry about you in the water. I spend half of my dives lately counting heads, making sure some joker hasn't swum off into the deep."

"Are they that inexperienced?"

"Not really. A few of them like to brag they were Navy SEALS, and they might have been, but it's a good long time since then and I would wager they have not been keeping their skills sharp. Plus, it's too easy to forget to monitor your gauges. There's too much to look at and the water is so clear it's easy to go too deep chasing a fish you want to take a picture of. They're not like Rose here. She's an excellent buddy."

Max nodded. "Ah." He lifted his right hand. "I vow to be a good little diver, sir."

"Too right, you will."

Then Max grinned at him and added, "At least when you are around."

George closed the back of the Rover and said, "Time to get a move on. Talk to you later, Rose."

"Have fun, guys." I waved and went back to Seaview to start the laundry.

**

When Iggy got home later that afternoon, I was making supper. He gave me a kiss and said, "I stopped at my house to find George and Max just coming out of the water from a dive. I talked to them as they got out of their gear and dried off. They wanted to rinse their gear in the garden hose, so I let them while I went inside to fetch three beers."

"That was nice of you."

"I am a nice guy. George asked if he could use my bathroom and while he was inside, Max packed his gear, pulling a manila envelope from his bag. It had an official-looking seal on it. Max put the envelope on the passenger seat and covered it with his towel."

"Hm, sounds interesting. Did you see where it came from?"

"No. I wondered what it was, but did not like to ask since Max tried to keep me from seeing it. After they left, I mowed the yard and picked up some fallen palm fronds, then I locked up and came home. On the way, I saw George's Range Rover backed into an access road by the lighthouse. It looked like he was reading a letter. I wonder what kind of letter Max would have delivered by hand and in an official-looking envelope."

I looked at him leaning against the kitchen island, his arms folded across his chest. "That's intriguing. I'd love to know what it said."

CHAPTER 16

George

In service to Her Majesty,

    It has come to our attention that living on the island of Anguilla, British West Indies, is a former Soviet agent (Cover: university professor) by the name of Dimitri Roskova. Roskova was the lead suspect in the investigation into the leaking of information concerning the Army's research and development of an anti-gravity propulsion system being conducted at a facility outside Boscombe Down in Wiltshire.

    During our investigation after the discovery that vital formulae and the diagrams of prototypes had been leaked, all trails pointed to a senior technologist on the project, a woman named Talia Shoreham. It was determined that Ms. Shoreham (37 years of age & unmarried) was the sole member of the group, aside from the principals, who had access to both formulae and diagrams. The investigation revealed that Ms. Shoreham, a lonely spinster according to co-workers, had taken a night class offered by her local university in Russian Literature taught by Dimitri Roskova.

    Approximately halfway through term, Ms. Shoreham and Roskova were meeting at a café in the nearby town alone. Employees of the café reported that Ms. Shoreham and Roskova engaged in lively discussions pertaining to the material covered in the course and not much else. No other meetings between Ms. Shoreham and Roskova were witnessed or reported. Close questioning on numerous occasions of Ms. Shoreham's *acquaintances did not produce any further information about their relationship. She came to the head of the suspects list when it was learned that in the week afterward; she met a last time with Roskova, again in public at the café, and upon the day after that meeting, she ended her life by her own hand.*

Shortly after the discovery of the leaking of the project information, Roskova's faculty exchange term ended, and he returned to Moscow.

In view of the fact that the Army researchers are still laboring to develop an anti-gravity propulsion system and have discerned hints from their opposite numbers in Russia that they too are near to perfecting a similar system, we would like you to insinuate yourself in Roskova's confidence and determine whether he did indeed use his position and Ms. Shoreham's infatuation with him and all things Russian to steal this information.

We would appreciate your immediate action in this matter. We anticipate hearing from you soonest. This is a matter of national security.

If you are discovered during the pursuit of this matter, we will, of course, disallow all knowledge of you or your actions.

M.

CHAPTER 17

George and Susan

"You were a long time," Susan said when George walked in. "Did you drop off the tanks to be refilled?" It surprised her when he walked straight through the kitchen without a word. She looked up from assembling a salad with leftover roasted chicken for their lunch. "George?" She watched his retreating back cross the living room and disappear behind the curtain over the door of the little room off the dining area he called his snug. Susan saw his hand swing behind him as if he were slamming a door. She waited a minute and then followed him. She stood politely at the curtain. "George? Are you all right?"

No answer.

"May I come in?"

George's voice rumbled toward her. "I would rather you did not."

"Did you and Max have an argument?"

"No."

She left the doorway and started back toward the kitchen and her salad. She got halfway, turned around, walked back, and flung the curtain aside.

George looked up from his desk, where he was staring down at a piece of paper lying on the surface.

"What is that?" she asked.

"A letter."

"From whom?"

"My new handler."

Susan felt her stomach twist and her whole body turn cold. "Your new handler? What do you mean?"

He laid his hands down softly on either side of the paper. "Just what I said. This is from my new handler. She's giving me a job to do."

"Where?" Susan held her hands clenched tightly into fists protectively at her waist.

"Right here," he said.

She let out a long breath. "I was afraid they were sending you to the Middle East."

"No, they want me to do a job right here." He paused; his lips pursed as if he had tasted something nasty. "And I don't want to have anything to do with it."

They were both silent, each of them thinking about how their enjoyment of retirement had been destroyed.

Susan spoke first. "Dimitri?"

He nodded.

"What can I do to help?" she asked.

"Stop fighting with Irina."

"You know about that?"

His smile was small and sad. "Of course, I do. Just like I know that bitch Billie Holland-Smythe deliberately set us up at her party."

"Now, George, you don't know that for a fact."

He kept talking. "And I know she couldn't wait to report our arrival to her bastard of a brother, Bertie."

"And Bertie used to work in your office."

"Yes. I always thought that even in the profession of tale carriers, Bertram Scott was the epitome of tattletales. He took a perverse pleasure in exposing traitors. Never once did he express admiration for our adversaries, who did the same job only from the other side. It was obvious he thought we were in the right and everyone else was wrong. A petty and vindictive man. It's a good thing he's dead, or I'd have it out with him."

Susan gulped at the menace in her husband's voice and sat in the chair across the desk from him. "How will my stopping fighting with that pretentious bitch help?"

George had to smile at her vehemence. "It will lower her guard, allowing me to more openly make friends with Dimitri, making my job easier and much quicker."

She squinted at him. "What do you mean more openly? Have you already been making friends with him?"

"Of course I have, dear. When else have I ever had a friend with similar work experience? All the men I worked with had covers that did not allow us to fraternize naturally. We didn't all live in an enclave and our supposed jobs were too disparate to allow for believable contact. None of us even went to the same schools, which could explain a friendship. Only when we arrived here did I find a man I felt had similar life experiences and would understand me. That is Dimitri."

Susan was horrified. "You haven't told…"

His answer carried a load of scorn. "Of course, I haven't. And neither has he. But we had similar general experiences, we could share that at least." She started to speak, but he held up a hand to silence her. The silence stretched long and unbearable, and then he muttered. "And now I lose even that."

She reached across the desk and put her hand on his. "I will do what I can to help." The sound of feet coming up the broken coral "lawn" reminded them of their guests. "I had better finish that chicken salad," she said as she rose. "You take them out to the patio and serve drinks. I made a pitcher of sangria. It's in the fridge."

He turned his back to the curtain that acted as a door, leaned over and dialed open the safe that was fitted into the credenza behind his desk. With the letter back in its envelope and safely on the shelf, he checked the desktop for any stray items. He pushed himself out of his chair, grunting as if he had suddenly aged ten years. He shuffled to the patio like an old man.

As soon as George had poured the sangria, Max lifted his glass and walked to the end of the patio facing the ocean.

Harriet picked up her glass and went back into the kitchen, saying, "I'll just keep Susan company."

George sat, his untouched drink making a ring of condensation on the glass top of the table.

Max sat down opposite George as Harriet left. George felt Max's eyes on his face. "Looks like the news was as bad as you expected."

"It was."

Max sipped his drink. "I know I shouldn't ask, but are you going to accept?"

George picked up his drink and downed it in one long swallow. "I don't see a way around it. We are told that we take a lifetime oath, you see. And they take pains to remind you of it when you retire."

"Same with the Navy," Max said.

George was silent while he poured himself another drink. "This stuff is refreshing." He sipped. "Gives me a bit of retroactive sympathy for the chaps who got called back while I was still active. Explains a lot about the shell-shocked look about them too."

"Anything I can do to help?"

George shook his head. "Turns out I had already begun. We'll just go on as normal. You're on holiday, after all."

Max opened his mouth to respond, but the sound of their wives bringing out the lunch silenced him.

The meal began with very little chat beyond compliments to Susan for making such a delicious salad.

George assumed that Susan had said something to Harriet because she didn't seem confused by the lack of cheerful conversation. He roused himself to get the group to think of something else. "So, Harriet, are you ready to have Susan take you round the local bazaars this afternoon?"

Harriet looked up in surprise and then smiled. "I think so. I've been saving a few pence that Max doesn't know about." She smiled at the faux frown on her husband's face. "Don't you worry, love." She patted his hand. "I won't break the bank for a few trinkets." Then she turned to Susan. "Didn't you mention an art group meeting today?"

Susan nodded. "Yes, but not until seven this evening. We will have plenty of time to cruise through the shops, such as they are, before then."

***

Their shopping trip seemed cursed. Everywhere she turned, Susan saw one of Irina's groupies.

In Malabar there was a trio of the women who made certain to sit around Irina at Literary Roundtable meetings as if it were their job to cordon Irina off from attack. Susan thought of them as Larry, Moe, and Curly, the Three Stooges of the expatriate women. They were Polish and evidently felt some sort of loyalty toward one of their former oppressors. As soon as they spied Susan, they stopped talking and crossed their arms over their not inconsiderable chests. Their glares followed Susan around the store as she and Harriet flipped the racks, discussing which of their daughters, daughters-in-law, and granddaughters might like what they were seeing. It was no better in Littman's; at least one of Irina's supporters was in Littman's jewelry, another one in Littman's upscale gifts, and a pair of them in Littman's touristy gift shop. Littman's had covered all the bases to serve the needs of each and every visitor to the island, no matter what their economic status.

Irina herself was in Mama Vita's, the bargain clothing store at the end of the street. Mama Vita's was just too small for the three of them to be in, so Susan pulled Harriet back out onto the street and across to Island Fashions, saying, "She won't follow us over here. I understand the Russians' pension is barely enough to survive on much less shop in this expensive store."

Harriet kept her mouth shut and just nodded.

CHAPTER 18

Rose

Trisha was an energetic addition to the guests at Seaview. She was up early running on the beach. One morning, she took the launch out to Sandy Island to snorkel. She rented a kayak from The Hook and paddled all around Road Bay one afternoon.

On Sunday, she came down to Johnno's for the jump-up. Before Iggy and I left, I saw Julius the local gigolo dancing her around to a slow song, talking in her ear the whole time, but she just thanked him for the dance and found another partner.

On Monday Silas came in to beg a muffin and said, "That Trisha danced every dance and with just about every man in the place. I think she was the last one to leave the floor at the jump-up. She is the one who can give Edward a run for his money."

"I don't know where she gets her energy. She seems to be in constant motion." I dried the last plate and started putting the breakfast things away.

Geneva leaned on the kitchen island, smiling at Silas. "That girl is going to burn herself out if she is not careful. I have never seen someone move around like she does."

Trisha came into the kitchen holding her water bottle. "I'm going to fill this up and go for a hike. I hear there's a trail that starts at the end of the road here in Sandy Ground and winds up the hill and along the cliff above the water. Have you hiked it? I'll bet the view is amazing." She put the water pitcher back into the fridge and turned to leave, waving goodbye over her shoulder before any of us had the chance to respond. "See you all later."

My other guests that week were more sedate, a little less manic in their vacationing. There was a middle-aged couple from New Hampshire who spent their days driving around to all the cultural sites they could find. I told them about the petroglyphs at Sandy Hill Bay and they were excited to visit. They visited The Old Valley with its cobblestone streets, shops with traditional crafts, and quaint cafes. One evening, they took Trisha with them to a program of indigenous music and dance that all three of them seemed to enjoy immensely.

The remaining two guests were retired teachers who were friends of Miriam and Jane's. They left right after breakfast and came back just before I locked up for the night. Betty and Linda were very complimentary about what I served for breakfast and said that the beds were the most comfortable they'd slept in on vacation in years. I asked them to be sure to put that in their review. It was just the publicity I needed.

I was happy that Seaview had been full for the last weeks. Every time I checked my bank balance, I felt even happier. Iggy had been busy, too. He'd begun to get a lot of phone calls from the expat community for minor jobs, like fixing light switches and rewiring plugs. Adding to his bank balance made him happy, too.

***

I invited Susan and Harriet over to Seaview for lunch one afternoon shortly after Harriet and Max arrived. Harriet told me she was especially happy to be away. Her mother had been ill most of the last year and since Harriet lived the closest, she was the sibling who spent the most time caring for her mum. Her sisters and brothers had helped when they could, but it was Harriet who drove Mum to the doctor's visits and to the hospital for her treatment and then spent the next two days staying with her to make sure she didn't die of the cure. Harriet said she was tired, too tired to face living with Susan and George for their vacation month, unwilling to engage in endless conversations, and felt guilty when she said that she needed time alone. So, it was with gratitude she embraced Susan's suggestion that she arrange a bungalow for them to rent, near to Susan and George's house, but still apart. Harriet knew that Max and George would spend the month speeding around the island scuba diving and fishing, so she was looking forward to having a few days to herself to read or just sit and loll under a palm tree with a glass of iced tea. She had written to Susan telling her how much she looked forward to having a few hours alone and was relieved when Susan wrote back that she totally understood and had not planned a month-long whirlwind of activities, anyway.

Harriet said she was happy that she wouldn't have to keep her company face on all month and lightheartedly embraced the tiring travel to the island. "I was disappointed that Anguilla wasn't the lush, flower-filled island of my dreams, but after a few days I decided that the sparse vegetation was easier on the eyes." She said she loved her little bungalow with its full kitchen and many windows that let the island breezes blow through. She thought she could happily spend the rest of her mornings sitting on the covered patio watching the sunrise and listening to the birds.

After that outpouring of words, I felt like I knew too much about Harriet, but she was Susan's friend, so I chalked it up to her way of over sharing.

We were just finishing up our lunch out on the patio when Harriet touched my arm and said, "Rose, there's a man poking around in your refrigerator."

I glanced in through the screen door to see the man pull a white basket out and set it on the kitchen island. "Oh, that's one of my guests. They're allowed to keep a basket of lunch food in there, so they don't have to go out for every meal. I have a microwave on the sideboard in the lobby for them to use to reheat leftovers, you know, doggie bags too. It works out well for everyone."

"You're very trusting," she said. "Aren't you afraid they'll eat your food?"

"Not really. On the whole, people are pretty honest. Oh,

there are some who try to pull a fast one and wheedle their way into cooking in my kitchen, but that's expressly forbidden by the Health Department, and I don't want to step over the line. I keep a grill out here for their use if they want to cook."

Susan chimed in. "That's why you and Max aren't staying here, Harriet. There's no place to cook, and you said that you wanted to make meals."

"Does each room have an *en suite* bathroom?" Harriet asked.

I shook my head. "No, there are two bathrooms, one in the center of each side of the hall. People have to share, but there are sinks in the corner of each room for washing up, shaving, and toothbrushing. It seems to work out well for my guests."

"Oh no, I wouldn't want to share a bathroom. You never know what germs people have. Sorry, Rose."

"No apology needed, Harriet. It's not for everyone. I charge a little less than places where each room has its own bath, so the people who stay here get a bit of a discount for the inconvenience." I gathered up the lunch plates and silverware onto a tray. "I'm going to carry this inside. Anyone want more iced tea or lemonade?"

Susan stood up, too. "No thanks. We're going over to Miriam and Jane's to play bridge for the afternoon. Sorry to eat and run."

"No problem. Enjoy your afternoon." I set down the tray and walked around the table to hug Susan. "Thanks for coming and bringing Harriet." I turned and hugged Harriet, too. "It was lovely to meet you and get to spend a little time with you. I'm sure we'll see each other again before you leave for home. How long are you staying?"

"Until the end of the month."

"Then I'm certain we'll meet again. Probably at a cookout."

Susan and Harriet picked up their bags and walked to the side of the yard and out through the gap in the bougainvillea hedge, waving as they turned into the road. I carried the lunch things into the kitchen and washed the dishes right away, so they didn't attract bugs.

Geneva came into the kitchen carrying the broom and dustpan. "I cannot stay ahead of the sand that gets tracked in. No matter how often I sweep, there is always a pile of it to throw back out onto the beach." She walked into the back room to hang the broom and dustpan on the hook, then came back into the kitchen. "I can finish washing those dishes, Mrs. Rose."

"I'm nearly finished. You can either dry dishes or you can leave for the day. I think we have everything taken care of."

"I will dry the dishes and then go down to see Silas."

The budding romance between Silas, who helped refurbish Seaview, and Geneva, my housekeeper, made me very happy. They were two wonderful young people, and I was enjoying watching the slow dance of their courtship. I also wondered if I had the same sappy smile on my face when I saw Iggy that Silas had when he caught sight of Geneva. Iggy's emotions were always more controlled than mine.

***

Phones rang all over the island, helped along by Harriet's confidential conversations with nearly every expatriate on the island, me included. Harriet spent most of her afternoons when she was resting in her bungalow chatting on her cell phone to each of her new best friends, swearing us to secrecy, and then detailing her suspicions that George spent his working life as a spy.

"And I'm sure he was a big one, one of the higher ups. He was always jetting off to places like Moscow and Warsaw. Hotbeds of commies, those places are."

I didn't believe in spreading gossip, but I'm sure the wires hummed with that little tidbit and others, claiming that Dimitri and George had been long-time enemies, spying on each other throughout their careers.

Because of her years of living next door to Susan and George, and that her husband, Max, had been in the Royal Navy and had a top-secret clearance, Harriet's words were taken as fact. I suspected she had a vivid imagination and a convincing way of confiding things that made what she said believable. I couldn't imagine that George and Susan wouldn't be angered by Harriet's gossip.

Like dominoes falling, rumors flew from lips to ears around the small island. Both George and Dimitri's reputations surged or fell depending upon where the sympathies of the teller lay.

"My dear, I heard Dimitri shot George years ago. Susan nursed him for months, vowing revenge on Roskova. That's why she and Irina are always at loggerheads."

The expatriate women latched onto the juicy gossip details that greased the phone lines around the island.

"Did you hear Susan had an affair with Dimitri? That's why Irina hates her."

"George should retaliate and have a little, well, you know, interlude with Irina."

"With Irina? I can't imagine her climbing down from her high horse far enough to actually have sex."

"Oh, you're terrible, but I love it." These, of course, were Susan's friends.

Irina's followers were different. "I heard Dimitri shot George when they were both working as spies years ago."

"I heard that too. I'll bet Irina wishes Dimitri's aim had been better."

A gasp and a giggle. "What a terrible thing to say!"

"But I'll bet she does."

All of that filtered down to me through overheard talk at the market or whispers at parties. A few people called to clue me in to what was being said, but since I wasn't retired and not really an active part of the expat community, I assumed what I heard was just the tip of the iceberg. And since I didn't pass any of it on, I was the end of the line for a lot of gossip.

Art League and Literary Roundtable meetings became even more divided. No longer did women circulate around the room, discussing art or books and sharing news. Now there was a definite "no-man's-land" down the center of the gathering, no one willing to risk censure by crossing over to the other camp. Only Miriam, Jane, and I sat in that "no-man's-land."

CHAPTER 19

Rose

A birding tour group from Hungary visited the birdwatchers. Four of the Hungarians stayed at Seaview. I was worried at first about what they'd expect for breakfast. I looked online to see what a traditional Hungarian breakfast comprised and found it was bread and sausage and jam. That fit pretty well with my standard breakfasts, so I stopped worrying. Like I had with other early rising guests, I set up the coffee pots the night before so all they had to do was flip the switch to have fresh brewed coffee before they set out at first light. I left plates of muffins and sausages in the fridge that they could microwave, so they didn't go off with empty stomachs on the days that they left for their dawn outings. I didn't want hungry Hungarians complaining about me.

The leader of the tour group spent his first afternoon in Anguilla snoozing on a towel on the beach. I was worried that he would get sunburned, but he said that he never got too much sun. It turned out his usual vacation spot was a lake in central Hungary with northern latitude sun, not the intense sun of the Caribbean. When he came in from his nap, he was red as a lobster and in some pain. I sent him up to Vista Market for some aloe lotion, which helped with the pain and diminished the heat of the burn. He was much more careful during the rest of his stay and his example kept the others from also getting too much sun.

They came back from Johnno's in the evenings, laughing and singing in Hungarian. A couple of them praised the comfort and cleanliness of the accommodations. One of them, a man who looked like a university professor with thinning light brown hair and sparkling brown eyes, kept flirting with me. I assumed that was the regular way he treated waitstaff and store clerks. I smiled at him but didn't think I was giving him any encouragement, treating him with the same detachment I treated the rest of the guests.

He told me his name was Dominik, and he was a widower. "I have a successful practice in Budapest. You would like it there."

I smiled at him and said, "Maybe someday my husband and I will visit."

He grabbed my hand as I served his breakfast. "You could come home with me on Saturday. We would be very happy."

I looked around at the other guests, who were studiously staring at their plates. No help there. I twisted my hand from his grasp and stepped back. "No, thank you. I'm a newlywed and am very happy here with my husband." And went back into the kitchen.

While I was doing up the breakfast dishes, I felt arms slide around my waist. I said, "You finished work early, Iggy, but I'm glad you're back." I hummed my pleasure and leaned back into an unfamiliar chest. Whirling around, I pushed the Hungarian away. "Dominik, stop that. I am a married woman, and I'm not interested."

"Do not be that way, baby. Okay, then we can be sweethearts for just one week. Your husband will not even know. He is off working." The middle-aged man who evidently thought he was a legendary lover raised his hands and reached out to me. "I can make you very happy if you give me the chance."

"No. No chances. I am not your baby. I'm not anybody's baby. Now go... watch birds."

He ducked between my dripping hands and clasped me around the waist again. His puckered lips grazed my cheek, and I tried to push him away.

"Let me go."

He held me even tighter. "You will not get away from me. I can take care of you."

I looked him in the eyes and said, "I told you no." Then I raised my leg and kneed him in the groin.

"Oof," he said and let me go to grab his privates.

The voice of the group leader came from the door into the lobby. "Come, Dominik, you have picked the wrong woman again. It is time to go birdwatching."

My would-be lover looked up from his crouch, raised a hand, and said in a croak, "Coming. Give me a minute."

I fixed the leader with a stern look. "You get control of Dominik, or I'll have to ask you all to leave."

He grunted and gave a brief nod.

I thought it would be a good idea to warn Geneva about him, so she didn't get manhandled, too.

***

When the local birdwatchers hosted a sunrise pancake breakfast for the visiting tour of European birders, I was invited. I had just sat down with a plate of banana pancakes and a cup of coffee when I saw Irina arrive to catch Dimitri standing alongside George, one serving coffee and tea, the other offering various juices. She was incensed and started berating her husband in front of everyone about being seen with the Brit.

"Irina, dushka, it was not my fault," Dimitri said as he escorted her to a seat with the leader of the tour group. "Jeremy asked me to pour the coffee and what could I say? No, my wife wouldn't like it? It's too early to make an embarrassing explanation like that."

"What do you mean 'too early'?"

"Too early in the morning, dear. Now, can I get you a cup of tea and some of Bibi's delicious banana pancakes?" He introduced Irina to the tour group leader, an earnest bespectacled and sunburned man from Hungary who was a fan of Irina's poetry, knowing that a morning's flattery would dilute her irritation at seeing him standing next to George. I was standing in line for more coffee when Dimitri came to get the tea he had promised his wife. He leaned toward George and said, "That was close."

"Uh, huh. I'm ignoring you from now on today, friend." George poured more guava juice for one of the Hungarian lady tourists with a smile. "Your wife may be beautiful, but I'm afraid of her."

"Me, too."

***

That night I came home from another Literary Roundtable meeting in a rotten mood. "I'm so tired of the backbiting and sniping the women are doing."

Iggy put down his book. "Maybe you should stop going for a while."

I sat down next to him on the loveseat in our apartment sitting room. "I don't feel like I can. I want to stay in touch with the expat women and Literary Roundtable and the Art League are basically the only places that I see them. Aside from chance encounters in the markets, that is."

"Do you think they will forget you if you are not at the meetings?"

I snuggled into his shoulder. "I don't know. We aren't really a part of the expat community."

Iggy laughed, jiggling my head. "I am their pet native electrician."

"Don't say that."

"Well, it is true. They only invite us to their parties and cookouts because they want to stay in my good graces when their lights go out or their stoves stop working. I can see how virtuous they feel about having a native friend. They go out of their way to be friendly and not prejudiced, but their long-held feelings come through. I am not of their class, and it shows. I only get invited because you get invited. No other Anguillans are ever at their parties except the servers and the musicians."

I stood up and paced. "Oh, I hoped you hadn't noticed that. I heard that Billie Holland-Smythe tries to pretend that she is friends with Geneva's sister Minerva, who is Billie's housekeeper.

Billie calls her Minnie and wants her to sit and gossip when she brings her breakfast tray, but Minerva does her best to preserve her dignity and doesn't unbend."

Iggy threw back his head and laughed. "I know Minerva. Mrs. Holland-Smythe will never get her to answer to Minnie. She is too much of a lady for that childish nickname."

"Do you think I should be more formal with Geneva?" I stopped pacing to look at him. "I think it makes her uncomfortable when I ask her to share lunch with me. I'd like her to be a friend and an employee, but I feel that's not the way things go in this society."

"You should be more formal with her. That is what she expects. You can offer her lunch, but do not be offended if she declines."

"Okay, I'll try. I wish you were a snorkeler or a birdwatcher, then you could join the men's groups and maybe they'd accept you as an equal instead of the condescending way they treat you now."

Iggy stood up and grasped my upper arms. "That would not help. I would stick out even more in those groups. Those men are much more educated than I am, and they would talk down to me or talk around me while still pretending that I am their equal. Nice try, but it would not work."

"But all the Anguillans I have met welcomed me with open arms. Or am I fooling myself that they treat me the same way they treat each other?"

"You are fooling yourself a little. It will take a long time for people to get used to you and see Rose instead of a white American woman who married a native man."

I shrugged out of his grasp. "It shouldn't make any difference. People are people, no matter the color of their skin. We all started from the same place in Africa, so we're all related. I don't understand why skin color is such a divisive thing. White people spend hours outside getting a tan and then they look down on people whose skin is naturally that color. I just don't get it."

He stepped in front of me and used his finger to tilt my chin up so he could look me in the eye. "I know you do not. That is one of the things I love about you."

I slid my arms around his waist. "I'm tired. Let's turn in. I'm tired of all this fuss and bother."

***

Low voices woke me in the wee hours. One was the gravelly voice of Dominik, and the female voice was oddly familiar, and one I would never expect to hear in Seaview in the middle of the night. I crept through the kitchen to where I could peek into the lobby. There Dominik stood in his bathrobe, kissing Irina Roskova. It was all I could do to keep from gasping. He carefully unlocked the front door and, lit by the glow from the porch light, pulled her into his arms, his hand loosening her hair from its clasp. They shared a passionate embrace before he let her go. Both of them murmured their affection for each other. One of her hands reached up to stroke his cheek, and then she was gone. Dominik watched her walk away before carefully closing the door and relocking it. In the light of the small lamp on the registration desk, I saw his satisfied grin as he headed to his room.

"Good night, Rose," he said as he reached the top of the stairs.

I inhaled and retreated into the dark kitchen. He must have seen me in the doorway because I hadn't made a sound. I knew I would blush when serving his breakfast in the morning, and I imagined he would wear a look of self-satisfaction that he had made one conquest on the island.

Had they met at the birders' breakfast that morning and been drawn together? Were they old lovers surprised to see each other again and couldn't resist one last tryst? The cold and self-contained Irina I was familiar with from the literary and art groups was in vivid contrast to the soft and passionate woman I saw leaving my bed-and-breakfast in the middle of the night.

I hurried back to bed, but had some trouble falling back to sleep. What would happen if Dimitri found out?

CHAPTER 20

George

After midnight that night, Susan awoke. She padded barefoot to the top of the stairs and saw a dim light coming from the end of the dining area. She knew that meant he was in the snug on his secure line, communicating with his handler.

***

In the days that followed, George made sure Harriet and Max were having the holiday they expected. He also stopped Susan from asking every time he had been away from home how things were going.

"But I want this to be done."

"As do I," he told her. "But you must let me do my job my way and not ask questions. *Secret* agent, remember?"

"Yes, I remember," she said with a laugh that threatened to turn into a sob.

"I'm back to being one, my love, at least for a little while, but I'm going to insist that this will be the last."

"Can you?"

George frowned into space. "I'll try. If I can get the information they are looking for, perhaps they will be more agreeable."

"I hope you're right. This is not the retirement I imagined."

He stepped in front of her and wrapped his arms around her, squeezing her tightly to his chest. "You have been an excellent wife. I will do my best to finish this job quickly and insist that they leave us alone to spend our declining years together."

She pulled back to look him straight in the eye. "I, for one, am not declining."

He smiled down at her. "Neither am I, but we don't have to tell my handler that, now do we?"

They stood in their embrace for a few more minutes, reveling in the last quiet moment they would have for a long time.

***

The next few times George saw Dimitri at the snorkelers and birders' meetings, he was much more aware of the Russian's behavior. He was trying to discover if Dimitri had received a similar letter from his own handlers, but Dimitri seemed the same as before. George tried to be the same man he had been before the detested letter arrived, but wasn't sure he could be. He was glad that Max was on the island and gave him an excuse to move around introducing him to the other expatriate men.

"Jeremy and Mike, this is my neighbor from home, Max Fitzpatrick. He and his wife Harriet are visiting for a month."

Jeremy thrust his hand out to shake. "Nice to meet you, Max. I hope you enjoy your stay on our little island."

Mike clapped Max on the shoulder. "Welcome."

George talked to Dimitri as he had before, trying not to seem more guarded, but wasn't sure how successful he was. He took Dimitri aside at the snorkelers outing. "Dimitri, I don't want Max telling Susan that you and I are friendly, so I plan to ignore you while he's on the island."

Dimitri seemed to understand. "I will say nothing to Irina about it, either."

George knew he could not get Dimitri alone while Max was on the island; the responsibilities of being host required George to pal around with Max. At first, that responsibility delayed his opportunities to probe into Dimitri's relationship with the sad and unfortunate Ms. Shoreham. Then George realized he could say something to Max in Dimitri's hearing to pave the way for a broader discussion. Max's youngest brother had attended the University of Hertfordshire at the same time Dimitri was there on his exchange, although Roderick was in the Math Department. Asking how Roddy was doing would be a good segue into asking Dimitri about his time there.

An unexpected opportunity came at the next birder's meeting before he had worked the subject into conversation when Max and Dimitri were together. Max decided he was not interested in bird watching enough to get up before dawn to drive up to Windward Point. So George called Jeremy to ask him to tell Dimitri that he could pick him up.

As he idled the Rover a block from Roskova's house, George felt guilty but also a familiar tingling he recognized as the adrenaline surge he could count on just before embarking on a new job. He had always thought of his missions as "a job." He felt that calling them missions gave them a false weight, like he was expected to act like that poseur, James Bond.

Everyone who had ever watched one of those fantastic movies thought espionage was littered with nubile women in bikinis eager to remove said bikini at the drop of a martini. People thought all spies had watches that shot bullets or poison, an Aston Martin sports car that either sprayed oil to make pursuers slide off the road or flew, and a pen that was a radio.

George's favorite Bond gadget was a tiny mouthpiece with what looked like a pair of CO_2 cartridges attached that allowed Bond to breathe underwater. He heard the military had called the movie producer asking where the technology had come from. His faith in the leaders of England's military had fallen quite a few notches upon learning that. How gullible could they be? he wondered.

His thoughts were cut short when he saw Dimitri turn the corner, his binoculars swinging on his chest, a bottle of water in a pouch on his belt, and an enormous hat clamped on his head.

"Good morning, George," he said when he opened the door. "Did your friend Max decide this was too early?"

George chuckled. "Yes, he did. Remember, he's on holiday.

I couldn't very well drag him from his bed and order him along."

Dimitri looked up from latching his seat belt. "No, I suppose you could not. I cannot say I am sorry he did not come. I have missed our little chats these past weeks."

George felt a small pang of guilt. He was not enthusiastic about his job and wished Max had never handed him that envelope. "I've missed them too," he said.

Driving up the island in the pre-dawn darkness, they talked about the birds they hoped to see. Rumor said there was a Caracara nest near the cliffs, and everyone hoped to be the one to spot it. George kept the conversation rolling on mundane lines like the jump in petrol prices and how hard it was becoming to find good meat. They talked about the snorkeling group's plans for a big barbecue the next week that Dimitri had volunteered to chair. "Mike has promised to bring some of his special sauce for us. I am very fond of that sauce."

George said, "I think everyone is. Susan wheedled a jar from Ali, and she puts it on everything. I'm afraid to walk from the shower to my closet without a towel on, if you know what I mean."

Dimitri looked a bit shocked, the dashboard lights giving him a skeletal look, and then he burst out laughing. "Oh, George, you are terrible. Now I can never look at your beautiful Susan without thinking of her stalking you down the hall, a jar of Mike's barbecue sauce in her hand."

George chuckled along with him, happy that his oblique introduction of sex into the conversation had been so successful.

The sun had risen enough to turn the clouds in the east a rosy pink when they arrived at the designated spot. There were six cars there ahead of them and they could see Jeremy putting the teams together. George parked the Rover at the end of the row and got his hat, binoculars, and water bottle from the rear seat. He and Dimitri joined the group just as Jeremy finished pairing up the men standing in front of him.

Jeremy turned and said, "I guess you two latecomers will have to be team number seven." He pulled a sheaf of maps from his backpack and handed one to each team member. "You notice that I have divided our watch area into sections. Each section is numbered. The section number corresponds to your team number."

George was glad to see the numeral seven on a patch right up against the cliff facing the sea.

Dimitri nudged George. "You see, Jeremy has given us the best chance, I am thinking. The Caracara likes to nest high in trees, but I think being by the cliff gives them the air movement they need to lift their big bodies and their broad wings."

"I see what you mean. There are currents swirling around the cliffs, I'll bet."

The two men settled the hats more firmly on their heads to keep the sun off their faces and started hiking up the path to their section. They moved with quiet steps to avoid disturbing the wildlife. As they reached their area, Dimitri stopped and pointed toward the cliff face. "Look, George," he whispered, "a sea eagle. I think you have not seen one yet."

George slowly lifted his binoculars and pressed them to his eyes. "Yes, I see." He watched with rapt attention as the majestic bird floated on the rising morning breeze. "He barely flaps his wings," George said. "Makes me wish I could fly."

They walked on.

"Maybe that is why you like to scuba dive so much, George. You can pretend you are flying."

"Maybe you're right."

They spoke very little as they carefully moved back and forth across the area Jeremy had marked for them. Dimitri and George saw some promising nests in the trees, but saw no Caracaras. They were surprised to hear Jeremy's soft whistle, which was the signal that two hours had passed and summoned the teams back to the meeting point.

As they walked back, Dimitri hesitantly said, "George, when you were, um, working, did you ever have to, well, entertain a lady?"

Gotcha, George thought. "Oh, I did a few times. I was

always afraid I would have difficulty performing. You?" He could see Dimitri tug at his throat as if he had something stuck in it.

"Well, I did, yes. I was not so worried about performing. I have always been able to fuck like a Georgian." He laughed at his play on words. "I was more afraid that Irina would find out. She has the temper of a Cossack."

George chuckled. "I imagine she has. Susan never asked me about it. Did Irina?"

"No, thank god, she did not. I am not so good a liar to Irina. She can see right through me."

George elbowed him. "I'll bet you had some coeds circling around you, too."

"What do you mean?" Dimitri stopped walking to look at George.

"I remember when I was at university," George said. "Each of the professors seemed to have a gaggle of young women gathered around his desk after class. The girls would follow him to his office, chattering like magpies. Even I could see that at least one of them had a serious enough crush on him to be willing to earn a higher grade, uh, on her back, you might say."

Dimitri started walking again. "Oh yes, groupies. I had them. They were pests. I wanted to tell them to leave me alone, but no matter what I did, there was at least one in each class that followed me like a puppy."

"Tough job. There were no adoring young women in the British Fisheries Department, at least none that didn't smell like trout and river water." He looked over at Dimitri, who was smiling. "What are you smiling about? Remembering one in particular?" He made his voice low and purring, hoping to strike the universal locker room invitation to confession so he could get his distasteful job finished in a hurry.

But then his training came roaring back. Better to lightly skirt the subject to soften up his quarry, then, when he was not on guard, move in for the kill. Before Dimitri could answer, they arrived back at the group.

There was a flurry of activity as each team compared their

finds. No one had seen a Caracara, so none could identify a nest site. The day was not a failure, though. George saw his first sea eagle, with a witness, so he could put it on his life list. Jeremy and Mason counted three nesting pairs of Puerto Rican parrots that appear to be migrating from the nearby island of Puerto Rico.

Tom and Dan were to provide breakfast afterwards. They laid out a generous spread of hard-boiled eggs, one of Tom's wife Sheila's delicious cinnamon coffeecakes, and a box of bananas. They had pitchers of orange-pineapple juice and thermoses of coffee.

George circulated among the group, carefully giving Dimitri space after their talk on the walk back. He felt more in command of the situation now that circumstances had slowed the job and reminded him of his training. It was a jovial group, trading stories of sightings in the past, and watching the Magnificent Frigate Birds soar over the waves.

CHAPTER 21

Dimitri and Irina

Dimitri slammed the door when he got home.

"Dimi?" Irina looked up from her seat in the shade on the patio at the back of the house.

He stormed through the house, dropping his hat and binoculars on the table as he went. "I cannot do it."

"Do what?"

He sat in the chair across from her. "I cannot treat George as if he were a target. He is a nice man."

Irina stuck her pen into the notebook on her lap and closed the cover on the blank pages. "I am sure he is a nice man now. But you need to find out if he was the one who led that woman into stealing the plans for the communications system like they asked."

"But..."

"No. No buts. You must do it. Think, Dimitri, think. We cannot afford for you to displease them, the ones who sent the letter. They have long arms. They can still hurt us. If they are angry, maybe your pension will stop coming, and then where would we be, huh?"

Dimitri leaned his forearms on his thighs and stared at the cracked tiles between his feet. "I know, I know. It makes me feel dishonest now."

"Dishonest?" She leaned toward him. "Your whole working life was a lie. How can asking a few questions now make a difference?"

"It feels wrong, that is all." He composed his face before looking up at her. "I do not think I can do it, Irina. I will write a letter to Comrade, I mean, Mr. Ivanova telling him to find someone else, that I cannot do as he asks." He stood and walked into the house.

Irina watched him as he moved, stoop-shouldered and defeated, away from her. He looked like he had aged years in the last ten minutes. "Dimi, wait." She stood up and followed him, her leather-soled sandals making a scuffing sound on the tiles. "Dimitri." He turned to face her, looking tired and broken. "Wait," she said again, "do not write just yet." She touched his shoulder. "What if we both worked on this?"

"How could we?"

She was silent for a minute. He could see her eyes dart from side to side and almost hear her thoughts churning. "We can, yes, we can make friends with them. Yes, I will do this for you, for us. I will be more civil to Susan. I will even praise her ghastly photo art and if she reads any of her doggerel at the Roundtable, I will not destroy it, even if that is what it deserves." She looked at her beloved husband and saw a spark of hope grow in his eyes.

CHAPTER 22

Rose

It had been a long time since I hosted a dinner party. I'd had people in for a casual lunch a few times and there was the big end of construction cookout that I'd had last year, but tonight would be different. George and Susan Clemment were coming over for grilled lobsters. I had an ulterior motive. I hoped that having people over in a small group would make Iggy more comfortable at the expats parties we were invited to. I understood his reluctance since he was usually the only native islander there, aside from the staff.

"I do not feel like I belong," he said. "The people are overly friendly and go out of their way to talk to me. It makes me uncomfortable."

"Did you ever think that they talk to you because they're interested in you and what you have to say? That maybe they're trying to get to know you?"

"No. Most of them are trying to prove to me and to themselves that they are not prejudiced. They try too hard instead of just being themselves. It is like they line up to speak to the Anguillan man, coming over one after the other to say hello and how are you."

I leaned on the kitchen island. "Would you rather that they ignore you?"

Iggy let out a sigh. "Sometimes, yes. I am not interested in the things that they talk about. I do not golf or go bird watching or snorkeling. I am not retired. I am not as educated as they are."

"But you listen to the news and read the newspaper. You can talk about world events and things that are happening in Anguilla. People are interested in those things."

"Some of them are, but most of them want to gossip about other people in the community of expats, and I do not gossip."

"No, I don't gossip either. It makes me sad that so many people, the women especially, say mean things about each other. Like the division of the women who support either Irina or Susan. Why can't they just agree to disagree and get on with their lives? It shouldn't matter whose side you're on, but it does."

While we talked, we unloaded the bags of groceries that we'd bought that morning. I had tried to avoid being drawn into the small clutch of women in the IGA that were on Susan's side or those who were on Irina's side in Vista Market. I wasn't very successful.

Early that morning, Billy the fisherman had knocked on the back door of Seaview and sold Iggy four nice-sized spiny lobster tails. Now the tails were soaking in a bowl of fresh water in the refrigerator to leach out some of the salt before we put them on the grill that evening.

As he put the last of the vegetables in the crisper drawer, Iggy said, "What else besides lobster are we serving tonight?"

"We'll make a salad, and I thought I'd cut the kernels off the cobs of corn we bought and sauté them with a little butter, onion, and bell pepper. How does that sound?"

"Sounds good. How about I call Amy's Bakery to see if she has a baguette we can have too? I love her bread."

"Oh, good idea. Call her."

He made a quick call on his cellphone and while Geneva and I worked on washing the towels and cleaning the guest bathrooms, Iggy drove off on his bread errand.

As I took the towels out of the dryer to fold, I noticed that an appliqued leaf on one towel was coming loose. I set up the sewing machine on one of the lobby tables and got it reattached. After that, I gave all the towels and face cloths a good going over to make sure none of the other ones were suffering the same fate. I put the machine away and set up the ironing board in the backroom to press the napkins and placemats that got washed every day, too. Those were holding up well so far.

Geneva came downstairs after she finished cleaning the last of the bathrooms and swept the sand out of the lobby. "Every day, more sand gets tracked into the lobby. I do not know what we can do to stop it. Sandy shoes and feet are marking up the floor."

"I don't know how to stop it, either. I got those palm fiber doormats that are supposed to scrape the bottoms of shoes when people walk over them, but I think there's too much sand for them to handle. We can't ask people to take off their shoes when they come in, they'd just track sand in on their feet. I'm afraid the finish on the floor is doomed."

Geneva looked at me and sadly nodded her head in agreement. She put the broom and dustpan away on the backroom hooks. "May I finish the ironing?" Geneva said.

"No thanks, I'm finished," I said, unplugging the iron. "That's the end of today's laundry, too."

"Is there anything you need help with for tonight's dinner party?"

I shook my head. "It's all under control. Iggy and I can make the salad, and I've made a key lime pie for dessert. The only other thing to do is sauté the corn and I'll do that right before the guests arrive. Take the rest of the day off if you'd like."

The younger woman removed her apron and hung it on a hook. "I think I will stop down at Johnno's, seeing if Silas is working today." She pulled a small mirror out of her purse and patted her hair into place, then applied lipstick.

I smiled but said nothing. It seemed like Silas' regular visits to cadge muffins or offer to fix things around Seaview were paying off.

Late in the afternoon I stood at the kitchen island with my biggest bowl and a sharp knife, cutting the kernels off the cobs of corn we got at the market that morning. Once all the kernels were cut off, I used a wooden spoon to break the clumps of kernels apart and sauteed them in butter with minced onion and bell pepper.

While I did that, Iggy tore up Romaine lettuce into a wooden bowl and cut up cucumber and tomatoes for the salad. "What time are the Clemments arriving?" Iggy asked.

"About six o'clock, so we have time to shower and dress before they arrive."

We heard a voice from the lobby. "Hurry up, Norma, we're going to miss the sunset."

From upstairs came an answer. "I'm on my way. Just a minute."

I heard footsteps hurry down the hall and start down the stairs. The hurried steps turned into a crash and a tumble.

"Oh my god, Norma, are you all right?"

Iggy and I hurried into the lobby to see a middle-aged woman in a heap at the bottom of the stairs. "Don't try to get up," I said to her. "Let's make sure you're not hurt first." Remembering my Medic First Aid training from a long-ago dive shop class, I started assessing the woman's injuries. She was breathing fine. There was no blood, and no bones sticking out anywhere.

"I'm fine, just embarrassed."

"Uh-huh, hold still for another minute," I said. "Let me make sure that nothing's broken. Does anything hurt when I touch it?"

"No."

But then I ran my hand down the woman's calf to her ankle.

"Oh! That hurts."

I turned to Iggy. "Go call the paramedics. It's probably just a sprain, but we can't be too careful." I turned to my guest. "I'm sorry, but you're going to miss the sunset today. Luckily, it'll set again tomorrow at about the same time, so you'll have another chance."

"Oh, for god's sake, Norma, why'd you have to fall down the stairs?" Her husband's tone wasn't very sympathetic.

"Because, Larry, someone was yelling at me to hurry. I was trying to hurry, missed a step, and fell." She folded her arms across her chest and turned away from him.

It didn't take long for the rescue squad to show up in their shiny new ambulance van. The two young men and one not-so-young woman were quick and professional in their assessment of Norma's injuries. They advised her to let them take her to the clinic, where she could have an x-ray to make sure that she hadn't broken her ankle. I was relieved when she agreed, worried that my liability insurance might not cover it if Norma had refused.

By the time they had Norma on the gurney and wheeled her out to the ambulance, Larry was in his rental car, ready to follow them. That way, he could bring her back to Seaview once her treatment was complete.

I looked at the clock when they'd left and sighed. It was a quarter to six, so we had no time for a relaxing shower before our guests arrived. "We'd better get changed," I said. "Susan and George will be here in just a few minutes."

"I will light the charcoal while you make the salad dressing."

"It's made," I said with a smile. "All I have to do is shake it up again and it'll be ready. Now let's get dressed in clean clothes."

We hurried into our apartment and changed. We stood crammed together in front of the bathroom mirror, combing our hair and making sure that we looked presentable. I liked the way we looked together, two handsome people growing older together.

"I will go out and get the charcoal started while you finish getting ready." Iggy said. Just as he put the grill lighter and fluid away, our guests arrived.

I glanced out the back door in time to see George escorting Susan around the bougainvillea hedge and into the backyard. "Oh good, we're having something grilled," George said. "I love grilled meat."

"Tonight, we are having spiny lobster. I hope that is an

acceptable substitute for meat," Iggy said.

"It is indeed."

Susan clapped her hands. "I love lobster. Is Rose inside? I made some planters punch I thought we could start the evening with. I'll go in for glasses. George, you stay here and keep Iggy company." She took the pitcher from her husband and went into the building.

"Yes, dear." He winked at Iggy. "Got to keep on her good side, you know. She's the one who really rules the roost."

"That sounds familiar. It is the same here. I just do as I am told, and we get along fine." The men laughed together.

"What's so funny?" I said as Susan and I came out of the kitchen carrying tall glasses filled with golden liquid. We each handed a glass to our husband.

George lifted his glass in a toast. "To building friendships," he said.

"To building friendships," we all repeated and sipped our drinks.

"Oh, that's good," I said. "Mango and pineapple?"

Susan nodded. "With a generous splash of rum, of course."

When the charcoal was ready, Iggy cracked the lobster tails and laid them on the grill. Susan brought out a tablecloth and silverware to set the table in the garden. It took a few trips to bring out the plates and salad bowls, along with the sauteed corn, the salad, the sliced baguette, and the melted butter. By the time the pie was sliced and served, everyone was full and happy.

A car pulled into the parking area, and I stood up to see Larry help Norma out of the car and hand her a pair of wooden crutches.

"Larry, why don't you two come in the back way? It'll be a lot easier than trying to use crutches in the sand, plus there are fewer steps to get inside."

"Thanks, Rose," Norma said. "It's going to take me some time to get used to using these things. I don't want to fall again."

I walked to meet them and made sure that their path to the back door was clear. "What did the x-ray show?"

"Just a sprain, no break, not even a hairline fracture the x-ray tech said. The doctor was a woman, and she was very gentle when she wrapped my ankle. Said I should use the crutches for the rest of my stay here and call the airlines to have a wheelchair meet us at the airports on the way home. What a pain to have this happen on vacation. I have to stay out of the water so I can't even go snorkeling."

"I'm so sorry, but I'm glad it isn't broken."

Larry stood by the door into the kitchen. "Come on, Norma, don't take all night. I want to go down to Johnno's and get something to eat. I'm starving."

Norma sighed. "Coming, dear."

I went back to join my dinner guests. They were curious about what happened, so I told them about Norma slipping on the stairs and spraining her ankle. "I'm very glad that it wasn't something caused by Seaview, so I'm not liable for her injuries or medical expenses."

"Although I wouldn't put it past her husband to try to get something out of you," George said. "He looks like the type."

I sighed. "Agreed. I'm going to call my attorney and insurance agent tomorrow to make sure that I'm covered on all bases."

***

George's instinct was correct. When I went out into the lobby the next morning to start the coffee, I found Larry crawling up the stairs on his knees, examining every step.

"What are you doing?"

Larry started and looked around. "Oh, hi Rose. I'm just checking to make sure that none of these steps are loose. Norma says that she missed a step, but I want to make sure it wasn't something else."

"Well, let me know if you find anything."

"I will."

I made the coffee and went back into the kitchen to take the muffins out of the oven so they could cool before breakfast. I cut up fruit to serve alongside the muffins and thought about frying up some bacon. Deciding that bacon was a good idea, I found a package in the fridge, pulled out a skillet, and started the burner. Iggy came out of our apartment and slid his arms around my waist.

"Good morning, beautiful."

"Good morning." I leaned back into Iggy's chest and relished the strength of his arms around me. "Be careful. I'm frying bacon. You might get spattered by hot grease."

As soon as I said it, a big drop of the bacon grease popped out of the skillet and hit Iggy's forearm. "Ouch!" He jerked his arms from around me and went over to the sink to run his arm under cold water.

I was right behind him. "Are you okay?"

"I am all right. It caught me by surprise. Do not let the bacon burn."

I stepped back to the stove and slid the frying pan off the burner. "It's almost done. Is your arm blistering? Do you need a doctor?"

"No, it will be fine." He held his forearm under the cold running water. "I will put gauze and tape on it to protect it, but I do not need a doctor."

"Okay, but keep an eye on it. I don't want it to get infected." I didn't want to have to deal with another medical emergency, but I'd certainly be more sympathetic than Larry. As soon as breakfast was done, I'd put in a call to my insurance agent to make sure I was covered for Norma's accident, just in case.

CHAPTER 23

Rose

The burn on Iggy's arm was taking a long time to heal. He kept it bandaged when he was working and uncovered it and let it breathe when he was at home. It was a pretty good size burn, about the diameter of a quarter. I kept wanting him to go to the clinic to have someone look at it, but he resisted. "I will be fine. It is just taking longer than usual to heal. Sometimes that happens in the tropics."

"I don't like it. What if it's getting infected? You've started sweating more, too."

Iggy chuckled. "We live in the Caribbean, and it is hot. Everyone sweats."

"You rarely sweat much, but I noticed in the last few days that you're sweating more, especially at night." I looked closely at his forearm. "Does the skin look discolored to you?"

"No, it looks like a normal burn."

"That's not a normal burn. It's too deep. I'm taking you to the clinic."

"No."

"It's either that or we go to the hospital."

"I am not going. You cannot make me go when I know I am fine."

I threw my hands up in frustration. "Fine. Don't come crying to me when your arm falls off." Tears filled my eyes, and I walked away before he could see them.

That night, Iggy woke me up. He was shivering and

sweating. "Rose, I think there is something wrong. Maybe you are right, maybe my burn is infected. We need to go to the hospital."

I was instantly awake. I leaped out of bed, put on the clothes I had taken off just an hour before, and helped Iggy dress. We hurried out to the car and headed to The Valley where the Princess Alexandra Hospital was located. I was relieved to see the red neon Emergency light lit over the door. I parked the car and helped Iggy get out. He was unsteady on his feet. The young doctor, whose nametag said Champion, was quick to get Iggy into an exam room and asked the nurse to take his vitals. The doctor asked me what happened, and I told him about Iggy being burned last week and the burn not healing.

"Oh, that is not good," Doctor Champion said and went back into the exam room to see for himself.

I followed him and stood just inside the door, watching as he rolled up Iggy's sleeve and removed the bandage. I could see that the burn was inflamed and looked much worse.

"You need IV antibiotics, Mr. Solomon, and right now." He whirled on his heel and nearly crashed into me in his haste to get the medicine started.

An hour later, Iggy was in a bed in the men's ward with an IV in his left arm pumping antibiotics in to combat the raging infection from his burn. I sat beside him, holding his hand and assuring him he would be all right soon.

Doctor Champion came into the darkened ward and pulled the curtain around Iggy's bed. "Mr. Solomon, I am going to give you a sedative so that you can rest. Mrs. Solomon, you need to go home. You cannot stay here all night. Come back in the morning."

I gripped Iggy's hand tighter. "Oh, but I want to stay with Iggy. I want to make sure he's okay."

"Go on home, Rose," Iggy said. "I will be fine here sleeping, and you have guests you need to make breakfast for. Come back after breakfast. I will still be here."

"You'd better be." I leaned over and kissed his forehead. It was hot and dry. I looked at the doctor.

"Normal," he said before I could comment. "A night with the strong antibiotic we are giving him will make a big change. Come back in the morning and see for yourself."

Doctor Champion escorted me back to the Emergency door and watched until I was safely in my car. It was a long drive back to Seaview, with only the stars and a crescent moon to relieve the darkness.

I lay in bed for a long time, watching the ceiling fan slowly rotate, hoping that the antibiotic would work fast so that my beloved Iggy would be back beside me soon. I pushed away the thought that I could lose another husband. Memories of Jim's last trip to the hospital kept me awake.

***

Iggy didn't come home the next day or the day after that. The infection spread all over his body, and he needed days of intravenous antibiotics to combat it. Once I got the guests fed and Geneva started on the chores, I hurried to the hospital to sit by his bedside. I watched him sleep. He was so still; I put my hand on his chest to feel his breathing. It barely rose and fell, but the movement made me feel better. It was quiet in the ward; no one was in the three other beds. I was lonely sitting there with my sock knitting in my lap and no one to talk to, but I didn't want him to wake up alone. I felt lucky that I had Geneva willing to shoulder more of the work at the bed-and-breakfast, so I didn't have to worry.

Every once in a while, Iggy mumbled something in his sleep.

I couldn't understand him. "What, Iggy? What did you say?"

But he didn't respond.

He lay like that all the first day and part of the second day he was in the hospital. I would have been more worried, but Nurse Ingrid said, "It is good for Mr. Solomon to sleep. His body heals better, and the antibiotics will work harder if he rests." Hearing that reassured me. I got a lot of knitting done.

When I was on my way in to sit with Iggy, I saw Susan and George coming out. "What are you doing here?"

"It was time for me to have my blood pressure and hemoglobin checked," Susan said. "I have to keep track of it if I want them to keep renewing my prescriptions. Why are you here?" She noticed my knitting bag and looked at me with a raised eyebrow.

"Oh, Iggy got a grease burn on his arm and it got infected, so he's here getting IV antibiotics."

"How is he doing?"

I shrugged. "Right now, he's asleep all the time when I'm here, but they tell me that's normal, that it's a good sign. I want him to wake up so I can tell he's getting better."

"Maybe I'll stop by and see him in a day or two," George said.

"I'm sure he'd appreciate that."

By the third day he was restless and by the fourth day he was sitting on the edge of his bed plotting how to remove the IV and sneak out.

"I cannot stand just lying here staring at the lizard on the ceiling."

That made me look up. "There's a lizard on the ceiling in your hospital room?"

"He only comes out at night."

"Ah, well, that's okay then. You need to stay here getting that stuff pumped into you so that you get better. The longer you're on this strong antibiotic, the sooner you'll be well. I brought you a book and some magazines. Maybe they'll help pass the time."

He took the bag of reading material and set it on the foot of his bed. "I wish I was home. I wish I was working. There are jobs I am missing." He started to stand, but I pressed him back down.

"I know. I called the people on the calendar and told them you were in the hospital and would contact them when you get released."

Iggy grunted. "George stopped."

"Did he? I saw him and Susan when I came in a couple of days ago. What did he have to say?"

"Not much. Just feel better soon. He brought me grapes. How are things at Seaview?"

"Good. Lonely without you, especially at night." I started to cry. "I miss snuggling with you."

He put his arm around me and tugged me down onto the bed beside him. "I will be home soon, and we can snuggle all you want. In the meantime, we can have a little snuggle right now."

A gravelly voice came from the far corner of the ward. "That your hoochie mama, Ignatius?"

I jumped in surprise and stood up. "Who's that?"

"Oh, that is old Quint. He is a fisherman who lost his leg in a boating accident and cannot keep his stump clean, so he comes in here every few months for a round of antibiotics and wound care, so he does not die of the infection." Iggy turned toward the old man in the corner. "This is my wife, Quint, so keep your opinions to yourself."

"Be nice, Iggy. He's just a bored old man."

"No, he is not. He is a dirty old man, and I will not have him talking about you like that."

***

On the fifth day, Doctor Champion said that Iggy could come home. Iggy was so excited I thought he could have run back to Seaview faster than I could drive there. I went by the pharmacy in the hospital to get the prescription antibiotics that he would have to take for at least two weeks longer. Then I went back to Iggy's room, hoping that it would be time to go.

"Why do I have to take pills for so long?"

"To keep killing the bugs until your arm is fully healed. You had a severe infection," Doctor Champion said.

"I will take the pills every day just like it says on the bottle, but what I really want to know is, can I go back to work?"

The doctor crossed his arms over his chest, then rubbed his chin with his right hand. "I predict you will not have enough energy for much work for a week, but you can start back doing small jobs on Monday if you are feeling all right. How does that sound?" He left the room with a wave. "The nurse will be in to give you your instructions."

Nurse Ingrid came in a few minutes later with a sheaf of papers and a bag of what turned out to be bandages and salve. She went through every line of every page of the discharge papers and handed me the bag of supplies. "You must change the dressing twice a day, morning and night, and make sure that the wound stays covered at all times and does not get wet. We do not want to see Mr. Solomon back here with a renewed infection." She waggled her index finger in Iggy's face. "You need to be a good boy and take care of yourself. I have faith that Mrs. Rose will see to it."

I looked at the supplies in the bag. "Are you sure that the wound is healing?"

"Yes, ma'am, it is healing nicely. The skin around the edges is regrowing, and the center is no longer weeping, all signs that the infection is vanquished."

"Let's hope so. I missed him. Thank you." I held out my hand to shake, but she swept me into a hug that almost had me in tears.

Nurse Ingrid heard me sniff and held me away from her. "You take care of yourself, too. Make that Geneva carry some of the load."

"She does a lot, and she's done the lion's share these past few days. Thanks for your good care of Iggy and you take care of yourself. I hope I won't see you again soon."

She laughed a big, full-throated laugh that rang in the ward. "I hope I won't see you too." She offered Iggy a ride to the door in a wheelchair, but he politely declined.

I picked up the small suitcase with Iggy's things in it.

When we got outside, Iggy took a deep breath. "I am so happy to be out of there. They are nice and took good care of me, but their food is not as good as yours and Quint is not who I want to share a room with."

On the drive back to Sandy Ground and Seaview, Iggy leaned forward and kept a hand on the dashboard, as if doing that would make the ride shorter.

Geneva was in the kitchen when we came through the door, and she rushed over to Iggy. "Oh, Mr. Solomon, Mr. Iggy, I am so glad to see you. I have been praying that you would be well, and I see it worked."

Iggy leaned down and touched his cheek to Geneva's cheek. "I thank you for your prayers. I am certain that the Lord held me in the palm of his hand and sped my healing journey."

I was tempted to roll my eyes at the dramatic tone of the last statement, but I could see that both Iggy and Geneva were true believers, so I busied myself getting something out for our lunch.

"Oh, Mrs. Rose, I have made some lunch for you and Mr. Iggy." She reached into the fridge and pulled out a plate wrapped in cling film. "I brought some barbecued chicken from Captain Mike's. It will make good sandwiches on Amy's coconut bread."

"Thank you, Geneva. That's very thoughtful of you. Barbecued chicken sandwiches sound delicious."

I'd have to think of some special way to thank Geneva for all the work she did while I was sitting in the hospital, hoping for Iggy to get better.

CHAPTER 24

Rose

After all the worry about Iggy in the hospital, it was a relief to get back to my guests. It was hard to watch my guest, Norma, who sprained her ankle on the first day of their stay, try to navigate the stairs to their bedroom for the rest of the week. She would sit on the bottom step and scoot up one step at a time to get up there with Larry following her, carrying her crutches. I could see how impatient he was, but he held his tongue most of the time. Coming down was even harder to watch. She would basically hop down one step at a time, holding the banister and one crutch. It looked to me as if she would overbalance and fall headlong down the stairs, but she took her time and made it. I let her use the back door to leave and enter the bed-and-breakfast because using crutches to go down the front steps into the sand would be more difficult. By the end of the week, she had figured out how to crutch in the sand and she and Larry went down to Johnno's or the Barrel Stave for supper most nights. I think they did a lot more car touring than they had planned that week, too.

On the Saturday morning of their departure, Norma stayed in the lobby after breakfast and sent Larry up to finish packing and carry their cases back downstairs. She asked me to go up and look around to make sure that they had forgotten nothing. Larry didn't like it, but he only complained a little before she silenced him with a look, especially when I came back down carrying a phone charger and hairbrush.

"I'm so sorry you fell down and sprained your ankle,

Norma," I said. "But it looks like you made the best of an unpleasant situation."

Norma gave a little sigh. "I had planned to go snorkeling out at Sandy Island but had to be content with sitting over at Johnno's watching the sunset and touring around in the car. We stopped at the craft market and that was fun. I bought some trinkets to give to my friends for Christmas."

"That's good. We used to call those vacation trinkets 'sweet somethings' in my family." I handed Larry their bill, and he handed it to Norma for her to look over before he gave me his credit card. "Everything all right?"

"Just fine," Norma said. "Thanks for a lovely week, Rose. Your breakfasts are to die for, especially the mango lime muffins."

"Those are Iggy's favorites too. I'm glad you liked them."

Larry bent to pull up the handles of their suitcases. "I wasn't sure I'd like the egg casserole things or the muffins, but I liked them just fine. Maybe we'll come back sometime, and Norma won't fall down the stairs."

"Good, I'd like that. Safe travels." I handed Norma a couple of brochures. "Here. Tuck these into your bag and give them to friends or leave them in a coffee shop. Thanks."

They turned and headed out the back way as the other three guests came clattering downstairs with their suitcases and carry-ons.

These were the writing friends from Milwaukee just finishing their second stay at Seaview.

"How was the writing this week?"

They looked at each other and Laurel said, "It was better than I'd hoped. I've been stuck lately, had a bit of writer's block, and being down here with all the time to write and few distractions helped a lot."

"That's great. How about you, Pam and Carol?"

Pam said, "I worked on rewriting a novel manuscript that's been rattling around for years, and I think I made some progress."

"I wrote a couple of new short stories. Nothing finished but rough drafts. I'm happy with that," Carol said.

I beamed at them. "That's excellent. I'm always happy when writers tell me they've had good luck writing at Seaview. Let me know when you get things published so I can order copies to add to my library." I gestured to the shelf beside the registration desk where I shelve novels and journals that showcased writing done at the bed-and-breakfast. "There's plenty of room for you three on there."

I handed out their bills and got them all checked out. "Thanks again for coming back. I hope to see you again sometime."

"Oh, we'll be back," Laurel said, and the other two women nodded their agreement.

Geneva and I spent the rest of the day cleaning and prepping the rooms for the new arrivals, who would come in on the afternoon flight. I made up four cheese and fruit plates, covered them with cling film, and stored them in the fridge until the new guests arrived. I made sure that there were a few splits of wine in the fridge to go with those little welcome plates.

We were barely finished with the cleaning and laundry when the first couple arrived. They were a husband and wife, Simeon and Milly Lincoln, and they didn't look like any of my previous guests. Simeon had long black hair worn in a low ponytail and oval wire-rimmed glasses that reminded me of the ones that John Lennon wore. Milly had purple hair cut very short and lying close to her head. They both wore blue jeans and wife-beater tee shirts, and they looked exhausted.

"Welcome to Seaview," I said. "You look like you had a long trip."

Simeon leaned his forearm on the counter. "All the way from London in one day is a long trip. The time change is brutal."

"Well, let's get you checked in and you can rest up from your long flight. I have a cheese and fruit plate and a split of wine to get you started relaxing." I quickly got them registered and escorted them to the salmon room. I was sure they'd both be sleeping before they'd finished the wine.

The other three guests for the week came in together. They were two women and a man—Debbie, David, and Denise; all friends and it was the first time they'd been to Anguilla.

"We like to snorkel and play beach volleyball. Do you have that here?"

"You can snorkel out on Sandy Island right offshore and there's beach volleyball at Shoal Bay up the coast a few miles. I'll show you on the map once we get you checked in."

It didn't take long to get them registered, scan their credit cards, and hand out maps and tourist booklets. Geneva showed them to their rooms and carried up the welcome plates and wine.

In no time, the three of them were back downstairs with bags of snorkel gear off to catch the launch out to Sandy Island.

I was finishing up at the registration desk and reminded them to be sure to apply sunscreen.

"Oh, we will," Debbie said. "We won't ruin our week by starting off sunburned."

There wasn't a sound from Simeon and Milly's room all evening. No footsteps, no sound of conversation. I figured they were sleeping off their jetlag and I would see them at breakfast.

***

Once I heard movement and running water upstairs, I went out and started the coffee so that the aroma of brewing coffee would let the guests know that breakfast was on the way. Milly was down first.

I saw her pouring coffee and leaned through the doorway to say good morning. "I hope you slept well," I said.

"I did. We did. Sim opened the window a little so we could hear the waves on the sand. Very restful." She carried her coffee mug to the front door and turned to ask, "Is it all right if I take my coffee out onto the front porch?"

"Of course. Breakfast will be ready in about twenty minutes, so you have time to enjoy that first cup in peace."

"Thanks. We left right after our gig ended and hopped on

the plane. Flying all night and most of the day yesterday was brutal. I'm glad we're here."

"Good. I'm glad you're here too." I wondered what kind of gig they had. They must be some sort of entertainers because I'd never heard another profession talk about their jobs as gigs. I went back to the stove to make sure the sausages didn't burn, turned off the burner, and covered the pan so they'd stay warm while the muffins finished baking.

The three Ds came down for coffee and stood around the pot talking about their plans for the day. Simeon slouched down the stairs wearing his jeans low on his hips, barefoot, and without a shirt, poured himself some coffee, and stood looking around.

I carried the tray of place settings into the lobby. "Milly's out on the front porch if you're looking for her."

"Thanks, mate." He headed out the door, and I heard the scrape of a rocker on the wooden floor.

Soon the muffins were baked and cooled enough to serve, so I put them in a couple baskets lined with napkins, blotted the scant grease off the sausages, and carried it all out along with butter for each table. "Breakfast."

The three D's chose a table and sat down. "Oh, this looks good," Denise said.

"What kind of muffins are these?" David asked.

"Orange blossom."

Debbie took one from the basket and held it to her nose. "Oh, it smells delicious." She peeled off the baking paper, buttered it, and took a bite. Her eyes closed in pleasure. "And it tastes as good as it smells. Thanks, Rose."

Milly went upstairs and came down with a shirt for Simeon. "Shirts at meals, please."

I was relieved because I had been trying to think of a polite way to ask Simeon to put one on. "Before you all go off for the day, I wanted to tell you about the weekly jump-up tonight at Johnno's Beach Bar a few doors down from us. You're all welcome to come to the party. It's for tourists and locals alike. And it's a lot of fun."

Simeon asked, "What's a jump-up? Sounds like a rave."

"Not quite. A steel drum band plays and everybody dances, and I do mean everybody. Just about the entire island population shows up, locals, tourists, expats. It's a nice mix of people. Johnno makes a mean rum punch, and we usually order bar snacks like conch fritters and plantain chips. He doesn't serve burgers on Sunday nights, only snacks. I recommend going down around five o'clock if you want to find a seat because the tables fill up fast."

Everyone nodded and said they'd think about it.

I noticed that Debbie and Denise kept looking at Simeon and Milly and then looking away. There was a lot of whispering going on at their table, too.

"Do you think it's really them?" Debbie said as I put fruit bowls in front of each of them.

"I don't know, Deb," Denise said. "I can't imagine they'd stay at a place we can afford. You'd think they'd be in some swank hotel. Maybe they just look like them."

Evidently, they thought they recognized the British couple.

Iggy came into the lobby for coffee. "Good morning. I am happy that you all made it to Seaview without too much trouble."

Debbie looked up from her coffee and smiled at him. "Are you the handyman?"

"This is my husband Iggy."

"Oh, I'm sorry. I thought... I didn't know you were married." She had the grace to look embarrassed over her gaffe.

"No problem. You'll see him around. Enjoy your breakfasts."

I followed Iggy back into the kitchen. "Well, that was kind of rude, wasn't it?"

His voice was low and a little sad. "Happens all the time."

When I went out to clear the tables, the muffin baskets were empty. I'd put in two muffins per person, and it looked like they'd each eaten two. I was glad that I'd included the sausages and fruit because these guests were hungry.

Iggy helped me wash and dry the dishes and pans from making breakfast. We got interrupted by Denise, David, and Debbie wanting more precise directions to Shoal Bay to see if they couldn't get a beach volleyball game started. I wished them luck and sent them on their way with the Anguilla directions they'd need to find their way, since many of the roads didn't have signs on them. Oh, there were road names on the maps, there just weren't signs on the roads themselves. Maybe I'd bring that up at the Chamber of Commerce meeting when I finally got brave enough to go to one.

Once we got all the dishes and pans put away, I hung the wet towels on the bar and slid my arms around Iggy's waist. "All the guests are out. We could have a little romance if you're in the mood."

He pulled me in close. "I am always in the mood for that. You do not have to ask me twice."

CHAPTER 25

Rose

In the afternoon, all the guests were back at Seaview, taking turns showering, and getting ready to go to the jump-up. The three Ds came down first and took off toward Johnno's in high excitement. They said they'd had a good afternoon playing beach volleyball at Shoal Bay with some locals and some other tourists from California who all said they'd be at the jump-up. Now they were ready for a real Caribbean party. "This is going to be great," Debbie said. "There'll be people there we already know."

Milly and Simeon came down just as Iggy and I were leaving for the jump-up.

"We weren't sure if we wanted to go to the party, but it sounds like a fun time, so I convinced Sim to go for a while. We're still pretty jet lagged, so we might not stay too long," Milly said.

"That's all right. Stay as little or as long as you like. It's a fun party for the locals and tourists alike, so there's some of every kind of people there."

"I'm craving the music," Simeon said. "I need new inspiration." He looked at me from under his lowered brows.

I got the impression he thought I should know who he was, but I was clueless. I probably should have made time to do a little online research. Iggy and I walked down the beach to Johnno's with them. I was happy that the three Ds had commandeered a table and had extra chairs, so Milly and Simeon could join them if they wished. We joined our usual friends at the big table against the wall. They had saved places for us and had even gotten our first drinks.

"Yours is the one with the umbrella, Mrs. Rose," Edward said. "I knows that you like not so much rum in your drink, so I asked Johnno to make it for you."

I reached over and laid a hand on his shoulder. "Thanks, Edward. I appreciate your thoughtfulness."

The beach bar was filling up with a mix of tourists and locals. I waved to Susan and George across the room. When the music started, Luke asked me to dance. He twirled me onto the quickly crowded dance floor, and I saw Denise and David dance past, looking like they were having fun. Susan and George moved into the center of the crowd and started dancing like they'd been doing it all their lives. I saw Simeon and Milly dancing in the corner. I thought it looked like they were trying to stay out of the crush.

Suddenly, a young woman's voice called out, "Oh my god, it's utter chaos!"

I looked around at the well-behaved crowd and wondered what she was talking about.

Half of the dancers stopped moving and just stared at where she was pointing while the steel band played on and the rest of us kept dancing.

"Where?"

"Is it really them?"

As one, all the young women, locals and tourists alike, surged toward the corner where Simeon and Milly were dancing. I turned my head to catch sight of them being engulfed by screaming girls. "Oh my, they look like they're in trouble," I said to Luke. "Dance us over there. Maybe we can help them."

Luke nodded at Silas and Melvin, who came over and the three of them pushed their way through the edge of the crowd to stand next to Milly and Simeon. I followed them, using their bulk to help me get close to the corner, too.

"Do you need help? These three are friends of mine. Can they give you a little space?"

Milly was backed against the corner post of the beach bar and Simeon was trying to keep from being crushed. He looked at me and nodded.

The three Anguillan men started forcing a little space around them and shouting at the crowd to back up. The music stopped and everyone was watching what was going on in the corner. I heard Simeon say that if they'd back up, he'd talk to the band and maybe they'd sing a song or two. That moved the young people away, giving them breathing room. Silas, Melvin, and Luke escorted them through the crush and up to the band. I stayed out of the way and watched from a distance.

The steel drum band members obviously recognized Milly and Simeon because they were acting a little star-struck, too. One of the band members left the bar and came back in a few minutes with a small amplifier and a cord with a microphone. They got it plugged in and adjusted before Simeon announced they were going to sing a little Bob Marley.

Even I recognized that name.

A hush fell over the crowd, the buzz of excited voices stopped, and everyone waited for the song to begin. The steel drums played the intro and Simeon and Milly came in right on cue. They sang songs I remembered from my college days and then some songs I didn't recognize. The band and the singers sounded like they had rehearsed together, and the crowd stood in ranks watching and listening to the impromptu concert.

Milly and Simeon sang five or six songs, each one greeted by cheers and applause. By the second song, everyone who knew the words was singing along and I could see by the light in Simeon's eyes that he was having fun. "Thank you from Utter Chaos!" Simeon said at the end of their set. "Please grant Milly and me a little peace. This is our first break in two years, and we need the rest. We were glad to entertain you tonight, but beg your forgiveness if we say goodnight." He handed the microphone back to the band member by the amp, took Milly's hand, and they threaded their way through the crowd and out onto the beach.

A few of the young women, locals and tourists alike, trailed after them and tried to follow them, but George blocked their exit. "No following them. They need to experience the hospitality of Anguilla, not be mobbed by fans. Leave them be." I could see the disappointed slump of the girls' shoulders, but they nodded and turned back.

I watched Simeon and Milly walk up the beach toward Seaview and thought that it was good that I'd gotten into the habit of keeping the bed-and-breakfast's doors locked because I didn't want any of Utter Chaos' fans sneaking into the place to bother my guests.

Iggy and I didn't stay too much longer at the jump-up. We were both tired from the week and Iggy wasn't fully recovered from his burn infection and hospital stay.

I smelled cigarette smoke when I unlocked the door and was ready to chastise someone, but then I realized they were out on the back porch and stood in front of the screen door. Not wanting to startle them as I crossed the kitchen, I said, "Please step away from the door. I'd rather not have smoke blowing in."

"Oh sorry. We didn't think you'd mind if we stood back here in the dark."

"I don't mind. I'd just rather not have the smoke smell. I quit years ago, but every once in a while, the smell tempts me to have just one more."

"It's a terrible habit," Milly said. "But it could be something much worse, so I don't harp on quitting too much. If it affects our singing, then we'll consider it."

"Can I get you something to drink?"

"No thanks. We poured ourselves some iced tea when we came through the kitchen. I hope that's okay."

"That's fine. The tea and cold water are there for guests. Thank you for singing for us tonight. I've never heard of Utter Chaos, at least not that I know of, but I like reggae and loved your songs. And now Iggy and I are turning in. Please be sure to lock the back door and put on the deadbolt when you come in for the night. Good night."

It had been a busy day and eventful evening. I was tired. I went into our apartment to find Iggy already in bed and nearly asleep. I hurried to brush my teeth and wash my face, put on my nightshirt, and slide into bed. Iggy patted me as I curled up next to him and we both were asleep in minutes.

***

There was a gaggle of teenage girls clustered at the foot of the steps when I went out to drink my first cup of coffee on the porch. "Can I help you?"

They shuffled from foot to foot and giggled. One girl said, "We want to see Simeon."

"Didn't he ask for privacy last night before he left the jump-up?"

"We weren't there, and we just want to see him. Milly too, of course."

"But mostly Simeon," I said.

They all nodded.

"We are not leaving until we see him," the leader said. "You cannot make us leave because we are on the beach, not on your property. The beach is public." She was bold, standing a little apart from her friends and staring straight up at me.

"And how would you like it if someone invaded your holiday?"

They looked like they didn't understand what I said. "We want to see Simeon," the spokeswoman said again. "And we are not leaving until we do."

I drained my coffee mug and looked down at them. "Fine. Just don't get sunburned and don't come up the steps."

I went inside to find Milly and Simeon with mugs of coffee headed to the porch. "There is a small group of young women out there who say they aren't leaving until they see you."

He looked at Milly and shrugged. "Might as well get it over with." And he led her to the front door.

I heard a couple of strangled screams as Simeon and Milly went out. They talked for a few minutes. I heard Simeon's low voice while I laid the places. When I went back out to serve the cheese omelets, they were inside and waiting at a table.

"How did it go?" I asked.

"Fine. We signed autographs and asked them to give us some peace."

Milly added, "And to spread the word that we need space."

***

Three nights later, I woke up hearing noises outside. I wondered what was going on. It wasn't outside my window. It sounded like it was in front of the hotel. I slipped out of bed and pulled on a pair of shorts.

"Where are you going?" Iggy asked from the bed behind me.

"I hear something out front and I'm going to investigate."

"Wait for me."

We crept through the kitchen and into the lobby without turning on lights.

A whispered voice came from the ground, "Be careful. Do not fall."

The sound of stealthy footsteps came from the second-floor gallery on the front of the building. "Which room is his?" said a girl's voice from above.

"I do not know, but there are only two rooms, so one of them must be the right one," said a female voice on the ground. "Can you peek in the windows?"

Iggy put his finger over his lips and indicated that he would go upstairs and out onto the gallery. I stayed at the front doors of Seaview, ready to open them on his signal. When I heard the gallery door scrape the floor, I opened the front door and stepped out.

"What do you think you are doing?" Iggy and I said together.

The girls screamed and the one on the ground took off at a dead run. The girl on the gallery started climbing over the railing.

"Oh no," I heard Iggy say. "We will not be responsible for you falling and breaking your neck. You will come down through the lobby and out the front door like a grown person."

He escorted a shamefaced teenage girl down the stairs and out the front doors. There was no sign of her compatriot on the ground. "You need to act with respect for Rose's guests, even if one of them is a musician. And you cannot be climbing around on the building trying to peek in the windows. If you try again, we will call the police and charge you with trespassing. I know your parents and they would not appreciate knowing you were trying to break into a hotel. Now go on home and think about doing better."

We watched her walk down the beach toward the pier, her shoulders slumped and her steps stomping the sand.

Iggy turned to me and said, "Maybe we need to hire a night security guard while the musicians are here, or we will have utter chaos every night."

"Oh, excellent play on words." I put a hand on his arm. "Let's go back to bed. The alarm will ring too soon as it is."

CHAPTER 26

Rose

At the next meeting of the Art League, I stood talking to a new expat member. She introduced herself as Jessica Livingston.

"Hi Jessica," I said. "It's nice to meet you. Where are you from?"

"We're from Woodstock, Georgia, outside of Atlanta, Barry and me."

"I've only been through the Atlanta airport, and I've seen nothing of the city. Did you enjoy living there?"

"Lived there all my life, so I didn't know anything different until we moved down here to Anguilla."

"How did you happen to settle here?"

"We came on vacation to St. Martin one year and took the ferry over to explore Anguilla and fell in love with the island and its people. What about you?"

"I moved here two years ago, after my first husband died. It had been our dream to refurbish and reopen Seaview, my bed-and-breakfast on the beach in Sandy Ground, and after Jim passed away, I did it myself. That's where I met my second husband. He was the electrician I hired to rewire the hotel."

"It sounds like he helped with more than the hotel," she said, leaning toward me with a small leer.

I leaned back, not liking her inference.

"What part of the States is he from?"

"He's not from the States. He's a native of Anguilla."

Her smile was suddenly stiff. "Oh, well, bless your heart."

She looked around. "There's my neighbor, Christina. These are her artworks displayed tonight. I think I'll go talk to her. Nice to meet you, Rose." She was gone between one breath and the next.

It took me a minute to realize that she might have a problem with me being married to a man who wasn't white. Part of me wanted to run after her to tell her Iggy was a good husband. That any woman would be glad to have him. But then I thought, no, if she feels like that, she's not worth my time and effort. Next time, I'd be ready to get that reaction.

I moved toward where Miriam and Jane sat in the middle of the room, waiting for the meeting to start. I looked up to see Irina standing in the doorway looking at the women gathered. Her eyes followed Billie Holland-Smythe swanning around in her art patron mode. Billie was one woman who had a costume for each of her personas. She could look artistic, literary, regal, or wealthy.

"Being the richest of the expatriates on the island gives her an elevated view of her worth," I heard Irina say to the woman next to her. "Billie enjoys making messes and delights in the discomfort of others, especially those whom she feels are beneath her in either status or wealth."

I had to agree with Irina. Look at the way Billie persisted in calling her housekeeper Minnie when everyone knew that the tall, dignified woman preferred to be called Minerva.

I saw Irina's gaze travel past Billie to land on Susan and Harriet, Susan's friend from home. Harriet's name was old-fashioned enough to set Billie on the path of putting her in what Billie saw as her place. No matter what Harriet's status truly was, Billie would find just the right words to make her feel somehow less than she really was, or to doubt her own self-confidence.

Irina stepped into the room, greeting acquaintances, and worked her way to Harriet and Susan, where they stood admiring a painting by Christina Huckaby.

I thought Christina was a genuine artist. She could, with just a few lines, sketch a scene that everyone could recognize, and still make you see things you hadn't noticed, like how the light makes drama where you'd never notice if she hadn't painted it. There were a few of her sketches on display tonight. Christina had watercolors on exhibit, too. These paintings were riots of color with no defined edges that nevertheless depicted recognizable objects. That one had to be the tumble of bougainvillea that trailed over the wall in front of a house just down the road from Seaview and the others were scenes from the annual sailboat regatta on Anguilla. Then there were the underwater pictures. The viewer had to lean close to discover that Christina had laid on swaths of acrylic color and then used something sharp to scribe shapes into the canvas.

I couldn't resist walking over to look at the art in time to eavesdrop on what Irina said next.

Irina leaned toward Harriet, who was peering at one of Christina's fish pictures, and said, "I think that one is my favorite."

Harriet jumped back to look at Irina, unsure of how to answer. "I, I can't really see what it is."

Susan leaned across her friend to smile at Irina. "It's the reef, Harriet. I think it's one of her best, don't you, Irina?"

"Yes, I do," Irina said. "It differs from your altered photos of the reef, Susan, but is just as interesting."

"Why thank you, Irina, but I don't consider what I do on the computer art. It's really more of a trick than it is artistic."

Irina looked surprised at that. "You do not think of your pictures as art?"

"No, not at all." Susan laughed. "A clever eight-year-old could easily do what I do and do it better. I'm too old to learn many new tricks, especially on the computer. I'm amazed that people like them as much as they do, but I guess people jump on new technology before its value is proven, don't you think?"

She went on. "I keep expecting to be unmasked as a fraud at any moment. I made a few when I was first playing with the computer program for storing and cropping digital photos, exploring the features you might say. Mason James from the Cinnamon Art Gallery saw them on my wall and thought they might go well in his shop. I let him take a few to sell cheaply and the rest, as they say, is history."

Irina looked stunned by the humor and honesty on the British woman's face. "I think they are interesting, but not really art."

Susan nodded. "My feelings exactly."

Harriet's head had been bouncing back and forth during the exchange like she was at a tennis match.

Susan turned to her. "Don't you agree?"

I could see the question put Harriet on the spot, not sure if she should defend her old friend's artwork from criticism. "I enjoy Susan's works, but they're too fuzzy for me. I like those sketches." She pointed to the framed art in front of them. "I like a picture I don't have to figure out."

Irina laughed. "Spoken like a Russian, Harriet. We like things orderly and straightforward, none of that fuzzy impressionism for us."

Susan spoke up. "But what about Marc Chagall? He was a Russian, and his work is anything but straightforward."

Irina said, "Touché."

All three of them laughed. I suspected Harriet laughed because she wasn't exactly sure who that Chagall chap was and what his paintings looked like, and Susan and Irina because they had been polite to each other, and it hadn't been so difficult after all.

The three women moved together down the row of art on display, sharing likes and dislikes about each one, leaning back from some and peering closely at others. They traveled around the room in a bubble of quiet astonishment, every other woman in the room having heard how they felt about each other many times over the previous months.

I followed the trio, wondering why Irina was friendly to Susan and Susan was being nice to Irina. What had changed?

CHAPTER 27

Susan

A kind of vacuum settled over the expatriate women at the Art League meeting. No one was quite sure she had seen what she thought she saw. Had that really been Irina being polite, nice even, to Harriet and Susan? Maybe Irina had decided not to be rude to Harriet since she was a guest on the island, and it was just a coincidence that she and Susan were together then. No, that wasn't likely since Harriet was the Clemment's friend and guest. Of course, Harriet would be close to Susan while she was on the island. Harriet had come to visit her. There was just as much consternation in Susan's camp over seeing her exchanging polite remarks with her archenemy.

No one looked more astonished than Billie Holland-Smythe. She must have been congratulating herself on the success of publicly introducing the couples and the enmity it produced in the wives. Now, the wives had inexplicably called a truce. Billie walked over to where Susan and Harriet were sitting. "I've decided to host a luncheon to welcome Harriet to Anguilla. Minnie will be happy to get it organized, I'm sure. Let's plan it for one day next week." She beamed down at the two women. "I will get invitations out tomorrow. You'll be hearing from me," she said, walking away with a slightly evil smile.

***

"That wasn't so hard," Susan said as she and Harriet drove away from the first Art League gathering that she had truly enjoyed since arriving.

"What?" Harriet's head lolled against the headrest.

"Being nice to the Czarina. I told George I would, so his mission would go more smoothly."

"Mission?"

"Harriet, pay attention!" Susan glanced over at her friend to see her eyelids at half-mast and her jaw slack. "How much wine did you drink?"

Harriet turned to face her in super slow motion. "Oh, I don't know, three or six glasses?"

Susan laughed. "No wonder you can't focus. We'll talk about it tomorrow."

"Mmmmm." And Harriet was asleep.

It was a good thing the island was small, so Harriet wasn't so passed out that Susan didn't have too much trouble rousing her friend when they got to the orange bungalow. Max was smoking on the patio when she pulled in and helped get his tipsy wife out of the Mini. Susan supported Harriet into the house and held her upright while Max stripped off her clothing, leaving her in her underthings. They eased her into bed and went back to the patio. Max picked up his pack of Nevadas, the god-awful cigarettes from Curacao.

"Smoke?"

Susan shook her head. "I was determined to quit when we moved here, one drag and I'm sure I couldn't quit again." She pushed the pack toward him. "You go ahead, though. I rather enjoy watching other people smoke."

Max chuckled and shook one out of the pack and lit it. "So how was the bun fight?"

"It wasn't a bun fight, as you so coarsely put it. It was an Art League meeting."

"Were there any men there?"

She shook her head.

"Then it was a bun fight."

"Chauvinist."

He shrugged that off and looked at her expectantly. "Well?"

She picked up his lighter and began twisting it with her fingers. "It was fine. Christina Huckaby had her drawings and paintings on display. She's very talented, way more than many of the artist wannabes on the island, including moi."

He blew a stream of smoke at her. "That's not what I meant. How did it go with the Czarina?"

A laugh sputtered from Susan's lips. "How did you know I call her that?"

"It stands to reason, doesn't it? She's a Russian and you think she's an egotistical bitch. What else would you call her?"

"True." She put down the lighter and clasped her hands in front of her as if she were making a report in school. "Well, Harriet and I were looking at the art and Irina came right over to us. I introduced her to Harriet, and she was very nice. We commented on Christina's works and said which ones we liked. And then Irina, well, she actually compared them to my photos. That astonished me."

"Why?" He stubbed out his cigarette.

"Because she has spent every other meeting letting everyone know how much of a hack she thinks I am. I straight out told her I didn't think I was an artist. That what I do is child's play and that any eight-year-old could do it and do it better. I think that was the key to her unbending."

"How so?" He lit another cigarette, and Susan had to clamp her teeth to keep from saying "another—so soon?"

"Well, after I said that, she walked around the rest of the display with us, and she was actually fairly nice. I wonder how long the ceasefire will last."

CHAPTER 28

Rose

I overheard Billie suggest the garden party at the Art League meeting. It turned up on the social calendar, and I received an invitation. I really didn't have the time to spend sitting around Billie Holland-Smythe's pool for an afternoon, but I couldn't resist going to see what would happen.

Since Anguilla is a desert island rather than a tropical one, the climate thwarted Billie's plan to have palm trees and hibiscus around her pool. She had to settle for potted palms and a cactus fence with bougainvillea growing over it in a multitude of colors. Her landscape designer had installed a white nylon sunshade, like a sail, that could be drawn out with a series of pulleys to shade the tables. He had also planted a windbreak of tall candelabra cactus to deflect the persistent trade winds from blowing the tableware, food, and guests down the hill.

For her spur-of-the-moment luncheon to rekindle the Cold War, at least on Anguilla, Billie chose a palette of soft yellow and lilac for her decorations. Tired of the saturated reds, corals, and turquoises that so many decorated with, she said that those colors made her feel overheated. She preferred the soft pastels, thought them more ladylike, cooler, more appropriate for a ladies' luncheon.

In the invitations she sent out she asked her guests to come in garden party formal, hoping that they all understood that meant pale colored dresses with flowing skirts and strappy sandals. Billie relied on two of the invitees to keep the grapevine humming. She made certain to mention to them emphatically that she was aiming for a certain overall look for this party, so she depended on them to get the word out. She did not want to see one of her guests emerge from their car in a garish Hawaiian print sarong with flip-flops. At first, I thought I'd wear my wedding dress, but the flowers on it were red, not in Billie's color scheme. I had a pastel yellow sundress that looked okay on me now that I had a tan. I would wear that with some sandals, also not red.

Billie knew perfectly well that, alone among her guests, Irina would look dreadful in soft, pale colors. Someone with the Russian's dramatic pale skin and stark black eyes and hair would look like she was in the final stages of consumption. Billie didn't care.

I overheard Minerva tell Geneva that Billie thought making Irina look bad was the least she could do for king and country.

***

Four days after having the idea at the Art League meeting, twenty women arrived at Billie's mansion for a garden party. Irina had taken the Katherine Hepburn route. She was tall, slender, and leggy like Miss Hepburn, so she wore cream trousers and a cream silk shirt with the sleeves rolled to the elbow, looking as if she had just come off the tennis court. She had on a pair of gold sandals that added the right touch of glitz. And rather than wear the wire and stone jewelry she usually wore, she had unearthed some more traditional jewelry to wear with the subdued ensemble. Not quite ballsy enough to seat Susan and Irina at the same table, Billie had her staff arrange three large round tables that each seated eight on her spacious stone patio near the pool. The food was served buffet style. I was sure Billie thought that offered many more opportunities for Irina and Susan to bump into each other. When the cocktail time had passed and neither woman had flared up or stormed out, Billie was reduced to stronger measures. She insisted that Harriet and Susan sit with her; it was only natural that the hostess sits next to the guest of honor.

Susan gripped my wrist and said, "Please sit next to me. I don't know what Billie is planning, but I need the moral support."

I wasn't sure I wanted to be anywhere near the fireworks that were sure to erupt from the women's proximity, but I agreed.

What took a bit more maneuvering was to lure Irina to sit on her other side. When the remaining guests saw the four of them sitting side by side at a table with me on Susan's other side from Harriet, no one sat in the empty seats.

"Tell me, Harriet, how are you enjoying your stay on our little island?" Billie said to the woman on her right.

"Oh, we're loving it, Billie. Thanks for asking. Max loves racing around the island in George's Rover and meeting all the diving and birding chaps. Of course, he'd rather dive than tramp around chasing a bunch of foolish birds, but he says, when in Rome..."

Susan looked a bit strained her friend would pass along a remark that her husband had obviously made in private. She moved Harriet's glass toward herself and got up to pour her friend a cup of coffee.

Billie chuckled and said, "I wouldn't want to get out of bed in the early morning dark when on holiday, either. Did Max work with George? Is that how you came to be friends?"

Harriet opened her lips to answer, but Susan laid her hand on Harriet's arm and said, "No. Actually, Max was in the Navy. He was the commander of a submarine. Our families lived next to each other, and our children were school chums."

"You sent them to private school, of course," said Billie.

"No." Susan shook her head. "They went to the district schools just like the rest of the children in the neighborhood."

"But with George's prominent position in the government, couldn't you afford to send them to better schools?"

Susan hoisted a puzzled look on her face. I could see the effort it took her to paste it there. "Billie," Susan said, "I don't know where you're getting your information, but George was an executive in the British Fisheries Department. He wrote reports on annual catch counts and legislation about limits and other boring things, including touring fish processing plants all over the country." She smiled at the memory. "I used to make him burn his suit when he came home from one of those tours. He prided himself on being a hands-on manager, not one of those government inspectors who presses the flesh with the bigwigs, peeks through the door of the plant, and then goes off for a two-martini lunch. Not my George. He'd be in there among the fish guts and the fish scales, quizzing people about their working conditions and if they had any safety concerns. He'd come home smelling of mackerel or whatever fish was in season, and I'd march that suit right out into the garden and set it alight."

We looked at her in astonishment.

"Well, not the most cordial of welcomes, I'll grant you, but I got so I hated the smell of fish. Still do." Susan's eyes fell on the mound of conch salad on her plate and realized her gaffe. "Of course, this perfectly prepared luncheon on your lovely pool deck isn't even in the same universe with the squalid conditions of the places George was forced to work in." Susan raised her green eyes to meet Irina's black ones. "Don't you think this is a lovely luncheon, Irina?"

A tiny smile touched her lips and Irina said, "I do. Thank you so much for inviting me, Billie."

Billie sat back in her chair, defeated, and I thought, good for you, Susan, for deflecting the nosy old bat.

Naomi Minten took me aside when I was getting a refill of sparkling water. "How is it sitting up there with the warring women?"

I glanced around to make sure no one could overhear. "It's fine. Susan and Irina are being polite to each other and Harriet seems unaware of the tension Billie is trying to resurrect."

"Well, I think you're brave. You couldn't pay me to sit up there in the blast zone."

The meal went well. Everyone complimented Billie on the

menu, and Susan and Irina maintained their irritating cordiality despite Billie's best efforts. She even sidled up to Susan at the bar when they were both getting refills and said, "Getting friendly with the enemy, aren't you?"

To which Susan replied, "Not at all. Irina is quite bearable when you get to know her. I'm sorry we got off on the wrong foot earlier."

Not at all what Billie hoped for, I was sure. She fared no better when she tried to goad Irina into criticizing Susan, but then Billie and Irina had never really got on very well.

CHAPTER 29

George and Dimitri

George wasn't the keep-in-touch half of the marriage. He relied on Susan to send chatty emails and letters to family and friends. But the increasing pressure of having to sneak around to spend time with Dimitri called for desperate measures. So, George, who was great at writing reports on missions, sat at his computer fumbling over an email to his son.

> *Dear son, Please ship me a wireless-capable laptop and two wireless routers. The laptop doesn't need to be new. One of the refurbished ones your firm has lying around would do just fine. Be a good chap and don't mention this to your mother. And don't put your return address on the package. I don't want her to ask questions. We are fine. Thanks, Dad.*

And then he hit "send." He sat watching the cursor blink, wishing he could unsend it. He hated to embroil his son in the mess he had created, but knew no other way to get another wireless laptop on the island. There weren't any computer shops like at home.

It seemed to George that what was carried in stores was completely arbitrary, almost as if when a shipping container arrived, the merchants lined up and the contents of the container were handed out, one piece at a time, in a rotation. He would follow Susan into a clothing store and see a pile of video disc players stacked in a corner. The grocery store had a shelf of off-brand hand tools, and the bakery seemed to have one of everything; a radio, a few CDs, a handful of tee shirts, two or three cheap ceramic statues, a small box of candles, and a garden rake. The random nature of most of the island stores' inventory puzzled him. Didn't they plan what they ordered and stocked?

He was sure that Susan had let slip to both their children that Dad was back in his old job. He suspected they knew what it meant. That was why he felt confident that his son would respect his request not to tell Susan and would get the laptop and routers to him as soon as he could.

In just about two weeks, a package notice was in George's mailbox. He slid the note into his pocket, told Susan that he had to run into town, hopped in the Rover, and took off. He drove past Dimitri's place tooting his horn twice and then parked around the corner. Within fifteen minutes, he saw Dimitri in his side-view mirror turn the corner and walk toward him.

Dimitri came up on the passenger side and opened the door. "Sorry it took so long to get here, George. Irina did not want to let me out."

"That's okay. I'm not in any hurry."

"What is up?"

"I got a notice of a package. I think it's the laptop and routers."

Dimitri got in, eager to be more in touch with George without all the hassles and tricky coordination of signals. The men drove into town, careful to avoid places where someone who would report back to their wives might see them. They scouted the streets around the post office and George parked in a lot behind the auto parts store. Dimitri stayed in the Rover while George claimed his package. He was back in view in about a half hour, lugging a medium-sized box bound with miles of tape and dotted with *Fragile* stickers.

Dimitri hopped out and opened the rear hatch for his friend. "Here, it will be easier to open back here," he said.

George smiled at Dimitri's eagerness to have what was in the box. He pulled a box cutter from his pocket and carefully slit the tape. He opened a garbage bag. "Scoop out the packing peanuts into here. I need to get one router out of there. Then we can repack it and relabel it with your address. I will take it back inside and tell them they gave me the wrong box."

"Will that work?"

"Of course it will work. They're always screwing up like that, putting mail in the wrong box or handing out packages to anyone who asks."

They carefully corralled the packing material in the garbage bag, chasing any of the packing peanuts that wafted away into the vehicle or tried to escape across the parking lot. Neither man wanted to admit it to the other, but they both hated littering and were in the habit of patrolling the beaches and roadsides for it. George annoyed Susan regularly by pulling over to pick up large items blown by the roadside.

"Oh, for God's sake, George," she would have said, "there are people whose job it is to pick up that stuff. Can't you just leave it? It makes the car smell."

George would just smile and nod and continue picking up whatever he had stopped for. "You know, Susan, vegetation would grow over this stuff before the sanitation workers get to it. Besides, you've seen the signs: Keep Anguilla Clean. That makes litter everyone's job. I'm just doing my job."

Susan would roll her eyes and mutter under her breath, "I married Sir Galahad when I thought I'd married Sir Lancelot."

George would smile at her and lightly place a hand on her knee. "I wager my Sir Lancelot tendencies outweigh the Sir Galahad ones by a mile."

She would smile and have to agree while delicately removing his hand from its sly trip toward her lap.

Dimitri crowed with delight when he spotted the laptop thickly wrapped with bubble wrap.

He reached to pull it out, but George stopped him. "Better to leave it wrapped. That way you can unwrap it at home and if Irina sees you can tell her it came to help you keep tabs on me."

"Good thinking." He stirred the remaining packing around until he found one of the wireless routers. He pulled it out and handed it to George. "How are you going to explain this to Susan?"

George tapped the side of his nose. "No need. I always unpack boxes at the post office because Susan is death on clutter. I'll just tell her it's from the office, that it will help me track your movements or some such. She's so involved in sniping at your missus she won't question me."

Dimitri shook his head. "It is the same at my house. I think I could bring home one of the island's wild goats and as long as Irina thought it was a way to get back at Susan, she would accept it."

They both stood in silence, considering the hostile ripples still flowing out from the bombshell that Billie had dropped on the four of them at her party weeks before.

George was the first to come back to the present. "Damn that Billie. Without her interference, this charade would not have been necessary."

Dimitri nodded. "Da. We could have become friends, and our wives would have tolerated each other, and we would have had peace."

They repacked the laptop in its carton, making sure that George's son hadn't packed a letter in it, and then he relabeled it with Dimitri's address. George took it back into the post office, waited in line, and handed it over, telling the clerk that it had been delivered to him by mistake. He dropped Dimitri off a block from his house and went home to set up the router.

By the time Dimitri picked up the package the next day, he would have the router set up and running so they could keep in touch without the danger of their wives or anyone else with a wagging tongue catching them.

***

Dimitri took George's lead and unpacked the laptop and remaining router at the post office, leaving the carton there to be recycled. He didn't want to give Irina the opportunity to peel back George's quickly applied label to see that it was originally sent by the Clemment's son to George. Irina was already suspicious enough of everything and everyone since the Brits had arrived in Anguilla. He didn't need to add fuel to that fire.

As soon as he walked into the duplex with the bubble wrapped equipment under his arm, she was by his side. "What is that, Dimitri?"

"Oh, you are here, my dear," he said, feigning surprise. "This came from headquarters so that I can better keep in touch with them and intercept George's emails."

For the first time since Billie had ambushed them at her king's birthday party, Irina laid her cheek on his shoulder. "I am sorry that this is happening to our idyll. We were having such a good retirement here until they arrived, and now you are back at work." She turned and glared toward George and Susan's house. "I hate them."

Dimitri put his hand on her cheek and patted it. "Do not hate them, dushka. It is not their fault that we both ended up here. I think headquarters is mad to expect me to gather information from George. He is as wily as they come, and besides, our countries are now friends. At least we are supposed to be. What can the Russian government possibly want to know that they cannot get by merely asking?" He hated lying to his wife, but his lifelong profession made lying natural to him. Now that he had a wireless laptop and router, he and George could keep in closer touch, not risking discovery by one of the island busybodies who were all too eager to carry tales to one of their wives. He pressed his lips to Irina's forehead. "I need to go up to the Eastern Store today. There was a letter enclosed telling me to get a shredder."

"Of course, you must do as they say. We cannot afford to have your pension cut any more than they have already."

Dimitri carried the still-wrapped items into the back bedroom where they had made a small office and laid it on the desk. When he had peeled back the last layer of bubble wrap, he was horrified to see a note from George's son saying he hoped this laptop did the trick. If Irina had seen the note, the trick would have been done all right. He could not imagine how angry

Irina would be to know that he and George were perpetrating a ruse over their wives so that they could spend time together. Dimitri shook his head. The intrigue was addictive, and the dishonesty was too easy after his life of deception. He loved it. He would be sorry when they finally told the truth.

***

George was sick of the deception, sick of skulking around the tiny island of Anguilla where everyone knew everyone else's business. He was tired of lying to Susan, having to mind everything he said to her. It was what he had retired to get away from and here he was back in the saddle and, what was worse, it was a saddle of his own making. He was ready to tell the truth and take the consequences, but he had to talk it over with Dimitri. Both of them had to agree to break their silence because he knew Susan could not keep that bombshell to herself. She would be so angry that she would shout his duplicity from the rooftop. He should send Dimitri an email after Susan went to bed. He was lucky that England was in an earlier time zone, so she didn't ask questions when he stayed up later to get in touch with his handler on the secure line or when he was up before dawn decoding the night's dispatches. She hadn't complained about the expense when he bought a shredder at the Eastern Store, either. He was mortified and struggled to keep his face still when the gregarious woman at the register commented about there being a run on shredders because a nice Russian man had been in earlier buying the same thing. She caught him by surprise, and he almost shushed her. As it was, he got an odd look from the woman because he had jerked when she said it. Ten years ago, a reaction like that would have gotten him killed.

CHAPTER 30

Rose

I had been bugging Iggy to learn to scuba dive so that we could go diving together, but he was strangely reluctant. He could swim, I knew that because we went on midnight swims together, so what was the hold-up?

I hadn't seen many Black people diving, just my previous guest Warren come to think of it, so maybe that was it. Maybe it was because he was an islander and few, if any of them dived. Well, there was Dougie at Tamarind, he dived all the time. I wondered what made him different.

Then I got to thinking about how to make Iggy feel more comfortable in the crowd of expats and make them more comfortable with him. They appreciated him as an electrician but didn't seem to see him as a man or a friend.

I didn't see the racial thing, never had. Oh, I noticed when people's skin was a different color, I'd have to be blind not to, but the color of people's skin didn't make a difference to me. There was my knitting friend Lomira and the other local women who came to knit nights. They were just regular women with the same concerns that I had—groceries, kids, and husbands. No matter the race, those things were the same.

Suddenly Iggy's arms tightened around me and he said, "Stop grunting and huffing and go to sleep."

"Sorry, I didn't realize that I was making noise. I'll go to sleep. I promise." I untangled myself from his embrace and moved to my side of the bed.

***

The cookout was the usual get together of the expat community and I wanted to go.

"They did not invite me," Iggy said. "So, I do not think that I should go."

"Oh, don't be silly," I said. "I'm sure they meant for both of us to go to the party."

He shook his head. "I do not think so. If they wanted me at the party, my name would have been on the invitation too."

I dropped my hands in exasperation. "But there isn't an invitation. It's a single piece of paper. A flyer advertising the cookout. Susan handed it to me at knitting the other night and said, I hope that you and Iggy can make it. 'You and Iggy' she said, so you are invited."

"I will think about it. You know that everyone else will be white, that I will be the only islander at the party, except if someone brings a servant along, like Minerva coming with Billie Holland-Smythe."

"Minerva isn't a servant, she's Billie's housekeeper. There's a difference. Just like Geneva isn't a servant, she's a housekeeper."

"But she is your servant. She is subservient to you, depending on your goodwill for her employment."

"Oh, you're making me confused, splitting hairs about the relationships between employer and employee. I'd be happy to sit down for a meal with Geneva. We have lunch together often, well, when I can convince her to sit down with me."

"Yes, when you can convince her to sit down with you. Do you not notice how uncomfortable she is when she does that? You are forcing her to face and break the class barrier when you sit down with her to eat. She feels like she needs to be under you, not alongside you."

"But I don't feel that way."

"No, you do not, but Geneva does. She is very conscious of her status in your house, just like I am very conscious of my status when we are at get-togethers with your friends."

I flung out my hands. "Maybe you should learn to dive or snorkel so that you could go on an outing with the expat community."

"They would not welcome me. I am part of the background. Besides, I still work at my job, they are retired. I cannot just down tools and go off gallivanting during the day like they do."

I moved closer to him and fiddled with one of his shirt buttons. "I wish you would learn to dive so that you and I could go diving together."

"I am not a good enough swimmer."

I looked up into his eyes. "You are a good enough swimmer. You swim better than I do. What's the real reason you don't want to learn to dive?"

He brought his hands up to clasp my wrists. "I am afraid. I did not want to tell you, but I am afraid of what might happen under the water. Big sharks, barracuda, running out of air, all those things could happen, and I would not know what to do."

I slid my arms around him. "Oh, Iggy, they teach you what to do about running out of air in class and big sharks and barracuda don't bother you. You're too big and noisy to be worth their trouble."

"What about the news stories of people being bitten by sharks?"

I squirmed a bit in his embrace. "Well, usually those are swimmers or surfers and they're on the surface and look like a seal, like prey. That's usually what happens."

Iggy grunted as if he wasn't convinced.

"This conversation has ranged far from the discussion of you and me going to the expat cookout tomorrow," I said. "I think we should go and see how it works out. If you're too uncomfortable, we can leave."

"Really? You would leave early if I felt uncomfortable?"

"Of course. I'm not staying someplace where you feel unwelcome. You're my date and where you go, I go."

***

That week, the cookout was at Little Harbour beach down at the end of an almost paved road that ended in the sand. There was a lot of room for parking and a nice flat area for grills and beach chairs. Iggy and I weren't the first ones to arrive, and for once it looked like one group instead of two. The men clustered around a pair of oil drum grills.

"Hey, Iggy," called George, "grab a beer and come join us."

Iggy waved and leaned down to my ear. "What am I supposed to do?"

I looked at him. "Get something to drink and go over to stand by George. See what the men are talking about and join in if you can. Laugh at the jokes if you can't."

Iggy walked across the sand, bent down to pull a beer from a cooler in the shade, popped the top, and went over to stand by George.

George put his arm around Iggy's shoulders. "Gentlemen, this is Iggy Solomon. His brother owns Johnno's Beach Bar, where you've all spent a few hours, I wager. He and his wife Rose own Seaview Bed & Breakfast in Sandy Ground. I know a few of our friends stayed there when they visited the island. Rose makes the best pimento cheese sandwiches I have ever eaten."

Hands reached across to shake Iggy's hand.

"Glad to meet you. My sister-in-law stayed at your place and raved about the breakfasts," said one man. "You'll have to share the recipe for the egg bake. She couldn't say enough about it."

Iggy sipped his beer and said, "Well, you will have to talk to Rose. Those are her recipes, and I do not know if she will share them. But I will agree, her egg bakes are my favorite, right after her mango lime muffins."

"Oh muffins. I could go for a muffin in the morning. Will she toast them for you?"

"I do not know. I have never asked, but it sounds like an interesting idea to try," Iggy said.

Another of the men said, "Are you retired, Iggy?"

Iggy tugged at his hair. "Despite the gray in my hair, I am

still a working man. I am an electrician and cannot seem to stop working."

A laugh rolled around the group.

"Yes, it's hard to quit when you love what you do."

"Do you scuba dive or snorkel?"

"No, I do not. I love to swim, but I have never dived or snorkeled."

"What about birds?" Dimitri asked. "Are you interested in the birds that fly through on their migration?"

Iggy turned toward him. "You stayed at Seaview last winter, if I remember."

"That is true. I am Dimitri Roskova. My wife Irina and I were visiting the island and fell in love with it, so we moved here in retirement."

"How do you do, Dimitri?" Iggy held out his hand to shake. "I enjoy seeing the birds, but I do not know their names or their habits. Maybe when I retire, I will learn."

I looked across the sand and watched Iggy in the group of expat men. He was the only islander in the group, and he was visible because of his color and because of his posture. I could see that George was trying to include Iggy in the conversation, but Iggy was giving short answers and mostly listening. That was okay. A good listener was always popular.

"Do you think your Iggy will fit in?" Susan leaned on my shoulder and whispered into my ear.

"I don't know. He doesn't really have a hobby that he can talk about. All he does is work. He's too busy for hobbies."

Susan nudged me. "I'll bet George can talk him into going along on one of their snorkeling outings. Iggy swims, doesn't he?"

"He does, but he's not real comfortable with a mask, snorkel, and fins."

"You know people will be happy to know an honest tradesman on the island, and I'm sure that Iggy can recommend other reliable workmen to the group."

"Yes, but that puts him and his friends at a disadvantage,

kind of like the hired help. Look around, Iggy's the only islander here."

Susan surveyed the group. "Yes, he is. Who else can we include? Maybe you know some people who would fit in."

I shook my head. "I don't really know. Dru Brooks is a friend of mine. Her father was governor of Anguilla for a time. She might fit in. The other people I know are business owners, like Iggy's brother, Johnno, and Rebecca O'Neill from the Barrel Stave restaurant, but I don't think that they would be comfortable in this crowd. Maybe I need to join Rotary or the Chamber of Commerce to build up a network of locals to offset this crowd of expats."

"Maybe that would be a good idea. See how you fare in a group that's decidedly the other color."

"Yeah, I'd get a little taste of what Iggy goes through. It's a wonder he asked me to marry him."

"Well, my dear, what happens in the bedroom has very little to do with what happens in the real world."

We laughed and nodded.

"So very true."

The men stood around the grills while two of them tended the ribs that were roasting.

"Did someone bring sauce? These are about ready to be turned again."

Mike Angerer got a jar of homemade barbecue sauce out of a cooler and carried it to the grill.

"It's my last one."

"Not the last one forever?"

"Oh no, but I need to set aside a weekend to make another batch. I have to collect jars from people I've given it to because jars are scarce on the island."

"I have jars," Iggy said. "I can never get rid of a good jar. You collect them and if you run short, let me know and I will give you some of mine."

Mike clapped him on the shoulder. "My man, that's the contribution that will earn you your own jars of sauce."

The other men looked at Iggy with new respect. They had to plead for a jar of sauce and not everyone got one.

The women looked up at the outburst of laughter from the men. "I wonder what they're talking about."

Ali Angerer laughed. "Either sex or sauce. That's our last quart of sauce. I'm sure Mike is talking about dedicating a weekend to making more. I just hope we can get enough tomatoes and molasses to make a full batch. You all need to dig out the jars and return them so that we can refill them. Jars are extremely hard to find on the island. Last time I had to order a case of them from Amazon and the shipping was brutal."

"I don't think Iggy would talk about sex," I said. "He's very private. It must be sauce. Is the sauce really that good?"

One woman exclaimed. "It's the best barbecue sauce you'll ever eat. I don't know where Mike and Ali got the recipe, but it's the bomb."

By now, they gathered around the tables where the side dishes were arranged, shifting the bowls around to group the fruits with the fruit salads and the pasta salads together. There was a bowl of corn salad that someone picked up and smelled. "Who brought real corn and where did you get it?"

"I've never seen corn on the cob on the island at this time of year."

Miriam spoke up. "Jane's goddaughter shipped us a dozen ears, and I knew that wouldn't be enough if I left the kernels on the cobs, so we cooked it up, cut it off the cobs, and made a salad with tomatoes, onions, and corn."

"Did you butter the corn?" one of the other women said. "I like a lot of butter on my fresh corn."

"No, we didn't butter it. I don't think butter would go well with the tomatoes, onions, and the splash of vinegar Jane put in there."

"Well, it looks delicious. Can't wait to try it."

By then, the men were calling out for trays to put the ribs on. Two of the women got pot holders and carried over a couple of baking trays for the men to load up with racks of ribs. When the trays got back to the tables, there was someone ready with a sharp knife to cut the racks into eating size portions.

"Where's the rest of the sauce for dribbling on top?" Ali asked.

Mike carried over a jar that was barely a quarter full. "Be sparing with this. It's the last of the last batch of sauce."

The men joined the women at the tables and the party got started. Plates got filled and people sat in groups of four and six, balancing their plates on their laps and setting their drinks alongside them in the sand.

"We need some of those lawn drink holders," someone said. "A lot of them."

Iggy got into line behind me. "I am going snorkeling with George tomorrow morning. I hope you do not mind," he said into my ear.

"No, I don't mind. Just you and George, or the entire crowd?"

"Just me and George. I told him I am not familiar with the gear, and he offered to take me out and help me learn. I thought that was very nice of him."

"Very nice indeed. Sounds like you might have made a friend today."

***

When we got back to Seaview, everyone was in an uproar. One of the beach dogs had gotten in through the kitchen door and had run all over the hotel, upstairs and down, pulling towels down from the bars in the bathroom and nosing around in the garbage cans. Geneva and Silas had chased it out, but Silas was bitten on the hand as he tried to grab the dog to get it to the door. Geneva had cleaned the bite and bandaged it when we returned.

I said, "I think you should go to the clinic since I am sure that the beach dogs don't get rabies shots."

Silas's eyes got round when I said that. "I do not want to go to the doctor. Geneva washed the bite and put salve on it. It will be okay."

Geneva insisted. "Mrs. Rose is right, Silas. You need to have it checked out and we need to remember which dog it was in case it acts mad."

"All right, I will go to the clinic." He put his hands up to stop the barrage of advice. "You can drive, but you are not driving my truck. We can go in your car, Geneva."

Geneva fetched her purse from the back room and pulled her car keys from it. "I do not want to drive your truck. It is too big and too noisy for me. We will be just fine in my car. Now come on."

Iggy had been silent, and I looked at him after the young people left.

"What? Something's bothering you."

"It is not good, not good at all, that Silas got bitten by one of the beach dogs. Usually, those dogs are submissive when you lay hands on them. That he got bitten could mean that it has rabies. Did they tell you what dog it was?"

A voice came from the doorway into the lobby. "I took its picture. That would help identify it." It was one of the guests. He held out his phone.

"Oh, I know that one," Iggy said. "It is not friendly and stays down by Old Reynaldo's house. I think I will walk down and talk to him about it." He went out the back door and turned left out of the backyard, headed to the neighborhood at the end of the road.

When they were all gone, I went upstairs and started cleaning up the mess the dog made. I sorted out clean towels and put them into the guest's room. I'd have to remind her to take her towels to her room when she finished in the bathroom. I mopped the floor in both bathrooms and swept up the sand that had shaken out of the dog's fur upstairs and in the lobby. In the kitchen, I scooped the garbage back into the can, swept up the spilled fruit peels and coffee grounds, and mopped the floor.

Iggy came back looking sweaty and disheveled. "We got the dog tied up at Old Reynaldo's place. He did not like it, but neither of us got bitten. I stopped at the police station to tell them that the dog had bitten Silas and that it was tied up so no one else would get hurt."

"What will happen to it?"

"They will monitor it for 10 days and if it does not show signs of rabies, then it will be released. Officer Micah called the local veterinarian. She will come pick up the dog and keep it under observation."

"Good."

CHAPTER 31

Rose

I was in the kitchen mixing up a batch of mango lime muffins when Iggy came home from his snorkeling lesson with George. He came in carrying a bag with his towel and some extra snorkel gear I had and set it on the kitchen island.

"Hey, don't put that sandy saltwater bag on the island. I just wiped it off."

"Sorry." He quickly removed it and used the hem of his tee shirt to wipe off the sandy mess.

"How did it go? Did you have fun? What did you see?"

"Slow down, Rose. Give me a chance to catch my breath. It went fine. George is an excellent teacher. We went to West End Bay in front of my house because it is calm, protected, and usually empty of people. It took me a little time to get used to breathing through the snorkel and even longer to stop tipping my head down so far that water would rush into the tube and choke me."

I stopped stirring the muffin batter to listen. "It took me a while to learn not to do that, too. What did you see?"

His eyes got big, and he spread out his arms. "I saw so many fish. Many big ones, Parrotfish and Grouper, even a Sea Bass. It is no wonder I have good luck fishing there. It is like a city underwater. I could have watched for hours. No wonder you love diving so much. There is so much to see. I never imagined it would be like that."

I could feel the size of the grin that stretched my cheeks.

"I'm so glad you enjoyed yourself."

"George invited me to come with them the next time the group has an outing. It is next Wednesday, usually a workday for me, but I think I will take the day off and go snorkeling. Do you think that will be all right?"

"I think that's a grand plan. Why don't we go over to Tamarind later and see if they have a rash guard shirt in your size so that you won't sunburn your back?" I finished stirring the batter, put the lid on the mixing bowl, and slid it into the fridge. "I'm glad you took an old shirt today, but you might feel more comfortable in the group with an official diving shirt rather than something headed for the rag bag."

He nodded his agreement. "I will hang my towel and swimming suit on the line and rinse off the gear you lent me. We should look for a pair of water shoes that are more my size too. My toes were a little cramped in these."

"Good idea." I was so thrilled that Iggy had enjoyed snorkeling with George enough to want his own gear and be willing to go along with the group next week. Maybe one of these days he'd agree to take a Discover Scuba class and decide to get certified to dive.

CHAPTER 32

Rose

Geneva and I finished the laundry early. There were only two rooms filled so far that week. Two more guests were arriving on Wednesday to stay until Monday. It was the first time a guest hadn't been there from Saturday to Saturday, and I felt like it threw my entire schedule into disarray. I wouldn't have those couple hours breathing room on Saturday between one group of guests leaving and the next arriving. I didn't realize how much I relied on those hours to decompress between departures and arrivals until they were gone.

The Saturday-to-Saturday guests were two couples who had arrived as strangers but formed a friendship and ended up doing everything together all week long. They hiked all the trails listed in the guidebook, some more than once. I put them in touch with Dimitri Roskova when they said they'd like to try birdwatching. He invited them to accompany the local group on their Friday morning ramble along the northernmost point of Anguilla. They were thrilled.

That meant that I got the coffee ready to turn on and baked muffins for them to reheat in the microwave, so I didn't have to get up before first light to feed them. They didn't seem to mind the self-serve breakfast.

***

On Wednesday morning, I dusted and aired out the two empty rooms to prepare for the arriving guests. They checked in just after lunch, saying that they'd flown in on the Island Air flight from Barbados and neither one of them was smiling.

"Welcome to Seaview. You must be Angie and Lisa." I said, hoping to generate a smile or at least erase the frowns.

"This place better be nicer than that dump of a hostel you booked us into on the last island."

"Oh, bite me, Angie. You were the one who found it and insisted we stay there. I chose this one. It's bound to be better."

I stood at the desk, entering their information, listening to them bicker. I handed back their driver's licenses and credit cards and said, "Let me show you to your rooms." I kept up a bright and cheerful monologue all the way to the turquoise and lilac rooms. Telling them about the colors of their towels matching their rooms, not to leave towels in the bathrooms, and that they were welcome to keep lunch foods and doggie bags in the refrigerator to reheat in the microwave.

"We can cook in the kitchen, right?" Angie asked.

"No, I'm sorry. It's against the Health Department rules for guests to use my kitchen. I have a grill on the patio you're welcome to use and there's a microwave in the lobby."

She looked daggers across the hall at Lisa. "We cooked at the hostel, but can't cook here? What did you think we would do, Lisa? Eat out twice a day?"

I slowly backed out from between them and left them arguing over their cheese and fruit plates and wine. As I reached the bottom of the stairs, I heard both doors slam almost in unison. The next few days promised to be interesting ones.

The next morning, as I was laying the table settings, I saw Angie leave the bathroom with only a towel wrapped around her. There was little left to the imagination. Well, if she didn't mind people seeing her undressed, I wouldn't say anything. Not unless someone complained. At breakfast, Angie and Lisa sat at separate tables with their faces turned away from each other.

When I put the plate down in front of her, Angie recoiled. "What's this stuff?"

"Shakshuka. It has sauteed tomatoes, onions, bell peppers, and garlic with a little spice and an egg poached in it. It's from the Middle East and is very popular with my guests." I set down a plate with some pita bread wedges on it. "People like to scoop up the tomato with bread. Try it. You might like it."

"It looks disgusting."

Lisa turned. "Oh, for god's sake, Angie. Try something new. You like tomatoes. You like eggs. Just try it. It's delicious."

The two couples at the other table watched the exchange with raised eyebrows. No one said anything. They just ate their breakfasts quickly and got up to leave.

From the kitchen, I could see Angie picking at her plate. She finally took a deep breath, scooped up some egg and tomato with the torn pita, and took a bite. I couldn't see her face, but her shoulders relaxed, so I knew it would be okay.

***

The next day, I was in my apartment doing a little cleaning when I heard a noise in the kitchen. Geneva was gone for the day, so it couldn't be her. Iggy hadn't returned from a job, so it couldn't be him either. It wasn't someone getting a drink from the fridge because the sound was wrong. I opened the door from my sitting room to the kitchen to see Angie stirring something in a saucepan. There were things strewn all over the kitchen island.

"What are you doing?" I asked.

"Just fixing some mac and cheese for supper."

"I'm sorry, but you can't cook in my kitchen. I told you that. It's against the Health Department rules and you could get me into a lot of trouble. Stop right now." I went over to the stove, turned off the burner, and faced her. I could feel my frustration building, but I took a breath and controlled my voice. "I'm tempted to ask you to leave Seaview, but I won't. Get out of my kitchen right now." I reached out to take the saucepan from the burner, but she was faster and clutched it to her chest.

"You can't be serious. You'd throw me out just for cooking in here?"

"Yes, I would. I'm new here and under a lot of scrutiny. If you wanted to cook, you should have stayed at Sydan's across the road. Anne has kitchenettes in her rooms." I could see that the heat from the pan was getting uncomfortable as she held it close. "Put down the pan and leave, please."

She slammed the pan down on the stainless-steel counter. "Okay fine. I'll just fast for the rest of my stay."

"Angie, you can get cheese and fruit and veggies at the market for lunches and pick up fresh meat to grill in the evenings. You just can't cook in my kitchen. It's against the rules."

Her face screwed up with anger, she said, "So you say. I think you just don't want anyone else in your precious kitchen. I'm outta here."

I watched her storm out of the kitchen, through the lobby, and up the stairs. Her room door slammed, and all was quiet. Looking at the mess on the kitchen island, I sighed, then re-wrapped and put away the block of cheese that Angie had appropriated for her supper, closed the plastic container of pasta, and put it away. I cleared the discarded packaging and used utensils from the kitchen island, dumped the curdled mac and cheese in the trash, and washed the dishes.

"Excuse me, Rose," Lisa said from the doorway. "Have you seen Angie? I took a walk down the beach and expected to see her out front when I got back, but she's not there."

"She's in her room. I caught her cooking in here and asked her to stop. She got angry and stormed out. It wouldn't surprise me if she was packing."

"Oh." Lisa blushed and took a step toward me. "I'm sorry, Rose. This trip hasn't been the dream experience we both thought it would be. A couple of our hostels were pretty rough, the food has been disappointing, and our money is running out faster than we thought it would. I know that doesn't excuse Angie's behavior, but it kind of explains it. I'll go talk to her." She turned and left the kitchen.

Monday couldn't come soon enough for me.

An hour later, there was a timid knock on my sitting room door. Iggy would have just come in and, anyway, he would have come in the back door. I crossed the room and opened it. Angie stood there looking pale and wringing her hands.

"I'm sorry, Rose. I didn't intend to get you in trouble. I didn't realize that you were telling the truth about the Health Department rules. I thought you just wanted to keep us out of the kitchen."

"Thank you for apologizing."

"Lisa went up the hill to Vista Market and bought some chicken. Could we please use the grill and charcoal to cook it?"

Iggy stepped in through the back door and heard her question. "I will get the grill started for you, Angie. Meet me out on the patio." He set down his tools, kissed my cheek, and went back out.

Angie stayed there.

"Is there something else?"

"Yes. Can we please use plates and silverware from the kitchen? We can't afford to buy that stuff and don't have it with us."

"Of course you can. I'll put it on the kitchen island for you, but you need to eat at the tables in the lobby."

"Okay. Thank you, Rose. We really appreciate it."

Lisa and Angie stood by the grill watching their chicken cook. Iggy had banked the coals to one side so that the outside of the chicken didn't burn while the inside stayed raw. He made sure that the women knew what he had done and why before he came back into the apartment to wash up after work and starting the grill.

"It sounds like you had an interesting day today."

I recounted the confrontation with Angie over cooking in the kitchen and thanked him for setting up the grill for them. "I don't think I could have been polite after Angie's tantrum this afternoon. I suppose I should be grateful that she's the first guest who tried to sneak into the kitchen and cook."

He put his hand on my shoulder. "Would you like to go out for supper tonight?"

"I would love to." I felt the smile spread across my face and my shoulders relax. "Let's walk down to the Barrel Stave and see what Rebecca's cooking tonight. Give me a minute to wash my face and change."

We had a lovely supper of grilled fish with sweet potato fries and a salad. Rebecca treated us to a slice of her luscious lemon cake to split for dessert.

***

Angie was on her best behavior for the rest of her stay, which was only another two and a half days, but it was a relief. She and Lisa took the launch out to Sandy Island and rented snorkel gear to paddle around on the shallow reef offshore. They used the grill again on Saturday evening to cook another piece of chicken, only asking for Iggy's help lighting the charcoal. "We don't want to burn ourselves," Lisa said. He was happy to be of service.

The other four guests left on Saturday morning to catch their flight to San Juan and then went on to their homes. At breakfast, they were teary at having to part company and already making plans to "meet in the middle" between their homes in a few months to get together again.

Geneva and I cleaned the sea side rooms and the bathrooms once they left. It felt a little odd not to clean the garden view rooms too, but we left them alone, figuring that I'd tackle them on Monday when Angie and Lisa left. Actually, we didn't have to rush to clean those rooms because no one would occupy them until the following Saturday.

Two more couples arrived on Saturday afternoon. One couple was Heidi and Hans-Jurgen from Germany. We'd met when we were all staying at Sydan's the year before while I was refurbishing Seaview. Anne Robinson, Iggy's sister, had sent them my way because Sydan's was full the week they wanted to stay.

"I know we can't cook in your kitchen, Rose, but we can make do with the microwave and the grill," Heidi said. "I can microwave and Hans-Jurgen will grill. It will work out just fine."

"I'm glad to see you again. I hope you enjoy your stay."

"Oh, we will dive every morning and go sightseeing in the afternoons," Hans-Jurgen said. "I read about some hiking trails in a new guidebook, and we are eager to seek them out."

I finished entering their information in the registration program and handed his cards back. "Be sure to arrange with Thomas to hang your dive gear in his gear locker. All I have are pegs on the back porch and they're much too exposed for security."

"Thank you for the information. I will do that when we go over to sign up this afternoon." Hans-Jurgen reached to pick up a suitcase and turned to me. "Maybe you can come diving with us one day while we are here."

"I'm sure I can arrange that."

They hauled their suitcases up the stairs. Geneva escorted them to the yellow room, explained about the towel colors matching the paint of their room, and gave them the cheese and fruit plate and wine we served to arriving guests.

The other couple, Gregg and Claudia, were from America and were exhausted. "We had to leave home at four A.M. to get to the airport in time for our flight. Then we had a long layover in Detroit, another layover in Miami, and a final two-hour layover in San Juan," Claudia said. "I need a nap."

"I'm not surprised. That's quite a trek to get here. Let me show you to your room and you can stretch out for a snooze." I picked up the fruit and cheese plate and a split of red wine and escorted them to the salmon room, giving my welcome spiel as we walked.

It felt good to have all the rooms filled again, even if the garden view rooms would be vacated on Monday.

CHAPTER 33

Rose

Silas stopped in Seaview after church on Sunday morning. "Uncle Iggy, are you coming to the car show?"

Iggy looked up from the lamp he was rewiring for a neighbor. "I do not know, Silas. I have seen all the cars around the island lately."

Silas shook his head. "I heard Henry is bringing out his 1957 Chevy Bel Air this year. You don't want to miss seeing those tail fins gleaming in the sun. It is a rare thing for him to get Justine out of the storage shed."

I was folding towels on the other side of the kitchen island. "Who's Justine? And why does he keep her in a shed?"

Silas and Iggy laughed. "Justine was Henry's daughter. She passed a few years back, but she loved that convertible, so he named it after her. Since she is gone, he rarely takes the car out, but this weekend is her birthday, so he will take it out for a spin. He said he would be at the car show."

Tears filled my eyes. "That's so sweet. Iggy, go."

"You come too, Rose. Get to meet more of my friends."

I thought about the laundry that needed doing and decided it would wait. "All right, let's go."

I changed my shirt and put on better sandals while Iggy put his tools away and washed his hands.

Silas left, saying he was on his way to pick up Geneva and would see us there. I put on sunscreen and grabbed a hat, assuming we'd be walking around looking at cars where there was no shade. I left a note on the registration desk telling the guests that I'd be out for the afternoon.

After a short, ten-minute drive into The Valley, we arrived. Iggy parked his truck at the end of a long line of cars and trucks, and we walked to the cars on display. The parking lot of the football field (what's called soccer in the States) behind the secondary school was full of classic cars and muscle cars shining in the strong Caribbean sun. There were a few souped-up street rods there, too. It was easy to see how much the owners valued their show cars. Quite a few of them stood with a chamois in their hands, ready to buff out any fingerprints left by too eager viewers. Having grown up in a family with a restored Model A Ford, I knew how particular classic car owners could be. There was a good-size crowd of people strolling along the row of cars on display. In the center of the row stood a gleaming red and white convertible with impressive tail fins and a white leather interior.

"Wow, that must be Justine. That is one beautiful car," I said.

Silas and Geneva walked up to join us. They were holding hands and Geneva looked very different from the way she dressed to come to work at Seaview. For work, she wore slacks and a blouse or a shirtwaist dress. Today she had on jeans shorts and a sleeveless shirt tied into a knot at her waist. Dressed this way, I could see why Silas was attracted to her. I had never noticed before, but she had great legs.

We walked slowly along, stopping to admire the individual cars and talk to their proud owners. Most of the muscle cars were the property of young men around Silas' age. The older men around Iggy's age were the ones with the classic cars and street rods. I was amazed to see Iggy transform into someone very different from the man I knew. He slipped into speaking a kind of Creole that was worlds apart from his usual careful speech. He introduced me as his wife to all the car owners, earning him some sly looks and a few fist bumps.

I touched Iggy's shoulder. "What are they saying?"

"Just congratulating me on our marriage." He gave my elbow a nudge to get me moving.

I thought he looked a little embarrassed, but let it go. Maybe once I'd been on the island longer, I'd understand the patois and not need a translator.

Iggy talked to the car owners and many of the locals attending the show. I stood by his side, not understanding most of what was said. They talked so fast and in a language I didn't know. I felt kind of like a third wheel.

When we'd seen all the cars and been up and down the row twice, Silas said, "Geneva and I brought a picnic. There is enough for all four of us. We would like you to join us."

Iggy and I looked at each other and nodded. "We would love to, Silas," Iggy said. "Where would you like to eat?"

Geneva spoke up. "Let's go over to Junks Hole Bay. There are tables there, wooden tables, so we won't have to sit in the sand or get it blown into our food."

"Good idea," Silas said. "Do you want to follow us or ride along and we will bring you back to your truck later?"

"I am not so old that I cannot drive down to Junks Hole. I know the way. We will see you there."

We drove out of The Valley and up the main road to Island Harbour and then off on the side road to Junks Hole Bay. I could tell it was a popular spot because of how deep the ruts and potholes in the road down to the beach were.

Geneva had made an excellent picnic. There were cold cut sandwiches, coleslaw, and watermelon. All four of us ate like it had been days since we'd seen food. "This is delicious, Geneva. I love coleslaw and this stuff is to die for. Would you be willing to share your recipe?"

She smiled and looked at me out of the corner of her eye. "I will only if you will share your recipe for banana bread. Every time you make it, the kitchen smells good for the whole day."

"Of course you can have the recipe. It's not a secret. I'll write it out and have it ready for you tomorrow when you come to work."

"Thank you, Mrs. Rose. I will bring the coleslaw recipe. It is from my grandmother, but is not a secret either."

Silas and Iggy walked off into the scrub to attend to the call of nature while Geneva and I packed the picnic things back into the cooler. There wasn't much left. I thought that Geneva and I had taken a baby step toward friendship that day.

***

When we were back in the truck driving across the island toward Seaview, I asked Iggy about the way he was talking at the car show. "What language was that? I've never heard you speak it before. You always sound so proper when you talk around me."

"Oh, it was just the island patois. The dialect I speak with my old friends and family when you are not around. I know you would not understand, so I leave off when I am with you."

"Am I a catch?"

"What do you mean?"

I turned in my seat to look at him. "Well, when you introduced me to the men with the cars, they gave you a sidelong look and a fist bump. So, I wonder if I'm a catch."

"I am glad that I caught you." He kept his eyes on the road, but reached over to pat my leg.

I pushed his hand away. "That's not what I mean. Did they think you had snagged a rich white woman to take care of you?"

He had a grace to look sheepish. "Probably. I will not tell them you scrimp and save just like the Anguillans. They think all Americans are rich. They see so many Americans and Europeans stay at the big resorts and dine in fine restaurants. Most natives think that all white people are rich. They do not meet people like you and Seaview's guests too often. I will let them think whatever they want to think."

"What if they ask you why you're still working so much?"

"I will tell them you are miserly and will not give me an allowance so I can be a man of leisure."

"Oh, thanks a lot."

We both burst out laughing. Iggy laughed so hard that he pulled over into a gravel lot so he wouldn't crash his truck.

When we had gotten control of ourselves, he pulled back out onto the road.

"Do you wish you had a car like Justine?"

He shook his head. "No. Convertibles are too hot to ride in with the top down. The sun beats down on you and fries your head. No, thank you. Besides, I have no place to park it out of the weather like Henry does."

***

When we got back to Seaview, all the guests were out. I was happy to have a few minutes of peace to cool off after being in the sun for so long.

For the rest of their stay, Angie and Lisa were model guests. They asked permission to use the grill each evening, effusive in their thanks to Iggy, who lit the charcoal for them each time. Angie insisted on washing their dishes after each meal. "I don't want to make more work for you, Rose. You've done enough for us as it is."

It was hard to remember how tired Claudia and Gregg were when they arrived by the way they spent their week in Anguilla. They were up before breakfast on Sunday and had already taken a walk around the neighborhood before I'd put the coffee on. Once they'd eaten, they left to spend the morning snorkeling off Sandy Island. They came down to Johnno's jump-up with us and were still going strong when Iggy and I left around ten. All week long it was go go go. It made me tired just watching them.

Heidi and Hans-Jurgen weren't around Seaview any more than Claudia and Gregg were. They went diving in the mornings and hiked and explored most afternoons. One thing guests like them did for me was give me extra activities I could recommend to my other guests.

The two couples went hiking together on the Katouche Valley Trail, down in the southwest corner of the island. They returned raving about passing through a tropical rainforest laced with soft streams and past tumbling waterfalls. Listening to them talk about their experience, I decided I needed to spend an hour at the Anguilla Tourism Board office to gather some new information to have on hand.

***

It looked like Angie and Lisa had a great time at Johnno's jump-up on Sunday night, the night before they left. Each of them danced with Edward a few times and they had lots of other partners clamoring for their attention all evening. I would never forget Angie's unhappiness when they arrived or her incursion into my kitchen, but I was glad that she seemed to have gotten over the mad she had on at first and enjoyed her stay at Seaview and on Anguilla.

Gregg and Claudia went down to Johnno's for the party with Heidi and Hans-Jurgen but weren't lucky enough to get a table. They leaned on the half-wall on the side of the beach bar and parked their drinks on the edge of the nearest table when they went to dance. It wasn't the most comfortable way to party, but they didn't seem to mind.

CHAPTER 34

Rose

I stole away on Tuesday to go diving with Heidi and Hans-Jurgen. It was a windy day, so the ride out was short and bumpy. Our first dive was on Paintcan Reef. It got its name from the myriad of colors of sponges and corals, mostly the sponges. The reef structure is larger here than on other reefs in the area and it's at a forty-five-degree slope that's the standard shape of a reef around Anguilla.

It was a little challenging to get geared up and walk from my seat to the gap in the boat's side where we made our entries, but Dougie and Freddy were ready to help. Walking always took a bit of effort with the heavy tank and weights on, but when the sea was rough, it made it that much more work. I tried to be one of the first ones into the water, as I was feeling a little queasy from the motion of the boat.

"I'll meet you at the mooring buoy," I told Heidi. "I need to get off this heaving deck or I'm going to heave myself."

"I'm right behind you," she said.

We staggered to the side of the boat, put on our fins and masks, and stepped off the side in a giant stride. It was such a relief to hit the water and float rather than having the deck tossing me around, even if it was rough in the water, too.

Dougie was already at the mooring buoy, and he was grinning at me as I swam over. He knew I got seasick when it was really rough and thought it was hilarious. "You should have come diving yesterday," he said. "The sea was calm as glass."

"Thanks for telling me."

When Hans-Jurgen arrived at the buoy, the three of us consulted on our dive plan as we bobbed in the waves and then descended into a swirl of fish. I don't know when I'd seen so many colorful fish in one place. There were Yellowtail Jacks and Bar Jacks swimming in small schools. Damselfish swam just above the coral protecting their algae gardens and Parrotfish of every color and type munched on the coral.

Heidi motioned me to come closer. She pointed at an opening in the reef where there was an octopus nestled in a niche watching us with one eye. As we approached, it changed color to match the mottled brown and tan of the reef and became almost invisible.

Hans-Jurgen swam up to us and had a tough time seeing what his wife was pointing at, but finally the octopus moved, and he saw it. He gave us a big okay signal, and we swam on into the slight current.

The three of us swam along in a loose group, each of us stopping now and then to see what was living inside a tube sponge or to watch the line at a cleaning station. It amazed me to see predators and prey lined up with each other so the tiny Cleaner Wrasses with their blue and yellow stripes could nibble away the parasites and algae that grew on their scales. Seeing the cleaning station reminded me of seeing George and Dimitri together at snorkeling group meetings. I just couldn't decide which one would be the predator and which one prey.

All too soon, it was time to turn back toward the mooring. Half of our air was gone, and we needed to swim to a shallower depth. The small critters lived on top of the reef. There were baby Spotted Moray Eels twined around the base of a purple tube sponge and a tiny little pea-sized Spotted Damselfish hovering by a sea fan. I motioned for my dive buddies to come see it, but before they could swim up a Bar Jack swooped down and ate it in one gulp. I jumped back in surprise and might have shed a small tear for the tiny life that was no more.

We made our way back to the mooring and ascended to

fifteen feet for our three-minute safety stop. I made sure that we were the last group to get to the surface so I could be the last one on board after the dive. It hadn't gotten any calmer or less windy during our dive, and I wasn't looking forward to another bumpy ride to the second dive site.

One by one, we walked across the deck to our seats along the gunwale, sat down and nestled the butt of our tanks in the holders. Once I had my mask, fins, and snorkels safely stowed beneath my seat, I carefully stood and changed my scuba gear to my second tank. I was very glad that it went quickly, so I could sit down again and not worry about losing my balance and falling.

Our second dive was at the shipwreck of the Catheley H. It's at about the same depth as Paintcan Reef, but Dougie asked us to be cautious about our depth and stay at the shallowest part of the wreck. And it is a wreck. It's in the worst shape of the regularly dived shipwrecks on Anguilla. It has abundant small fish and lovely sponges and feathery crinoids all over it, which I think makes it look like a fairy castle.

Again, I made sure to be the first one in the water and the strength of the current surprised me as I swam to the mooring buoy. "It's a bit of a challenge today," I said when I reached Dougie.

"It is. Do you have your safety sausage in your BCD pocket just in case?"

"I do. I never leave it behind." I patted my pocket where the easily inflated florescent orange plastic tube nestled. It was something I kept handy in case a current blew me off a dive site and sent me out into open water. The safety sausage would bob on the surface, showing the boat where to pick me up. "Just in case."

"Good."

When my dive buddies reached me, we descended to the top of the wreck and tried our best to stay in place. It was hard. The current was strong and wanted to push us past the shipwreck and out to sea. It was kind of funny, though. If we turned into the current and kicked medium hard, we'd stay in one place so we could look at the things growing on the ship. I especially enjoyed seeing the tiny pink polyps of Orange Cup Coral that looked like Silly Putty toes when they had their feeding parts retracted.

Heidi was good at finding things hiding in the nooks and crannies of the ship's wheelhouse. She waved us over and was wriggling her fingers in front of a Spotted Moray Eel. Just as she turned to beckon us closer, the eel lunged out of its hole, barely missing her fingers. She jumped back and nearly dropped the regulator out of her mouth in surprise. The eel's sharp, backward facing teeth would have sunk into her fingers and been almost impossible to get away from. I shook my head at her foolishness but thought maybe she'd learned something.

The current nearly pushed us past the shipwreck while we were all clustered together, making sure that she wasn't hurt. We turned facing into the current and kicked hard to regain our position over the wreck.

I checked my air and saw it was getting low. Time to swim to the mooring line and ascend. Again, we stopped at fifteen feet for a three-minute safety stop and that time we had to cling to the mooring line to keep from being blown away by the swiftly moving water. I was the last one on board and staggered across the deck to my place on the bench. I wasn't glad to be on the tossing boat, but I was glad to be out of the current.

Stowing my gear under my seat, I unzipped my wetsuit and peeled the top off, so I didn't get chilled on the ride back to shore. I was glad to have a dry towel to wipe my face and hair and my shoulders. The sun felt good as the boat raced ahead of the wind back to the beach in front of the dive shop. I thought about a day when Iggy would have taken scuba lessons and be able to come with me.

I waited my turn at the rinse tank, bagged my dripping gear, and headed back toward Seaview to hang my gear on the back porch pegs to dry.

As I walked away, Hans-Jurgen called out, "Rose, do you want to go down to Johnno's for a burger with us?"

Although a burger sounded tempting, I'd left Geneva alone all morning to deal with the cleaning and laundry and wanted to get back to help her. "No, thanks. I need to get back to work. Thanks for the invitation, though."

We waved goodbye. They walked past to get to the beach bar, and I turned in through the gap in the bougainvillea hedge to hang my gear, grab a quick sandwich, and see what was left to be done.

***

Wednesday night was knitting night. I was still holding them every other week and every time there were more people attending. Geneva and I made a big batch of cereal mix with butter, garlic powder, and Worcestershire sauce. It made the whole place smell so good that the guests came into the kitchen one at a time following their noses.

"Is that what I think it is?" Claudia said as she stood at the door from the lobby to the kitchen.

"It is. Would you like some?"

I took pity on them and gave each of them a paper bag with a couple scoops of it for them to snack on. There was still plenty left for the knitters. I put a big bowl of the cereal mix on the sideboard with a stack of paper cups alongside so that people could just scoop up the mix and eat it out of the cup, so they didn't have to get their hands greasy and then dirty their project. There were pitchers of iced tea, lemonade, and water, too.

Since I had left Geneva alone for most of the day before, I felt like I needed to do most of the cleaning for the knitting get-together.

On the dot of six thirty, the first crafters arrived. Word had gone around the island that Mrs. Rose welcomed all crafts, so now we had not only knitters and crocheters but quilters and embroiderers. I also kept the little ad running in the tourist newspaper, so most times there were a few avid knitting tourists attending too. Maybe some of them visiting for knitting would choose to come back to stay at Seaview. I just hoped I had enough snacks to feed everyone.

Lomira shyly showed off a gorgeous doily she'd crocheted for her table centerpiece. "Oh, that's beautiful," one tourist said. "I've never tried crochet but if that's what you can do, I might just have to give it a whirl."

Susan was busy knitting tiny fruits and vegetables for a grandchild that liked to play kitchen.

"Where did you get those patterns?" I said.

She held up a small cob of sweet corn she was attaching husks to. "On the internet, of course. I had to buy some of them, but most of them are free and there are many more crochet patterns for food, too."

"What kind of food?" one of the local women asked.

"Oh, pies and pizza and cakes. I've got a pattern for a hamburger and bun with lettuce, onion, tomato, and cheese. I swear there's a pattern for just about anything you'd want to knit or crochet," Susan said.

"They look like they would be popular at the church bazaar."

Several of the local women nodded and started conferring. I had a feeling that a cottage industry had just been born.

"What are you knitting, Rose?"

I held up my tube of knitting with double-pointed needles sticking out all over. "I'm making a pair of fingerless mitts for my grandniece. She's a big fan of those wizarding books and movies. I found a pattern on a knitting website for these that says these are like ones that were made by a character. I hope she likes them. She's ten."

"She'll love them," one tourist said. "I've got a ten-year-old, and she'd kill for a pair." She pulled out her phone. "What's the pattern name? I'll look it up right now and save it."

I showed her my tablet with the knitting app on it where I keep most of my patterns and projects. "It lets me count rows and repeats. I don't know what I'd do without it."

"Oh, that's handy. I'm writing that down too."

A couple of others asked for the name of the app and the

site where I find most of my free patterns. That's what I love about crafters. They're willing to share patterns and resources. They don't care where people are from or what color they are. If they've got needles or a hook in their hands, they're part of the crowd.

During the evening, people moved around to sit by other crafters. It made me happy to see them mixing themselves naturally by interest or project instead of sticking to their friends.

By the time the last person left, the cereal mix was almost gone, and the drink pitchers were empty. That mix is salty.

Iggy came out to help me rearrange the tables and chairs so that the lobby was ready for breakfast the next day. "It sounded like you had a friendly crowd tonight."

"We did. Every time we meet, there are a couple of new locals who come with friends and there are always a few tourists to mix in too."

"Was Susan here?"

"Yes. You should have seen what she's knitting. She's making little bitty fruits and vegetables for a grandchild who likes to play kitchen. So cute. Maybe someday I'll have a grandbaby to knit cool stuff like that for."

"Maybe."

"Wouldn't you like to be a grandpa? I know your niece and nephews have children that consider you a kind of grandfather. Maybe one day Will and Elizabeth or Marie and whoever she ends up with will make us grandparents. I'd sure like that."

"Do you really think they will want an island man to be their children's grandfather?"

"What will it matter? You're my husband and their stepfather. Of course you'll be the children's grandfather. You can teach them to speak Creole."

"They would not want that."

I put my arms around him. "I wish you would teach me."

CHAPTER 35

Rose

At the next Literary Roundtable meeting, Susan sat next to me in the middle of the room. I looked at her in surprise. "What are you doing here?" I said before I caught myself.

Susan sighed. "I'm tired of the division among the women on this island. I'm going to be civil to Irina if it kills me. And it just might. But now that Harriet has gone home, I'm making the effort."

"Good for you. What does Harriet's leaving have to do with it?"

"Nothing really." She shook her head. "I got tired of trying to avoid Irina and her groupies when we were out shopping and gave up."

That evening was a shocker for many of the expat women.

When Irina read one of her new poems, Susan said, "That's an interesting way to look at things. I wouldn't mind hearing that again." An audible gasp followed the statement, and a whisper spread around the room.

Irina said, "Thank you, Susan." And she picked up her notebook and reread the poem.

***

Now that Max and Harriet had gone home, George needed a dive buddy every once in a while. I was happy to oblige. One afternoon, we met at Iggy's house to do a shore dive off his beach in West End Village. It was hot standing in the tropical sunshine getting into my wetsuit and scuba gear, and it was a challenge to walk down the steps that Iggy had carved into the rock wall down to the beach when he was a young man. The steps were narrow and steep. I was glad that I could hold on to the wall as I descended. We walked right out into the shallows carrying our fins. It's much easier to stand in hip-deep water to put on my fins, plus I have my buddy's shoulder to hold on to, so I don't lose my balance. George was doing the same, using my shoulder for balance while he put on his own fins.

Once I had my mask on and secure, I swung my right arm back and around to catch my regulator mouthpiece, purged it to push out any water, and put it in my mouth to take my first breath. Submersion was such a relief. Warm water washed over me and crept inside my wetsuit, cooling my overheated skin. When I was totally underwater, I laid on the sandy bottom. I put tiny spurts of air into my BCD to adjust my buoyancy, so I was neutrally buoyant, not floating to the surface or sinking to the bottom, but able to swim along and stop to observe the life of the reef. George was patient with my slow preparations to dive, spending the few minutes looking around and deciding in which direction to swim.

The reef in front of Iggy's house was shallow, with small patches of coral where the baby critters lurked. Tiny eels twined around stands of fire coral, little butterfly fish with their baby stripes hid out under little sponges. As I swam nearer, they darted into their hiding places, but if I held still and hovered there, they came out to continue going about their business. We moved on into deeper water. We leveled off at about thirty-five feet, where the corals and sponges were full size. Orange barrel sponges the size of bushel baskets hosted small groupers, one in each. The purple tube sponges looked like organ pipes. They were three to six feet tall and clustered together like a bouquet. Tiny shrimp and brittle stars with their spiky legs lived there.

In the scooped-out place of a coral head a Damselfish tended her algae garden. She blew water across it to keep it healthy and drove off marauding Blue Tangs that swam down to snatch a bite. When the Damselfish swam up to drive the

Tangs away, a little crab darted out of hiding deeper in the reef and frantically plucked algae and stuffed it into its mouth. The Damselfish came back to chase away the crab, and the game started all over again.

We didn't have to swim far to see the life down there. A different type of fish or critter filled every square yard. From a hole in the reef a lobster waved its long, whip-like antennae. I thought maybe I'd stop over at Billy the fisherman's place when I got home to see if he had any lobsters for sale.

At the base of a small tube sponge, George spotted a red-orange Seahorse swaying back and forth in the surge. I wished for a camera.

We compared air gauges, and it was time to turn back to shore. We made our slow way back into the shallows, past the big orange sponges, past the small patch reef where the babies lived, to where the surge moved us forward and back as we spent the three-minute safety stop to let the nitrogen in our blood and tissues off-gas to stave off decompression sickness. Then we swam until I could stand with my shoulders and chest out of water to take off our fins and pull our masks down to hang around our necks.

"Excellent dive," George said.

"Yes. I'm impressed that you saw the Seahorse. It was so tiny and would have been easy to miss."

"I'm good at spotting small things."

I thought but didn't say, I'm sure you are.

The hardest part of the dive was the last part when we walked out of the water where gravity took hold again and made everything heavy. The climb up the rock steps was just as challenging. It was a relief to take off the BCD with the tank attached, peel off my wetsuit, and stand in the sun, feeling the wind in my hair. As we dried off with chamois towels, George and I relived the high spots of the dive. Afterward, we sat on Iggy's deck drinking water to clear the saltwater out of our mouths and sharing a few handfuls of the tropical trail mix I'd brought along. I told George that I really wished Iggy would take diving lessons so he and I could go diving together.

As we were packing our dive gear and loading George's SUV, I caught sight of Mrs. Whiting glaring at us over her fence. I waved and said, "Good afternoon, Mrs. Whiting." But she just huffed and turned away. I was sure that new rumors of me spending time with a man who wasn't my husband would spread in no time.

***

I was driving home from diving with George when I stopped at Happy Holiday Homes to see if the Dutch woman owner was in and had time to talk. She was, and she did. She introduced herself as Louise and said that she and her husband Mel had built the bungalows twenty years before and had run them ever since.

Louise showed me an empty bungalow, and it was lovely. It had a kitchen area with a full-size stove, a small refrigerator, and a sink. There was a living/dining area with a good size table with chairs, a small loveseat and chair, a bedroom with an air conditioner, and a bathroom behind the kitchen. Out back there were laundry lines for hanging wet swimsuits and towels and a nice, high privacy wall. On the front porch there was a small patio table and chairs and on the end was a water spigot with a hose, a rinse bucket, and pegs on the wall for hanging gear to drip dry.

"Come," Louise said. "Let's go sit on my porch and have some lemonade. You can tell me all about Seaview and how you brought it back to life."

We had a nice long chat about being an innkeeper and how interesting it was to accommodate the various guest personalities week after week. "Many of my guests stay for weeks or months," she said. "It makes it difficult to maintain a professional distance from them. Sometimes I don't even try when I really like the people, like the ones that come back at the same time year after year."

"I have a few guests who have come more than once. One is an author who stays for a month at a time and works on her novel the whole time. She says that the yellow room is her lucky room," I said. "How do you advertise Happy Holiday Homes?"

She took a long drink of her lemonade. "I have a website, and I'm listed on the 'Discover Anguilla' website under Accommodations. Most of my reservations come from that. Of course, word of mouth is also a good way to get new guests. How about you?"

"I have a website that my daughter set up for me and she maintains it too, so I only pay for the domain, not maintenance. I get guests from online searches for bed and breakfasts in Anguilla, and I have printed brochures I send home with departing guests and ask them to leave one at the gym or café where someone might see it. I've gotten guests that way, so I'm not stopping that practice even though the printing isn't cheap."

"What printer do you use?"

"I use Jacques' Printing in St. Martin. I tried to use Acme Printing here in Anguilla, but he never returned my calls and was always closed when I went by."

She laughed. "You mean Jake's Printing. He doesn't use the French pronunciation. That's how people know that you're an islander. Wiley, the guy who ran Acme was lost on a fishing trip a few months back and his wife hasn't gotten herself together to reopen yet. I'm afraid if she waits much longer, she won't have any business left. People will be patient, but won't wait forever."

"Oh, that's too bad. I lost my husband almost seven years ago, and it took me a couple years to get myself back on track. I'd like to get Seaview listed on the Discover Anguilla website too. Do you know how I can go about it?"

"You need to stop in at the Anguilla Tourism Board office in The Valley. They keep the listing of all the accommodations on the island. I think all you have to do is sign up."

"Thanks. I'll stop by the next time I'm in town."

We talked longer about guests, the difficulty being from another culture and trying to fit in, and the backlash from Mrs. Whiting's slanderous rumors of last year.

Louise said, "I don't know what you did to her to make her

take against you so hard. But it must have been something big to make her that angry."

"What I did was have Iggy Solomon fall in love with me and marry me instead of marrying her, even though he was never interested in her. They're neighbors down in West End Village, and she had her eye on him ever since his wife died. She's still not over it and I think some women still believe her lies. I was afraid that you would be the same."

Louise touched my forearm as it lay on the patio table. "I never believe gossip. You're safe with me."

I checked the time and realized that Iggy would be worried. "I've got to run. Thank you so much for chatting with me. I hope to see you at the Chamber of Commerce meeting or the new businesswomen's meeting. Anne Robinson promised to take me along to the next one." I dug my keys out of my shorts pocket and walked over to my car. "Thanks for the lemonade. You'll have to come to Seaview some day for a tour. Bye."

I drove across the island toward Sandy Ground, wondering if Mrs. Whiting would have fired up her rumor mill and started making phone calls about me diving with a man who isn't my husband before I got home.

CHAPTER 36

Rose

The next day I stopped in at Vista Market. Mrs. Richards was busy with a line of customers, so she didn't greet me as I entered. I went up and down the aisles, filling my basket. Three kinds of cheese, two loaves of Amy's coconut bread, two cartons of wine splits—one red and one white, a bottle of pinot grigio for myself, a little fruit, a few veggies, and a package of chicken parts from the freezer case. It made me happy that I could get the coconut bread at the market sometimes and not always have to drive to Blowing Point to the bakery. I took it all up to the counter to check out just as the last of the line of customers left.

"Good morning, Mrs. Richards," I said.

She looked at me with a squint. "I heard something, Mrs. Solomon, and thought I would mention it to you."

"What's that?" I noticed she hadn't called me Rose.

As her fingers sorted through my purchases, she said, "A little bird told me that you are having an affair with another man. A white man."

My heart sank. Word sure travels fast on Anguilla. I sighed. "No, I am not having an affair with anyone but Iggy. I went scuba diving with George Clemment yesterday. We dove in the bay in front of Iggy's house, there's a nice bit of reef there, and Mrs. Whiting was glaring at us over her fence. I assume that's where the rumor came from."

Her hand stilled on the cash register buttons. Her lips pursed, and she blew out a long breath. "Yes, Eleanora Whiting was in here first thing this morning and she could not wait to tell me what she saw. I was not so eager to believe her and told her I would ask you about it when you next stopped in."

"I'm glad you asked me. I really don't want to have to go around proving myself to everyone again. Will I have to battle her rumors every time I talk to a man that isn't Iggy? I'm glad that she doesn't come to Johnno's jump-ups because I dance with a bunch of different men during the night. Please know that I am not a loose woman, that I don't want any man but Iggy. I do have male friends, but none of them have my heart or any other part of my body."

She nodded, gave me a little smile, and told me my total. I paid her, bagged my groceries, and went out to the car.

Driving back to Seaview, I decided I would talk to anyone and everyone about this newest false rumor. Just when I'd started being accepted by the island people, this had to happen.

Iggy was just getting home from a job when I pulled in. He came out and helped me carry in the bags and box of food. I took a deep breath and told him about the latest rumor floating around about me.

"How was shopping?" Iggy asked.

"Shopping went well, but I have a new old problem."

"What do you mean?"

I kept unloading the bags and putting the food away in the cupboards and refrigerator. "Well, Mrs. Whiting saw George and me when we got out of the water after our dive yesterday. She decided that we're having an affair and has already started a new rumor telling people that."

"No! The woman will never leave it alone. I think she has lost her mind about you."

"It's you she's lost her mind about," I said. "She must think if she spreads enough rumors, you'll abandon me and go back to her."

"I was never…"

I put my hand on his arm. "I know you never cared for her except as a neighbor and friend, but in her mind, she was working her magic on you. She plied you with her good coconut bread, and I'm sure did other things to attract you to her."

He sighed. "Yes, she brought me supper sometimes. I suppose I will have to go back to telling everyone that the rumors are false. That I am only interested in you, and you are only interested in me. Maybe if we say it often enough, people will start to believe us."

"Maybe." I put my head on his shoulder and sighed along with him.

***

At the next Literary Roundtable meeting, Susan came right up to me and said, "I hear you're having an affair with my husband."

I looked at her in shock. My mouth dropped open, then I noticed the twinkle in her eye. "I'm not. Where did you hear that?"

"Oh, word gets around. Actually, I overheard someone talking about it in the IGA. Two local women were behind me at the meat counter and said something like, 'There is that woman whose husband is having an affair with Ignatius Solomon's new wife.'"

"Damn. I hoped that rumor would die before it got around. Mrs. Whiting saw George and me come out of the water the other day and I was certain that just this thing would happen. I talked to Evelyn Richards at Vista Market the next day and told her what was really going on. I hoped she would spread the word, but evidently Eleanora Whiting has a faster grapevine with a greater reach."

She reached out and touched my arm. "Don't worry, no one in our circle believes it, no one who counts, anyway."

Her elitist comment surprised me. I always thought Susan was a rational, tolerant woman who wasn't a racist, but I guess she had a little of that in her, just like so many did. "Susan, everyone counts, especially since I married an Anguillan and am trying to become a part of the island community. Despite what everyone is saying, I am not having an affair with George. I like him, but, sorry, ick."

Her eyes widened, and then she turned red. "I just heard what I said, and I apologize. Of course, everyone counts. I meant I am the one who counts, and I don't believe it." Then she looked at me out of the corner of her eye with her mouth crooked in a smile. "You think my husband is icky?"

"Oh, no... I, oh, Susan, you know what I mean." I smiled back at her. "George is a good dive buddy, but he's not my type."

CHAPTER 37

George and Dimitri

Once Max and Harriet went back to England, Dimitri concentrated on maneuvering the conversation around to whether George had anything to do with the theft of the communications system plans every time they were together. For his part, George did the same, hoping to find out that the Russian hadn't gotten overly friendly with the secretary of the department where the anti-gravity propulsion system was being developed.

Conversations in George's Rover were becoming more and more stilted as each of them worked to bring up the subject that was uppermost in their minds.

"So, tell me, Dimitri, you mentioned you had groupies when you taught at Watford. Any of them stand out?"

"Yes, there was one poor misguided woman whose grandmother was from Russia. She had a romantic view of life in my country. I worked to disabuse her of her silly notions, but don't know how successful I was. She was part of a group of women who met after class for coffee. I went along a few times but never stayed long."

George hummed but made no comment.

"What about you, George? Were there any young women that stood out to you?"

"Not really. Most of the ones I met were fish biologists, not very interesting, and they smelled funny." He laughed at the memory.

"No, not at your cover job. In your actual work. Anyone that you remember in particular?"

There was a long silence. Then George said. "We're both doing it, aren't we?"

"Doing what?"

"Our old jobs. You must have gotten a letter like I did."

It was Dimitri's turn to be silent. The SUV rolled over the potholed and rutted island roads while the occupants stared out the windshield.

"Da, I got a letter like you did. I did not want to do what they asked, but we are afraid that if I do not, they might stop my pension and then we could not live. Not here, not anywhere."

"How are we going to manage it? I want us to be friends. You're the only one I know who understands what my work life was like."

"Yes. I do not know what to do." Dimitri looked out the side window like he was afraid for George to see his face.

George stopped at the end of Dimitri's street and idled at the corner. "Did you get the anti-gravity propulsion system plans from Ms. Talia Shoreham?"

Dimitri turned to face George, a shaft of late-day sunshine lighting his face. "No, George, I did not. All I got from Ms. Shoreham was a flowery worded term paper romanticizing life in Russia. I wrote all over it in red pen, handed it back, and she stopped hanging around me. What about you, George? Did you steal the plans for the communications system from some low-level bureaucrat in the research department?"

"In all honesty, I saw the plans, but I'm not the one who got them. I don't know who did, and I don't know how he or she did it."

The men turned to look at the neighborhood out the windshield again. "We cannot tell our wives that we talked like this today," Dimitri said. "Irina would murder me in my sleep, or maybe she would not wait that long."

"Susan wouldn't be happy either. She's convinced that you're trying to pry secrets from me, even though I assure her you're not." He stopped talking and looked at Dimitri out of the corner of his eye. "Although I suppose that's exactly what we're each trying to do."

Dimitri nodded, still looking through the windshield. "We have both spent our working lives lying so much I am not sure that I know how to tell the truth."

"That's one way of looking at it. Are you telling the truth about Ms. Shoreham and the propulsion system?"

"As far as I know. What about you and the communications system?"

George snorted. "I've already said I'd seen it but not obtained it."

"Obtained is such a pleasant word. Much better than stolen."

A woman had appeared in the doorway of the house they were parked in front of. George saw her, waved and said, "We'd better move. That lady looks suspicious of us sitting here."

Dimitri picked up his water bottle, got out, opened the back passenger door, pulled out his snorkeling gear bag, and slammed the door. "Thanks for the ride and the talk, George. I will see you." He put his ball cap on his head and walked off toward his house on the next block.

George waved at the woman again. This time she lifted her hand ever so slightly in a return wave as he pulled away, turned the corner and headed home.

CHAPTER 38

Rose

My last guests to check in that Saturday were late. I hadn't heard the afternoon flight from San Juan come in and wondered if there was a problem. I called the airport and asked if the flight was in.

"No, the flight was delayed out of San Juan due to a big storm in the States. The plane, she had to fly out over the Atlantic a-ways to get around the storm and that has made her late."

I imagined the man's hand describing a big arc in the air when he said that the plane had to fly "out a-ways." "Thank you," I said. "I won't start worrying about my guests being late just yet."

"Oh, no, do not worry. The plane is supposed to be here in about one hour. You can rely on me."

I hung up the phone and smiled. Catch me relying on anything an airline employee told me about what time a plane would arrive. Air travel is notoriously unreliable when it comes to being on time, especially in the Caribbean.

Speaking of unreliable, Mrs. Whiting was working overtime spreading the rumor that I'm having an affair with George Clemment. Iggy said he's talked to most of his friends and anyone he does electrical work for and told them I'm a good and faithful wife. I've been talking at Art League and Literary Roundtables to anyone who looks at me sideways when I'm next to Susan, telling them that the rumor is false. Susan says she's doing the same. I despise how persistent these rumors are, despite all our efforts to refute them.

It was nearly dark when the guests arrived, tired and hungry. I got them checked in and escorted them to their rooms. Pete and Bunny were dragging, but perked up when I gave them a fruit and cheese plate along with a split of wine.

"This is great," Pete said, munching on a piece of Gouda. "But where can we get something more substantial to eat? We've been flying all day and haven't eaten since Atlanta, and that was a long time ago."

Bunny sagged onto the bed and sat there sipping wine and staring out the window. "I can hear the ocean, but it's too dark to see it. Is there a restaurant nearby where we could get something to eat?"

"There are restaurants and beach bars that serve food all up and down the beach. Most of them are an easy walk from here. It depends what kind of food you're looking for."

Pete looked at Bunny, and she nodded. "Nothing too fancy, but nothing too loud."

"If you walk down the beach to the left after you leave Seaview, there's Johnno's Beach Bar. He serves good burgers and fries, but it might be a little loud since it's Saturday evening. A few places farther on is the Barrel Stave. Mrs. O'Neill has a moderately priced menu and makes excellent grilled fish and salads. Most of the places have their menu posted outside the door. I'm sure you'll find something to your liking."

I could hear the other new arrivals moving around in their rooms. Diane peeked out their door as I started down the stairs.

"Ron and I want to go to supper, too. We heard you telling them about places to go. Can you tell us too?"

So, I repeated my restaurant spiel. As I was speaking, Pete came out their room door and said, "If you want to come along, why don't we all go together?"

"Great idea." Diane looked over her shoulder and said, "We're going with this other couple, Ron. Is that okay with you?"

Ron's voice rumbled from behind her. "Just as long as I get

something to eat. I'm starving. Are they ready? Let's go."

In a few minutes, four cheerful and hungry people came downstairs and left to seek food. They were all talking and getting acquainted. I thought it was going to be an enjoyable week.

***

The next morning, as I took the egg casserole out of the oven, I heard loud scraping coming from the lobby. I looked out to see Pete and Ron shoving two tables together.

Pete saw me looking and said, "I hope you don't mind, but we want to eat together, and these tables are a little small."

"No, I don't mind."

Lola and Ann, the two single guests, were at the third table, so everyone had a spot. "Are you happy sitting together?"

The two women looked at each other. "Yeah, this is fine. We're old friends."

"Oh good. Everyone have coffee?" There were a few murmurs of assent, and Ron lifted his mug in salute. I returned the salute with a smile and said, "Great. I'll bring out the food in a minute."

It didn't take long to serve the fruit bowls and plates of egg casserole. "There's more of the egg bake if anyone needs it or I can bring out a loaf of bread, butter, and jam if anyone would like toast."

Ron was nodding as I spoke. "I'll have toast. Toast is important."

Diane said, "Oh Ron, you're such a toast guy." She looked at me. "Ron has to have his toast every morning. With butter. And jam. He'll love you forever if you give him toast."

"Coming right up."

Either everyone had toast, or Ron had a lot of toast because the loaf of coconut bread was half gone when I went out to clear the tables. I thought I'd better send Iggy to Amy's Bakery early tomorrow to lay in a supply for the week. I'd have him go to Vista Market, but I didn't want us to take all of Evelyn's weekly supply on Monday morning.

***

All the guests trailed us down to Johnno's jump-up that evening at about five o'clock. For once, there were tables available, so everyone had a seat. It was fun watching my guests experience a true Caribbean party.

There was rum punch all around except for Ron. Ron had a beer or three. The women danced with each other and with a few locals. Edward, Silas, Luke, and Melvin made sure that the ladies had fun. Pete and Ron didn't dance to the fast songs, but they were quick to stand up to claim their wives' hands when a slow song played. I enjoyed seeing the couples enjoying a little closeness, talking and laughing as they danced.

Lola and Ann were popular with the locals. Those ladies really enjoyed dancing and barely sat through a song. Julius, the neighborhood gigolo, danced with each of them at least once, but it didn't look like either of them took him up on his offer to entertain them while they were on the island.

Iggy and I stayed at the party until about ten o'clock and then said goodbye to our friends and walked up the beach to Seaview. I looked down toward Johnno's as I waited for Iggy to unlock the door and saw the two couples following us.

As they walked nearer, I said, "Had enough party for tonight?"

"Oh yeah," Ron said. "We're not as young as we used to be. Parties like that are for young people. Three beers and two dances and I'm done for the night."

Diane laughed. "We don't party like we did when we were kids. I'm still tired from traveling all day yesterday and then snorkeling all day today. I feel a hangover coming on."

"I'll make sure that breakfast is easy on your stomach in the morning. And I'll have lots of coffee ready when you wake up."

"Can I have coffee in my room?" Bunny said.

"You can, if you can convince Pete to come down and get you some. I don't deliver. I'm getting too old for too much party myself." Everybody laughed. Then I made sure that the door was locked behind them. Even though Calvin Brooks, the lecherous plumber who harassed and assaulted me, had died a few months back and I had seen him buried, I still couldn't shake the need to keep the doors locked to keep him out. After saying goodnight to my guests and making sure that the lamp on the registration desk was on, I walked through the kitchen to turn the deadbolt on the back door.

When I walked into our apartment, Iggy put his arms around me and pulled me to him. "You know you can leave the door unlocked when you are home, right?"

"Yes, but I wasn't home tonight. I was down at Johnno's, and I won't leave the door open to invite just any passerby in to check things out. Do you leave your house unlocked when you're not there?"

"Sometimes I do when I forget to lock the door, and nothing is ever disturbed. You should have more faith."

I nuzzled into his chest. "I'd rather have good locks. Why are we having this conversation?"

"I just think that you forget you do not have to worry about Calvin coming in to fiddle with the pipes or put his hands on you."

"I remember, but I like that the guests know the place is locked so they are safe, and their belongings are safe too. It's simple safety and being a responsible innkeeper. Why does it bother you?"

He looked down into my eyes. "I want you to feel safe with me around and to remember that Anguilla is a basically safe place to live. You keep telling your children that you are fine, and I think you are not convinced in your mind."

I slid out of his embrace and went toward the bathroom. "I am fine. It's just going to take me a little while to get used to me not having to worry about Calvin anymore. I'm fine. Don't worry about me." Worrying about Mrs. Whiting and her rumors crossed my mind, but I pushed it aside and got ready for bed.

I hadn't finished brushing my teeth when Iggy came into the room ready for bed. He edged me away from the middle of the sink and reached for his toothbrush. He spread out his elbows and got in my way so I couldn't reach the sink to rinse my mouth. "What are you doing?"

"I am brushing my teeth," he said through a mouthful of toothpaste foam.

"Well, I need to finish brushing mine. Move over and give me room."

"You cannot make me." He peeked at me from the corner of his eye and couldn't hide his grin.

"Oh, yeah?" I pushed against his hip with my own and we had a little shoving match right there in the bathroom. I started laughing as we each struggled to displace the other one in front of the sink. I got a hand under the stream of water when he turned on the tap and splashed him in the face. He retaliated with a handful of water that he flung at me. "Hey, don't get my clothes wet."

"Well, take them off and they won't get wet."

"Okay." And I quickly stripped out of my shorts, tee shirt, and bra. "Now you."

He was even faster and soon we stood in the bathroom in our underwear, our chests heaving, and laughter bubbling out. The laughter turned to sighs as we embraced. I don't think I ever rinsed the toothpaste out of my mouth.

CHAPTER 39

Rose

I checked the community calendar in the local newspaper to find the date of the next meeting of the Chamber of Commerce. I planned to go to network with other small hotel owners on the island and also see if there were islanders who might fit into the expat community activities.

The next Chamber of Commerce meeting was in two days. I checked my calendar and had the evening open. The Chamber met at one of the restaurants on the island at five thirty in the evening, just after most retail businesses closed for the day. That month they met at Darling's, a quaint and homey little restaurant on the road to Shoal Bay. I had never been to Darling's, so I was glad to see the place and look at the menu.

There were a lot of cars in the parking lot when I pulled up. I parked at the end of a row of cars and walked across the road to the entrance. I was surprised at the number of people there, almost all of them locals. In the center of the room stood a man in dark slacks and a light blue shirt who seemed in charge. He was directing a woman at a nearby table to get people signed in and hand out nametags, although it looked like most people already knew each other. I excused myself as I made my way through the crowd to the table to get signed in. Silence followed me.

"Hi," I said when I reached the table. "I'm Rose Solomon. I own Seaview Bed and Breakfast in Sandy Ground, and I thought it was time I got acquainted with other small business owners on the island."

"Welcome, Rose," the woman said. "I am Charity Blackmon, Secretary of the Anguilla Chamber of Commerce." She pushed a clipboard toward me. "Please sign here with your contact information and make yourself a nametag."

I did as I was directed and stuck the nametag to my chest. I turned to face the room to find everyone staring at me. I took a deep breath. "Hello, everyone. I'm Rose Solomon and I look forward to getting to know you all."

A few people met my eyes with a smile, but most of them turned away.

I felt the sting of being one of the only two white people at the meeting. I sat next to Thomas, the owner of Tamarind Dive Shop, the only other white person there and realized that I felt more comfortable in his company. I thought the way I feel as a minority in this meeting must be the way Iggy feels at one of the expat events. How can we both work to feel more like we belong?

Once the regular program "How to best attract tourists to your business" was finished, I tried to network with other small hotel and bed-and-breakfast owners at the meeting.

One woman who owned a small hotel in another village slid in front of me as I tried to join the group. "We do not need an American interloper telling us how to run our businesses."

Anne Robinson, owner of Sydan's Garden Inn and Iggy's sister, was at the meeting. She drew me into the group of owners, saying, "This is my sister-in-law, Rose Solomon. She is a hotel owner too and deserves to be a part of this discussion."

Two women stepped aside to let me edge into the group. I felt the residual effects of Mrs. Whiting's lies and rumors of the last year that I was a speculator, didn't respect the Anguillan people, and was only interested in making money. And the latest one was that I was having an affair with George. I wondered if I would ever live them down. It was hard to stand there and see others whisper behind their hands while looking at me, but I stiffened my spine and stayed in the circle. I listened politely as people in the group complained and offered solutions, but I held back from participating. I was afraid that any suggestion I made would be misunderstood.

On the way out of the Chamber of Commerce meeting, I walked alongside Anne. "I don't know how I'm going to live down the damage that Mrs. Whiting did with her lies about me. More people believe her than believe me, even with Iggy going around spreading the truth, that I'm committed to building my business and committed to becoming part of the community in Sandy Ground and in Anguilla, and not having an affair."

Anne rubbed her hand over my shoulder. "The only way is to keep doing what you are doing. Shopping in local stores, paying your bills on time, hiring local workers. It is just going to take time."

I ground my teeth. "But it's so frustrating. I know I could help advertise their businesses and they could help me. Cecilia over at Scilly Cay told me that there's a businesswomen's group starting up on the island and I'd like to join, but I'm afraid that my reception will be the same as it was tonight, someone closing the circle against me. I can't always depend on having you around to rescue me."

"Well, I appreciate you sending people you do not have room for over to Sydan's. Word will get around. Are you still plying Evelyn Richards with muffins every week?"

"I am. I'm afraid if I stop, she'll go back to cursing my name and spreading rumors and lies. It's cheap bribery. Plus, it saves me from eating too many."

Anne left her hand on my shoulder and bent over, laughing. "I think I will have to talk trash about you to get in on the muffin bribery."

"No, no, don't do that. I'll bring you a muffin or two, I promise. Cross my heart."

"Well, if they are as good as Johnno and Silas say they are, I will appreciate it."

We walked across the road and into the parking lot. Anne stopped by her car. "This is me. I will let you know when the next businesswomen's group meeting is. You can ride with me, and we'll see if they try to cut you out."

"Thanks, Anne, I really appreciate it. I've got a contact at Blue Harbour Resort who lets me piggyback some of my ingredients orders onto their big orders. It saves me a lot of money. I put the flour, sugar, and cooking oil into aluminum trash cans with lids on them to keep out vermin. It's working pretty well."

Anne opened her car door to let the heat out. "That is a good idea. How did you think of that?"

"Cecilia again. She advised me to ask around to find a big resort that would let me tag along on their orders, and Blue Harbour agreed. I drop off muffins to their supplies manager too."

"You are going to get a reputation for giving out muffins for favors. That could be a good thing."

It was getting hot standing in the rays of the setting sun. I leaned over and kissed Anne on the cheek. "Thanks for including me tonight. I really appreciate it."

Anne kissed me back. "I did it for the muffins."

I laughed, waved goodbye, and walked down the road to my car.

***

Mrs. Whiting, who saw herself as my chief rival for Iggy's affection last year, ran into me at the IGA during my next shopping trip. Literally ran into me. I was picking out a few heads of romaine lettuce when a cart smashed into me, nearly knocking me into the bin of lettuce. "I beg your pardon," I said, and turned around to see Mrs. Whiting gripping her cart and winding up to ram it into me again. "Hey, stop that." I held out my hand to deflect her cart. "Just leave me alone. I can't help it if Iggy chose me over you. Go ram your cart into him if you're still angry about it."

"He is not here, and you are here flaunting your wedding ring." The look on her face was pure anger bordering on madness. "Does Mr. Solomon know you were at his house with another man?"

"I was scuba diving with a friend, not having an affair. If you could see how ugly your anger is making you, you'd stop." It might not have been the best thing to say, but I knew she was vain about her looks and thought reminding her of what that much anger did to her face might snap her out of it. It didn't. It only made things worse.

Mrs. Whiting reached into the bin of onions next to her and started hurling them at me.

I tried to duck and dodge away, but her cart and the edge of the lettuce bin hemmed me in. "Ouch. Stop that. You're making a mess."

The store manager rushed up to her and gripped her wrist. "Put the onion down, ma'am, we do not allow throwing food in the market." He was a middle-aged man with authority written all over him.

Mrs. Whiting struggled against his firm grip and then sagged as her anger drained away. She put the onion she was holding into her cart, abandoned the cart, turned and left the store empty-handed. The manager and I looked at each other.

"I'm sorry she caused such a fuss," I said. "I'll help pick up the onions."

"That is unnecessary, Mrs. Solomon, the produce boy will clean it up."

I shook my head. "No, I want to help. I feel like I'm partly to blame. It won't take long." Then it hit me. "How do you know my name?"

"Everyone knows about the lady who rescued Seaview and turned it back into a small hotel." He smiled at me. "I am glad to see you shopping in my store."

"It's a nice store." I tucked the romaine I was still holding into a mesh bag with the other lettuce I'd chosen, put the bag into my cart, and picked out the onions that had landed among the lettuce in the bin. The produce boy was already stooping to pick up the onions that had flown all over. He and I worked for a few minutes until we had chased down all the onions and put them back into the onion bin.

"I'm so sorry for making more work for you."

"Thank you for helping," he said with a smile. "That lady is angry with you."

"Yes, she is, and I don't know what to do about it."

He shrugged and went back to stacking carrots. I felt the eyes of the other shoppers on me as I moved up and down the aisles. At the meat counter, a woman I had never met said, "Mrs. Whiting sure has a mad on about you."

"That she does."

"She carries a grudge. I would be on my guard if I were you."

"Thank you. I'll keep that in mind."

The rest of my shopping trip was uneventful.

I stopped at the outdoor produce market under the big tree for a few vegetables as usual. I was relieved not to see Mrs. Whiting's car in the Vista Market parking lot. I took the box with a dozen various muffins out of the back seat and took it in to Mrs. Richards, the owner.

"Oh, thank you, Mrs. Solomon, I love your muffins," she said, taking the box and putting it on the shelf behind her, but not before peeking in to see what kinds were there. "Do I see a new kind in there?"

"Yes, there were apples at IGA last week, so I could make apple cinnamon muffins. I hope you like them."

"They had apples at the IGA? We hardly ever get them on Anguilla."

"I know. That's why I grabbed as many as I could. Do you have any of Amy's coconut bread?" I craned my neck to look down the aisle at the bakery shelf.

"Not on the shelf, but I saved the last one for you." She reached under the counter and handed me a bagged loaf of bread.

"Thanks for this, Mrs. Richards. My guests love this coconut bread. I tried making it but don't really have the touch to make bread. Mine is always dry and too dense. I don't know what I do wrong."

"Maybe Amy will give you a lesson one day if you ask her. And call me Evelyn."

"I might just do that. Thanks, Evelyn." I moved down the aisle, picking up some fruit and cheese from the cooler, a couple cartons of splits of wine for my arriving guests, and a bottle of pinot grigio for me. I needed a glass of wine after my adventures with Mrs. Whiting at the IGA.

CHAPTER 40

George and Dimitri

It was George and Dimitri's turn to organize the snorkelers' monthly activity. As the newest members of the group, it fell to them to plan the activity and get the information circulated. They emailed each other and searched forums on the internet. George got a chuckle when Dimitri wrote he thought they should go to a whole other island for the next meeting, just to get out from under their wives' scrutiny. George wrote back that he thought that was a good idea and suggested that they meet for an early morning breakfast at the Rose Inn the next day to plan it.

Dimitri arrived first and sat at their usual table with two mugs and a pot of strong island coffee already there. "I did not mean it really, George," he said as George sat down next to him.

"I know you were making a joke, Dimitri, but I think you might be onto something." George picked up the carafe, poured himself some coffee, and refilled Dimitri's mug. "After I got done laughing at the idea, I realized it was perfect. Have you noticed that Franz isn't running his inter-island ferry lately?"

"I saw it tied up at the customs dock the other day and wondered what it was doing there."

"He's had to have some heart surgery and his son, Davis, didn't want to let Ezra and his Rasta pals run it while Franz was laid up. He plans to start it up again in a few months when he's back on his feet and the docs say he's clear to work."

"What does the fast ferry have to do with my idea?"

George drained his mug and refilled it. As he did, their young waitress came and took their orders; both of them still got a lot of pleasure out of ordering eggs and sausages and fried potatoes, flaunting their wives' rules.

"So, what is your idea, George?" Dimitri said. "Don't keep me in suspense."

"Well, I was thinking, why don't we rent the ferry to take us all over to Dog Island to snorkel for the day, have a big beach barbecue, snorkel some more, and then come home in the evening? Make a proper day of it. That boat of Franz's is really more of a big pleasure boat than an official ferry. It would work great as a floating dive platform."

Dimitri was silent.

"Well? What do you think?"

Dimitri laughed and clapped him on the shoulder. "I think that is a capital idea, old chap."

George threw back his head and roared with laughter. "I'll give Davis a call and see about setting it up. We'll have to make sure there's a spot on the leeward coast of the island so that we can pull in close enough to offload the food and such without damaging the reef. I'm sure they sell charts at the Harbour Village Marina. I'll stop there on my way home and pick one up."

"You had better wait until we know we can rent the ferry before you go buying charts."

"But now that you've had it, I want to get this idea moving. You're a wicked man, Dimitri Roskova. You're going to land me in big trouble yet."

They both laughed at that and tucked into their platters of eggs that the waitress had just set down in front of them.

***

It didn't take George long to track down Davis to see about chartering Franz's fast ferry. By then Franz had come through the surgery and was resting at home and doing physical therapy. He insisted on being part of the planning. "I'm dying of boredom here at home," he said. "And I'm driving Maggie nuts too. She wants me out of the house and out of her hair."

Davis shook his head. "Ma is already trying to get me to drive Pop down to the office so he can bedevil the secretary instead of her. I'll bring Pop over, and we can make a plan."

"Uh, no," George said too quickly, earning himself a sidelong look from the younger man. "Susan feels the same about me being in the house all the time. Why don't I take you and your pop to lunch in the next few days, say to the Rose Inn, and we can hash it all out?"

Davis agreed and called his father, who agreed too. As he hung up his phone, Davis said, "Pop is looking forward to it. How's Wednesday?"

"I'll check with Dimitri and call you back, but that should be good. Pencil us in."

Wednesday saw four men, two islanders and two expats, seated in the dining room of the Rose Inn. George and Dimitri had been there enough that the young waitress brought their coffee without being asked. Franz was very specific about how he wanted his lunch prepared; he even asked that the cook come out to speak with him. "I am not in any hurry to go back and have more of my blood vessels scrubbed out, so I am watching what I eat," he said, nodding his head emphatically.

***

Preparations for their day on Dog Island went swiftly. The snorkeling group voted unanimously to rent Franz's boat for the day.

Both of their wives asked if there was a radio onboard and they were happy to say yes and get on with their outing. By that time, neither Irina nor Susan had raised too many objections to the fact that their husbands would spend the day together. The constant worry that their opposite number would spend the time looking to pry secrets from them had abated. Irina was especially casual when Dimitri told her about the day on the boat. She merely reminded him to take a hat and his "disgusting rubber suit" so that he didn't get sunburned. Susan waved a hand at George saying, "I've got a gallery showing coming up and you know cruise ship season is nearly upon us. I don't have time to go gallivanting off on a snorkel trip with you. Maybe I can go next time."

Thank god I don't have to tap dance around to discourage her from coming, George thought. He was sure that there was no way Irina would want to tag along with them. Dimitri had said that she hated to even go into the ocean, hated the feeling of salt water on her skin and the idea that creatures lived, died, and pooped in the water that was touching her. George thought it was pretty funny that someone as self-controlled as Irina seemed to be freaked out over a little diluted fish poop, but he was grateful all the same.

Plans for the outing went smoothly. Enough people signed up to cover the rental fee easily, and they received permission from the Marine Park office to tie up at the mooring they maintain on the leeward side of Dog Island. The last cargo freighter had brought six pallets of charcoal so they wouldn't have to cook burgers and hot dogs over a fire fueled by burning wood scraps and cactus carcasses. Davis arranged to tie up Franz' ferryboat at the pier just past the customs office in Sandy Ground, so there was plenty of parking nearby and lots of room on the pier for the mountain of gear they planned to take.

CHAPTER 41

Rose

A few days later, Iggy's sister Anne walked over from her guesthouse up the road from Seaview to tell me when the next Anguilla Businesswomen's meeting would be. She and I had talked about it a little after the Chamber of Commerce meeting I went to, and she promised to take me along with her to the next one.

"The businesswomen meet next Thursday at six thirty. Are you able to get away for it?"

"I'll make sure that I am." I checked the calendar on my phone and tapped it in. "I want to do everything I can to network with other women business owners on the island and, by my actions, disprove Mrs. Whiting's hateful rumors about me. I know that's what led the women at the Chamber meeting to shut me out."

Anne scratched behind her ear. "You are probably right. Eleanora Whiting has a big mouth and a lot of friends who believe everything she says."

"I hope that a few of the women who know me will be there and dilute the bad feelings those rumors produce. I know that Cecilia from Scilly Cay will be there. She's the one who told me about it. And Evelyn Richards from Vista Market seems to like me more."

"Of course she likes you. You bribe her with muffins every couple of weeks." Anne patted my arm. "I thank you for the muffins you give me, too. Pretty soon, you will have to have a muffin subscription plan to keep up with your muffin deliveries."

"If that's what it takes to be accepted, I'm glad to do it."

"Keep it up and you will get a reputation."

"Hey, do people bring snacks to the meeting? I could bring some muffins. I have smaller pans that I never use. They'd be great to feed a crowd."

Anne threw back her head and laughed.

"What's so funny? I want people to like me, and if you feed them, people like you. It's a proven fact."

"I will check with the organizer and see if you can bring some muffins to the meeting."

"Thanks. Find out how many people they expect. I don't want to run out before everyone's had one. Or two."

***

The next Thursday I walked down the road to meet Anne at Sydan's. She'd offered to drive since she knew where we were going. I took a large plastic container filled with little two-bite muffins with me to share.

We drove across the island to St. Andrews, where the group met in the church hall. The number of cars in the lot surprised me when we pulled in. "Wow, this is more than I thought would be here. I hope I have enough muffins."

"Do not worry, others will have brought something to share." Anne patted the top of the container on my lap. "I am certain that these will be very popular and help you make friends."

Anne was right. The muffins were popular. Several of the women came up to me asking about my recipe.

"So, Mrs. Solomon, how do you make your muffins so tender? Mine are always dry." This from the woman I was certain was the one who had cut me out of the circle at the Chamber meeting.

I smiled at her, even though I wanted to kick her in the ankle for believing the rumors about me. "I use flavorless oil instead of butter or margarine in the batter. Oil makes the batter softer. Or you can use half melted butter and half oil if all oil makes them too soft for you. And don't over mix them. That makes them tough."

"What is flavorless oil?"

"Vegetable oil, canola oil, coconut oil, but not olive oil. It's too heavy and will weigh down the muffins."

"Oh, thank you," she said and took another muffin.

"You're welcome. What's your name?"

She looked abashed. "I am Terese Whiting."

"Whiting? Like Eleanora Whiting?"

"Yes." She looked at me and then looked away. "Eleanora is my sister-in-law. I am sorry that she said all those mean things about you, and I believed her."

"You don't believe her anymore?"

Terese shook her head. "No. She is so fixed on you, she is not in her right mind. And Mr. Solomon went around saying that he was never interested in her even before you came. I know Ignatius. He is my cousin, and I believe him."

"Thank you for saying that. I'm trying to become part of the island community and the business community because I'm here for the long haul. What is the name of your place?"

"It is the Rose Inn in Island Harbour. I own it with my mother, Bonita, who is Ignatius' auntie."

I had to smile. The island was really like a small town. "I've been there. You have good food."

"Thank you." She turned to speak to another woman just as the chairwoman called the meeting to order.

I enjoyed the meeting. There was a lot of discussion about getting supplies and Cecilia repeated her recommendation that we see if we couldn't find a big resort to piggyback our orders on to.

I suggested that the small hotels, inns, and bed and breakfasts all pool our advertising dollars to have a bigger presence in the tourism brochures and on the websites. To my surprise, Terese Whiting seconded the suggestion, saying that she and her mother had been trying to think of ways to stretch their advertising money. There were seven innkeepers at the meeting, and we put our heads together once the main meeting program was over and made a date to sit down and work on figuring out how to make the most of our advertising expertise and budget.

"I'm sure that all together we can make a bigger splash than each of us can individually," I said.

Terese said, "Rose, since you had the idea, do you have any thoughts about what we can do?"

"I have a couple of ideas, and I can consult with my daughter who takes care of my website. She has good instincts for what works. The rest of you put on your thinking caps, and when we get together next week, we can brainstorm."

"I will get in touch with the publisher of the Anguilla Tourist brochure at the Tourism Office," Anne said. "She is an old school chum of mine and might have some ways that we can put our business names out in front of the public."

One of the other women raised her hand. "Pardon me for saying this, but we compete with each other. I am afraid that some will benefit at the expense of the others."

I nodded as she spoke. "That's an excellent point. How about everyone write up a list of what makes your place distinctive before we meet again so we can make sure that each of us has the same sort of exposure as the rest? How does that sound?"

A murmur of agreement rose from the assembled women. "That is right. For some of us, the location is the most appealing, others have extra amenities, and still others offer special discounts for special occasions," another woman said.

The discussion carried on for a few more minutes, and then people left in ones and twos. A few of the women came up to me and complimented me on the muffins I brought. More than one said they were looking forward to getting together to work on a group advertising campaign.

Anne and I walked together out to her car. I swung the empty plastic container by my side. "I guess the muffins were a hit. There isn't a crumb left."

"Yes, and your idea about an advertising group was very popular," Anne said. "I think tonight you made strides toward being an accepted member of the local community."

"I think so too. I can't wait to tell Iggy how the meeting went. I know he was nervous that I'd be disappointed in my reception, but it went well."

"It was good of you to offer to host the advertising meeting at Seaview. That will show people you are a part of the island landscape, too. Plus, I know they are eager to see how you have refurbished the place. Everyone was sorry to see it in such disrepair, but no one had the money to take on the job."

I laughed. "Or was foolish enough to try? You know, we had to take out just about every wall, wire, and pipe in the place. The only thing left of the original place is the reception desk and the pigeonholes behind it. And the outer shell, of course. Everything else is new."

By then we were driving through the dark across the island to Sandy Ground. We had the windows open, and the warm night air flowed through the car. "Thanks for driving tonight, Anne, and taking me along. I don't know if I'd have been brave enough to go on my own."

"You would have done it. You would have walked in with your container of muffins and fit in just fine." She pulled up and parked in front of Sydan's. "I can see that now you have your foot in the door with people you are going to be a part of the island life."

"I hope you're right. Thanks again for driving. I guess I'll see you next week at the advertising group meeting. I'll make little sandwiches." I walked down the road planning the snacks for the meeting and hoping tonight's warm reception of my idea would survive the scrutiny of the group next week.

CHAPTER 42

Rose

On Monday Geneva and I were cleaning the kitchen and doing the breakfast dishes when there was a quick knock on the back door and Silas came in. "Good morning, ladies. Would you have any spare muffins for a starving man?"

I smiled, kept drying dishes, and let Geneva find him something to eat. She was the one he wanted to see, anyway.

"There are some day-old muffins in the back of the refrigerator," she said. "I could probably freshen them in the microwave for you. Would you like something to drink?"

He crossed the kitchen to stand behind her while she reached into the fridge. "I would not say no to a glass of juice. Johnno and I have been cleaning the beach bar, and I am hungry and thirsty." He put his hands on her waist. "I have been missing you. Where did you go this weekend? You were not at church yesterday morning and not at the jump-up last night."

She shrugged off his hands and crossed to the microwave with the plate of muffins. "I went to Sint Maarten to visit my cousin Valentine yesterday. She has a new baby and was feeling lonely. I caught the early ferry this morning." The microwave dinged, and she removed the plate. "Here are your muffins. I will pour you some juice."

Silas settled down on a stool at the kitchen island and started eating. "Mrs. Rose, you make the best muffins I have ever eaten."

"Thank you, Silas. I'm glad you like them. My guests like

them too."

Geneva handed him a glass of juice and stood next to him, watching him eat, her eyes following his every move.

***

I left them in the kitchen and went upstairs to clean the bathrooms. We did them every day. With the guests sharing them, I tried to be scrupulous about sanitation to make them as comfortable to use as possible. Every day we swept up a handful of sand that got tracked in and I shuddered to think of the sand that washed down the shower drain, hoping that it didn't clog up the pipes.

I was on my hands and knees cleaning the floor in the white and green bathroom when I noticed that there was water on the floor behind the toilet. There was a curb across the shower, so I didn't think that much water would come from there. I felt under the toilet tank, and it was dripping from the bottom. Where was the water coming from? I didn't think the tank could overflow. Then I remembered when I was a kid in the hot and humid summer days, the toilet tank had condensation on it because the water in it was a lot colder than the ambient temperature. I checked and found that the toilet tank was wet up to the waterline. Dad had worked out a way to warm up the water a bit, but I didn't remember how. Maybe Iggy would know another plumber who I could ask.

"Mrs. Rose, you should let me do that." Geneva's voice came from behind me, and I jumped.

"You startled me." I turned back to mopping up the water off the floor. "I'm perfectly able to clean bathrooms. Did Silas go back to work?"

"Yes, he did, but only after he ate all the leftover muffins. I will get started in the other bathroom."

"Great. He's welcome to the muffins, then I'm not tempted to eat them. Say, do you know how to keep the toilet tank from sweating in the heat? I'm afraid that the dripping condensation will ruin the floor."

"My uncle put in a valve or something that lets a little

hot water into the toilet filling pipe, so the water warms up and keeps the tank from sweating."

I sat back on my heels. "Is your uncle a plumber?"

"No, he is not. He just knows how to do things."

"I think I need a plumber. I'll ask Iggy if he knows a good one. At least now I know what to ask for. Thanks."

It didn't take long to finish cleaning the floor as I crawled backwards out of the room, pushing my cleaning supplies tote behind me.

***

I left Geneva to finish cleaning the other bathroom and went downstairs to start the laundry. We changed the towels every other day and the sheets once a week or when a guest left. Today there were two baskets of towels to be washed. I started the first load and went into the kitchen to put away the dry dishes from breakfast.

I got it all put away and heard running water outside the kitchen door. I hurried out to find water cascading out of the washer drain pipe, flooding the back porch and patio. I pulled out the knob to stop the washer cycle and tried to figure out why the water wouldn't drain. The hose from the washer didn't seem to be clogged, so I tried to see if something was plugging up the drainpipe. It was too dark in there, so I used the flashlight app on my phone. I shined it into the pipe and jumped back when I saw eyes looking back at me.

"Why is there water all over?" Geneva said, coming through the back door.

"Because there is a big frog or something in the drainpipe."

"A frog? Frogs are pretty small here."

"I think it's a frog. Maybe it's a rat. Here, use my phone and look down there. Something's looking back."

"No, thank you, Mrs. Rose." She lifted her hand to refuse to take the light. "I will take your word that there is something inside that pipe. How are you going to get it out?"

"I don't know. Probably wait until Iggy gets home.

Hopefully, he'll know what to do." I shook my head. "This just isn't my day. First, the toilet tanks are sweating water all over the floors and now something has moved into the washer drainpipe. I don't have time for all of this." I felt my shoulders tighten and my jaw clench.

When I dreamed of opening a bed-and-breakfast on a Caribbean beach, I never thought of all the work it would entail and all the things that could and would go wrong. I had long dreamy hours of imagining palm trees swaying in the ocean breeze with happy, smiling guests begging me to let them stay longer. In reality, it was a lot of hard, never-ending work and I was glad to have Geneva to help me. Cooking breakfasts was the simple part. I had a few recipes that I rotated through, adding new ones every once in a while, but mostly I made the same things week after week. Muffins in various flavors, egg bake with whatever veggies and breakfast meat was available that week, my daughter-in-law Elizabeth's sheet pan French toast, Rudolf's Banana Bread, and omelets with sauteed onions, bell peppers, and cheese.

While I waited for Iggy to get home and fix the washer drain, I cubed some day-old Italian bread, spread it in a buttered baking dish, and assembled an egg casserole for the next morning. I had found some Polish sausage at the market that week, so I cut that up and then sauteed it with onions and peppers. I beat eight eggs with a cup and a half of milk. I spooned the sausage and veggies over the bread cubes, then carefully poured the egg and milk mixture over it all, topping it with three different shredded cheeses. I used three kinds because they were all too small to slice for cheese and crackers or grilled cheese sandwiches and I didn't want it to go to waste. Of course, I could have eaten it, but my waistline didn't need the help. I covered the baking dish with foil and slid it into the refrigerator to rest overnight.

"Why is the back yard flooded?" Iggy said as he came in the back door.

"Oh, I'm so glad you're home." I threw my arms around

him and gave him a big kiss. "Something is in the drain pipe blocking it so the water can't drain. I used my phone flashlight to see if I could figure out the problem and something was looking back at me. I think it's a big frog or maybe a rat."

"I do not think it would be a frog. The only frogs we have are Cuban Tree Frogs and they are not big enough to get stuck in the pipe." He took the flashlight off his tool shelf and went outside. I followed him to see what he thought was in there. Iggy bent over and shined the light down into the pipe. He quickly straightened up. "That is a frog all right, a mighty big frog." He looked again. "Not a frog, a cane toad. They are big and nasty. I do not know how I can get it out. Let me consult Old Reynaldo. He has experience with them clogging up his cistern pipes. I will be back." He handed me the flashlight and left to walk down the road to the goat man's house.

I had a bad feeling about it. I was certain that he would have to dispatch the toad because I couldn't imagine how he could lure it out.

I spent the time he was gone looking up cane toads on the internet. They sounded nasty. They secrete a toxin that can kill pets and poison people. Maybe we could entice the toad to leave the drain pipe with what it likes to eat. I checked. Insects—don't have any handy. Garbage—that I've got. I made shepherd's pie for supper, so I've got potato and carrot peels. I wondered if cane toads liked vegetables. There was some really old meat in the garbage. That sounded like it might be something a toad would like. Maybe I'd dig it out and put it by the pipe. It was smelly and a little slimy, just like the cane toad.

I decided it couldn't hurt, so I pawed through the garbage and found the rotten meat. I used a plastic bag over my hand to lift it out and carried it at arm's length out to the backyard and put it next to the drainpipe. Then I went back inside to give the toad some privacy. I peeked through the screen to watch and, sure enough, that cane toad crawled out of the pipe and landed smack on the meat. It ate. Just then Iggy came back into the yard and startled the toad, which hopped away into the bougainvillea and crouched there with its beady eyes trained on its abandoned supper.

"How did you know to do that?" he said.

"I didn't, but I looked up what they like to eat and had some nearly rotten meat in the garbage, so I put it by the pipe, and it lured the toad right out." I felt very smart and a little brave for feeding a poison toad.

"That is what Old Reynaldo said to do. He even offered me some of his garbage, but I said thanks and thought we could figure it out. He will be impressed that you did it all by yourself."

I buffed my nails on my shirt. "With a little help from the internet."

Iggy leaned over to pick up the meat, but I stopped him.

"Stop! Don't touch that. Cane toads secrete poison, and it could irritate your skin. Here, put this bag over your hand and pick it up." I handed him the bag that I'd used to carry the meat from the garbage can to the backyard.

He picked up the rotten meat and flung it over into the bougainvillea, where the toad could eat it in peace.

"Should we be afraid that the toad will get used to being fed here and hang around?"

"I will fix a screen over the washer drain pipe so that it cannot get down there again. It will not stay here long once the food runs out."

We walked together back toward the kitchen door. I turned to look at the toad, happily eating the rotten meat. "I wonder if cane toads eat rats. I wouldn't mind that."

Before supper, Iggy cut a square of screening he fitted over the washer drain pipe and secured with a hose clamp. He cut a slit in the middle just big enough for the hose from the washer to go through. "There. That should keep the toads out of the pipe."

Now that the pipe was clear, I started the laundry again. It would take most of the evening to get it done, but I needed the towels to be cleaned and put away because tomorrow was Saturday and sheet-changing day, which meant another big laundry day.

***

Geneva and I were busy all the next day. I spent the morning readying bills for the departing guests while Geneva washed the breakfast dishes and cleaned up the kitchen. Once everyone had checked out, we both headed upstairs to strip the beds, toss those towels down to be washed, and clean the bathrooms to be ready for the arriving guests.

The first to arrive were Jed and Carol Higgins. As she walked in the door, Carol screwed up her face and said, "What is that smell?"

I sniffed. "Lemon bathroom cleaner, I think."

"It smells vile. Do you use it all the time?" She folded her arms and frowned. "I am very sensitive to fragrance. Use something else."

I blinked at her. "It's all natural and organic. I have nothing else. I could use ammonia but that might smell worse. We can try to use it sparingly and open the windows when we clean. Would that be all right?"

"I suppose it will have to be."

Jed stood patiently while his wife surveyed the lobby. "Should I check us in?" he said.

She shrugged. "If you have to."

"You made the reservation. We might as well."

I entered their information in to the computer program and checked their room assignment. "Geneva will escort you to your room." I gestured to the young woman standing ready with the fruit and cheese plate and wine glasses in her hand. "It's the lilac room, Geneva." I handed her the keys.

"Would you prefer white or red wine, ma'am?" Geneva asked.

"White with cheese. What a foolish question." Carol turned away from the desk and followed her up the stairs.

Jed picked up two suitcases and trudged after them. "I'll be back for the rest," he said over his shoulder.

At the top of the stairs, Carol stopped. "No, we have an ocean view room."

"I am sorry, ma'am. The lilac room is a garden view room." Geneva gestured down the hall with the keys.

Carol scowled and put her fists on her hips. "Jed, go downstairs and tell that woman we want an ocean view room."

"I, uh, yes dear." He put down the suitcases and turned to come back down to the registration desk.

I met him halfway. "I'm sorry, but when you made your reservation, the two ocean view rooms were already reserved. The garden view rooms are the same size and have the same furnishings as the ocean view rooms. I'm sure you'll be comfortable in the lilac room."

"Well, I'm not," Carol said. "I don't want to overlook some parking lot or a weedy backyard. I want to see the ocean out my windows."

"Out the windows you'll see palm trees, the salt pond, and the sunrise. It is on the side by the parking lot, but you have to lean out to see it." I gestured for Geneva to continue down the hall and open their room for them. "You are welcome to sit on the front gallery at any time. You access it by that door down the short hallway there. It has a perfect view of the sea and the sunset."

"Hmph," she said. "We'll just see about that. I want to speak to the owner."

"I am the owner and the manager and the head of housekeeping. I also make the breakfasts, do the laundry, and anything else that needs doing around the place."

"Oh. Well, I suppose this will be acceptable. Which one is my bathroom?"

"The bathrooms are shared. There is a sink in your room for freshening up, toothbrushing, and shaving. People use the bathrooms for showering and toileting and be sure you take your towels with you when you use the bathroom and back to your room afterwards. The appliques on your towels match your room color. There are towel bars in your room to hang them to dry."

"You have got to be kidding."

"Ma'am, I told you all these things when you made the reservation. All of this information is in the email I send with your confirmation."

"Well, I didn't read all of that." She turned to her husband. "Did you, Jed?"

"Yes, Carol, I read it, and I told you all about it. You agreed we should stay here. Can we please get into the room so I can put these suitcases down, go get the other ones, and we can go out for a drink?"

Carol took the wine and a glass from Geneva. "We can go out after I finish the wine." She followed Geneva the rest of the way down the hall and went into the lilac room.

Jed followed her in and came right back out for their other cases. He looked at me before climbing the stairs. "She's just tired from today's travel."

"Of course." I smiled at him and as soon as he was gone, I shook my head. This promised to be an interesting week.

CHAPTER 43

Rose

The rest of the arriving guests trickled in. The Willards, a married couple, were in the yellow room, a single woman named Sarah Marsh was in the salmon room, and a single man checked in to in the turquoise room. They were all happy to be there and eager to get moved in and start exploring the island. Craig and Sandy Willard had been to Anguilla before. They stayed in an inland guesthouse, but said they wanted to be right on the beach, so they chose Seaview for their return visit. The single man, Raymond Langton, told me he was a writer when he made his reservation. Geneva and I moved the desk from the lilac room into the turquoise room, so he'd have a place to work.

"I hope you get a lot of writing done during your stay. What kind of books do you write?"

"I write crime fiction," Raymond said, looking up from signing the registration form. "Police procedurals, so I'm hoping to spend some time with the local cops to learn how things work on a Caribbean island."

"There's a police station not too far down the beach from here. I'm sure the officers will be happy to tell you all about their methods. Officer Micah has been a big help when I've needed him."

He glanced at me. "Have you needed the police often?"

"No, not really. A local man had a crush on me and wouldn't leave, so Officer Micah helped convince him to keep his distance." I wasn't about to go into detail about Calvin Brooks' obsession with me and how I had to swear out a restraining order to keep him at bay.

I heard a door close upstairs, and Jed and Carol walked down the hall and down the stairs. Carol paused behind Raymond and said, "Hello, handsome. Come here often?"

I saw the wine-induced spots of color high on her cheeks.

"Uh, no, this is my first time," Raymond said.

Jed reached back and took Carol's arm. "Come on dear. Don't disturb the man."

"I wasn't disturbing him. I was being friendly."

"Then don't be friendly."

She jerked her arm out of his grasp and pouted, walking out the door in front of her husband.

I finished checking Raymond in and said, "Let me escort you to your room. I have a fruit and cheese plate for you to enjoy. Can I get you some wine? I have red and white."

"I'll take the plate, but no wine. I'm a beer man."

"Luckily, I have a bottle of beer in the fridge. I'll bring it up after I show you to your room."

Once he was settled in his room and all the other guests were either in their rooms or out, I went back into the kitchen to start supper. Iggy and I had gone to a barbecue the night before at Dru Brooks' house and she'd sent us home with a mound of leftovers. So, I wrapped the ribs in foil and tucked them into the oven to slowly warm. I did the same with the johnny cakes. There was coleslaw too. I kept nibbling on it until I was afraid I'd eat it all, so I put it back in the fridge. I'd get it out when it was time to eat.

Dru had really come out of her shell since Calvin passed away. I'd never known her to be so happy and active in local affairs. She confided last night that she was thinking of running for a seat in the House of Assembly. Since her father had been governor of the island at one time, I thought she had a pretty good chance of knowing how the government worked.

I heard Iggy's truck pull up behind the bed-and-breakfast and patted my hair into place. I checked the time and was glad that his afternoon electrician job hadn't taken too long. When he came through the back door, I met him in the back room where he left his tools. "How did the job go?"

He walked over and put his arms around me. "Just fine. I was at Jeremy Minten's house, replacing a couple of plugs and light switches. Mice had chewed the wires." He leaned down and kissed me.

"Ugh. That sound awful."

"Everyone around here has mice, you know that. They are a fact of life."

"I know, but I rarely see them. I only hear them scrabbling around in the walls at night. Speaking of that, we could use more traps."

"I will pick some up at Henry's Hardware the next time I'm in Blowing Point." He sniffed. "Are we having leftover ribs for supper tonight?"

"Yes. And I didn't eat all the coleslaw, so there's some of that too."

"Good."

Iggy and I were sitting at the kitchen island having supper and talking when we heard voices in the lobby.

"No, I don't want to go upstairs. I want to go back to that beach bar and have another drink," Carol said.

"You've had enough drinks for today. It's time to stop. Do you want to go get something to eat?"

I heard the doors of the sideboard open and close.

"No. Isn't there something to drink around here?"

"Carol, for god's sake, stop digging around looking for liquor. We've talked about this. Slow down."

"You slow down. I want another drink. If you won't get me one, I'll go back to Jimmo's or whatever the place is called and find someone who will." She walked into the kitchen and stood with her hands on her hips. "Hey, Rosie, what does a girl have to do to get a drink around here?" She slurred her words and swayed slightly.

"I'm sorry, but we don't serve drinks. I don't have a liquor license."

Her eyes settled on Iggy. "Who's the handsome stud? Your boy-toy?"

Iggy stood up, walked around the kitchen island, and extended his hand. "How do you do? I am Ignatius Solomon, Mrs. Solomon's husband."

Carol grabbed his hand and pulled him into an embrace. "Hello, handsome. I'll bet you know how to show a girl a good time. What say we go down the beach and get a little drinky?"

Jed stepped forward, took Carol by the shoulder, and pulled her away from Iggy. "Carol, now you're just embarrassing yourself. Let these people have their supper in peace." He looked at me, his face flushed. "I'm so very sorry to interrupt your meal. Come on, Carol, let's go." He kept a grip on her upper arm and walked her toward the lobby.

"Ow, you're hurting me. Let go."

"I'm not hurting you. I'll let go when we get to our room." He looked over his shoulder and said, "I'm really sorry."

Her querulous voice faded as they walked up the stairs and down the hall. All the way, Carol was trying to convince Jed that they needed to go out for another drink, and Jed kept saying no.

***

The next morning at breakfast, Carol was pale and shaky. She held her coffee mug in both hands and sipped the hot brew carefully. I suspected she would be queasy, so I made muffins and fruit bowls that should be easy on her stomach.

When I carried out the food tray, she was sniffing the orange juice pitcher. "No mimosas?"

"No, sorry. Just plain juice." I served each guest a fruit bowl and put baskets of muffins on the tables. "Today, we have fresh baked banana walnut muffins with tropical fruit on the side. I hope you enjoy it." I went back into the kitchen to make myself some breakfast.

Iggy came out of our apartment dressed for church. "I am going to services this morning."

"Fine. Tell Pastor Davis I said hello." I walked over and

straightened his tie. "You look very nice."

"Thank you." He kissed my forehead, patted my behind, and left, jingling his keys as he walked to his truck.

I heard chairs scraping the lobby floor, so I grabbed a tray and went out to clear the dishes. Carol sat at the table alone with a mug of coffee still clutched in her hands.

"How was breakfast?"

She glowered at me from under her penciled-on brows. "I can't eat that muck."

"The muffins or the fruit?"

"Both. Don't you have anything civilized, like croissants?"

"I'm sorry. I don't know how to make croissants. People tell me my muffins are very good. Did you try one?"

"Jed didn't give me one."

I sat down across from her. "Well, there's still one in the basket. If I peel off the paper, would you like to try it?"

"I guess." She shrugged.

I carefully peeled off the baking paper and cut the muffin in half. I put the halves on the plate in front of her. "Would you like me to butter it for you?"

"No. My stomach's a little touchy this morning, but I need something to soak up all the coffee. I'll try a bite of muffin."

After the first tentative bite, she ate the rest of the muffin in short order. "That was okay. Is there another one?"

"Let me check and see." I gathered up the other baskets. "Yes, there's one left. Would you like it?"

She put a hand on her stomach. "Maybe not. Maybe I'll just go upstairs and..." She dropped the coffee mug, which bounced across the floor, stood up, shoving her chair over, and dashed for the stairs. She made it to the bathroom before heaving everything up. Thank goodness.

Jed rushed out of their bedroom and stood in the bathroom doorway; his hands braced on the doorjamb. "Carol, are you all right?"

In between heaves, she said, "I will be."

CHAPTER 44

Rose

I wasn't sure whether to mention the jump-up to Jed and Carol. After her stomach episode at breakfast, Carol spent a couple of hours in their room while Jed took a walk down the beach. After washing the breakfast dishes, I cleaned the bathrooms and swept the hall and lobby.

Carol leaned on the doorjamb of their room and watched me sweep. "Why are you doing that? Don't you have that native woman to do that kind of work?"

"Sunday is Geneva's day off and anyway, we share the work. I do most of the cooking, but she and I share everything else." I swept the sand and dirt into a dustpan and stood up. "Are you feeling better?"

"I'd feel better if I had a drink. Can I have another one of those little bottles of wine?"

I shook my head. "No, I'm sorry. I reserve that for welcoming guests when they arrive. I can't afford to hand it out when anyone asks. You could go up to Vista Market and buy your own bottle of wine. You're welcome to leave it in the refrigerator."

It was Carol's turn to shake her head. "No, Jed wouldn't let me do that. He says I drink too much and wants me to slow down. If I had my own bottle of wine, I'd probably drink it all in an afternoon." She looked over her shoulder at her empty room. "I should just go down to Jimmo's and get my own drink. I think I will. See you later, Rose."

I carried the full dustpan downstairs to empty in the trash. "It's Johnno's," I said under my breath.

In the end, I told all of my guests about Johnno's jump-up that evening and they all attended.

"We went to Johnno's jump-up last time we were here and wouldn't miss it," Sandy Willard said.

Raymond Langton was coming in from the beach and said, "What's so fun about it?"

"Oh, there's a great mix of locals and tourists and everybody dances with everybody else. There's one local man who is like a whirling dervish. I swear he danced every dance and with every woman in the place."

I said, "That would be Edward. He helped refurbish Seaview, and he loves to dance. He goes to all the jump-ups all over the island but says that Johnno's is the best."

Sarah leaned over the railing in the upstairs hall. "Is everyone going? I want to go, but don't want to go alone."

"Yes, we're going. Meet us in the lobby at five and we can walk down together."

"Do come," Raymond said. "I'll be here at five."

Jed walked through the group, saying nothing. He went into his room and came right back out. "Rose, do you know where Carol is?"

"She said something about going out for a drink. I think she went to Johnno's."

He looked stricken. "I told her to stay here." And he dashed down the stairs, pushed past the other guests, and ran down the steps to the beach.

Since it was after four thirty, the Willards, Sarah, and Raymond all went to their rooms to get ready for the jump-up.

Iggy and I changed and made our way down to the beach bar where our friends had claimed the big table and saved chairs for us.

"Mrs. Rose and Uncle Iggy, come sit with us," Silas said. "We have room for you at our table."

I was surprised to see Geneva sitting beside Silas.

"Hi Geneva, I'm glad to see you having some fun."

"Hello, Mrs. Rose. Silas convinced me to come and dance with him."

"Well, I'm glad to see you."

Just then, the steel band crashed into the first song. Edward took my hand. "May I have this dance?"

"Yes, you may." I took a quick sip of my rum punch and followed Edward onto the dance floor.

As we circled the room in the crowd of dancers, I saw Jed and Carol off to the side. It looked like they were arguing. Jed was tugging Carol's arm, and she was trying to pull away. When we got nearer, I heard her say, "I want to dance. Will you dance with me, Jed?"

Jed's shoulders sagged, and he took the drink from her, put it on the bar, and escorted her to the dance floor.

Carol shimmied out of his grasp. "No, I want to dance with an island man. They know how to dance." She reached an arm out and scooped Edward up and inserted herself between him and me.

I staggered back and nearly fell, but someone caught me from behind. "Stay on your feet, Mrs. Rose. You could get trampled." It was Julius, the local gigolo.

"Thanks, Julius. I'm fine." I walked back to our table and sat down next to Iggy. "Not dancing tonight?"

"I am waiting for a slow song so I can dance with my wife."

"That's an idea I can get behind." There were a few baskets of bar food on the table, so I made a paper plate with conch fritters, chicken fingers, and plantain chips.

I watched the dancers. Carol and Edward were moving slower than the rest of them. I could see that Carol was unsteady on her feet and Edward was trying to steer her toward a chair. Jed met them at the edge of the dance floor to help.

"No," Carol said. "I want to keep dancing."

"Sweetheart, the song is done," Jed said. "You sit here while the band takes a break."

"Get me another drink."

Jed went over to the bar and conferred with Johnno, who nodded and made a special rum punch, without the rum.

Carol took a big swallow of the fruity drink and nodded. "That's what I needed." She handed her glass to her husband, her head tipped toward her shoulder, and she slid out of the chair, passed out cold.

People backed away. Johnno came around the bar and Iggy went over to help. The brothers got the woman back onto the chair and conferred with Jed.

"I can carry her back to Seaview," Johnno said. "She's just a bitty thing." He scooped up the unconscious woman and left the bar with her.

They walked down the road, which was much easier going than taking the sandy beach route. Jed walked alongside, apologizing to Johnno with every step. Iggy went along in case Johnno and Jed needed help.

Iggy and Johnno were back in just a few minutes. "Well, that was interesting," Iggy said.

"Interesting is a good word for it. I wonder if she drinks like that at home or if it's a vacation thing."

"Oh, I think her drinking is an everyday thing. Jed said that he is trying to get her to go to a treatment center, but she refuses to admit she has a problem. He has taken away her car keys so she cannot drive drunk and injure herself or anyone else."

"I wonder where she gets the booze to drink all day."

"Has it delivered, I suppose."

The rest of the guests looked like they were having fun. Julius claimed Sarah's hand for the first ballad, but after that Raymond was faster to ask her to dance. By the time Iggy and I said goodnight, they were holding hands and gazing into each other's eyes.

I elbowed Iggy and nodded toward their table near the opposite side of the beach bar. "Looks like Cupid struck."

He looked where I indicated. "Or maybe it is too much rum, but I hope it is Cupid. We do not need more drama since we already have Carol."

"That's the truth."

***

Early in the week, I walked Raymond down to the police station to introduce him to Officer Micah and the other officers. The policemen were flattered that a writer wanted to know about their methods and practices. Raymond invited them to come down to Seaview when they were off duty and sat interviewing them in the lobby, taking copious notes.

But every evening, he and Sarah went out for supper together. It was fun to watch the budding romance. I just hoped it was more than a vacation fling for both of them.

CHAPTER 45

Rose

For the next few days, Carol seemed to maintain a moderate level of tipsy. She had a water bottle with her at all times and I suspected that there wasn't only water in it. Jed convinced her to take the launch out to Sandy Island one morning, but she came back complaining that there wasn't a bar out on the island, so she couldn't get a "real" drink.

By every afternoon, Carol was overly friendly to Iggy, Craig Willard, Raymond Langton, and any other man in her vicinity. Jed kept busy peeling her off men and apologizing to the women accompanying them.

On Friday morning, Jed came down the stairs so fast he almost slid down the last few steps. "Call an ambulance. I can't make Carol wake up."

My heart lurched. "Is she breathing?"

"Just barely. Hurry."

I pulled my cellphone out of my pocket and dialed 9-1-1. I told the operator that we needed an ambulance fast.

"What is your emergency?"

I looked at Jed. He nodded. "Alcohol poisoning. Hurry! She's barely breathing."

Jed turned and ran back up the stairs.

I followed him to see if there was anything I could do to help. When I got to the room, the floor was littered with empty tiny wine bottles that I kept for arriving guests. Carol must have raided the kitchen and grabbed all the little bottles she could find and taken them to her room. There was at least a dozen of them. Combined with the usual level of alcohol in her system, that much added had to be nearly lethal.

Jed sat on the edge of the bed near his wife's head. "Carol?" he said. "Carol, honey, come on. Wake up." He patted her cheek and kept putting his hand on her chest to make sure that she was still breathing.

I grabbed the wastebasket and gathered up all the empty wine bottles. I counted them as I put them into the basket. Fifteen. No wonder she wasn't waking up. I heard the siren getting louder as the rescuers approached, so I hurried down the stairs carrying the clinking wastebasket with me. I went out the back door and motioned them to come. "She's upstairs in the last room on the right. Hurry! I don't know if she's still breathing."

The rescue squad members pulled out their cases and ran through the kitchen and lobby, then up the stairs to Carol's room.

Jed was standing in the hall crying. "I can't make her wake up. She's barely breathing. Oh, please help."

They rushed into the room, and I heard them calling her to wake up. I started up to join Jed when one of them said, "She's stopped breathing. But I still have a heartbeat. No, no breathing, no heartbeat."

One of the paramedics pulled a defibrillator up onto the bed and started it. They shocked Carol once, twice, three times with no effect.

I reached Jed's side and put an arm around him. It was on the tip of my tongue to say that they'd save her, but I couldn't make myself.

One of them pushed open her robe, pressed the heel of his hand above the notch below her breastbone, and started chest compressions. The other one grabbed a bag and started breathing for her. He looked at me over his shoulder. "Come, you squeeze this bag every five seconds." We changed places. I leaned over Carol ready to breathe for her and he called for both of us to stop so he could listen with his stethoscope. "Nothing. Keep going."

We kept it up for nearly an hour with no results.

"I am calling it," said the senior paramedic, who was on the phone with the emergency doctor.

"No!" Jed said and fell to his knees in the hall, sobbing.

"I am sorry, sir, but your wife was just too far gone for us to save her." He turned to the other paramedic and me. "Stop breathing. Stop compressions." He looked at his watch. "Time of death is 9:47 A.M."

By then, the other guests filled the hall. Raymond stood in his doorway watching the drama unfold. He reached out to hold Jed's shoulder while he cried. Sarah Marsh and Sandy Willard were crying. Craig Willard had his arms around them, letting them cry on his shoulders.

The senior paramedic sent his partner down to bring in the gurney. "I will carry her downstairs. She is so light, there is nothing to her."

Everyone cleared the hallway for the removal of Carol's body. The paramedics carried her downstairs and gently laid her on the gurney. They zipped the body bag over her and rolled her out to the ambulance. Jed followed them. They left him with her while they returned for their equipment. "I am sorry we made a mess, Mrs. Rose."

"That's okay. I'll clean it up."

And then they were gone.

Jed rode in the ambulance with them.

I started cleaning the room. I gathered up the soiled sheets and was glad that I had put impermeable mattress covers on the beds.

The other guests went back to their rooms. I couldn't imagine going off to do fun vacation activities after what they had witnessed. One by one, they came out, each carrying a beach towel and a bag.

Sarah said, "We decided to go sit on the beach and think about Carol and Jed. Carol was a sad person, wasn't she?"

"Very sad. I wonder what made her so sad, but now we'll never know."

The Willards came out of their room to join Sarah. "Ready?" Sally said. "Is Raymond coming too?"

Sarah shook her head. "Not right away. He said he needs to reach his word count for the day and then he'll be along. He said no more than an hour."

The three of them turned and trudged down the stairs and went out into the sunny day.

**

Geneva and I worked quickly to remove all traces of what had just happened from the lilac room. We wiped the mattress cover with a strong cleaner and remade the bed with fresh sheets. We replaced the used towels, dusted the surfaces, and swept the floor. I found three more little wine bottles under the bed. What a shame. Before we left the room, I opened the windows to let the room air out to remove the smell of death.

We each cleaned one bathroom. When I smelled the lemon cleaner, tears came to my eyes when I remembered Carol's reaction when they arrived last Saturday.

Once the laundry was done, folded, and put away, I told Geneva to go home. It felt like there was nothing more important to do than remember Carol and wait for Jed to return. I was sitting at the kitchen island staring at my hands when Iggy returned from doing an electrical job for one of the expats. I couldn't remember who. I didn't go to meet him when he came in or ask about his day.

"Rose, what is wrong?"

I turned toward him and said, "Carol died."

He strode across the kitchen and enveloped me in his arms. "I am so sorry. How did it happen?"

I cried, and the words came out in little jerks. "She raided my wine stash. Drank almost twenty. Little bottles of wine. Feel like it's somehow my fault."

"How can it be your fault? You did not give her the wine or even show her where you kept it. Did you?"

"No. But she knew I had it here somewhere. Oh, Iggy, I can't imagine how Jed feels. He tried so hard to get her to stop drinking."

He held me even tighter. "But she could not stop. Drinking like that is a sickness and people die from sickness all the time. This was not your fault."

"I know, but I still feel bad."

"You may grieve for her, just do not blame yourself for what happened. Okay?" He held me away from him and looked me in the eye.

"Okay." I wiped my tears and tried to smile. "How was your day?"

"Not as eventful as yours, but I fixed all the burned-out lightbulbs and loose sockets for Mrs. Holland-Smythe. Minerva sends her greetings."

I checked the time. "Oh goodness, it's suppertime." I opened the refrigerator to see what I had I could quickly fix. "Looks like leftovers again."

"I do not mind."

CHAPTER 46

Rose

I was so nervous the afternoon of the advertising group meeting. Geneva helped me get the lobby ready for the group. We shoved the three tables together to make room for everyone to sit around them and have room for making notes. I found a stack of notepads at the back of the Eastern Store and bought some so that I'd have them to hand out. I collected pencils and pens in case everyone didn't bring their own.

We made pimento cheese and olive and nut spread into small sandwiches. Anne said that she'd bring cookies. I made a couple gallons each of sun tea and lemonade to serve for drinks. My guests that week were four single women who had gotten acquainted the day they arrived and had done just about everything together since. They seemed to be on a quest to eat at every local restaurant they could find and would come back late in the evening with tales to tell of delicious food and gracious hosts. I was confident that they'd be out when the innkeepers arrived and most likely not return until they left.

Geneva and I got all the sandwiches made before she left for the day, wrapped them in cling film, and stowed them in the fridge.

"Would you like me to stay behind and serve?" Geneva said.

"No, but thanks for the offer." I didn't want to appear to be setting myself above the rest of the women. "I'll serve the refreshments myself. I really appreciate your help to get ready for tonight and I will tell you how it goes when you come to work tomorrow." I was determined to do everything I could think of to make sure that Geneva knew how much I valued her help around Seaview.

Six-thirty arrived, and Anne knocked on the back door with her container of cookies. I let her in and at almost the same time, the other innkeepers started filtering in the front door.

"Welcome to Seaview," I said as they all filed in together. I was surprised to see Lomira, who worked in the shop at Tamarind Watersports, but didn't get the chance to ask why she was there. She hadn't been at the first businesswomen's group meeting I went to.

Every one of them eagerly looked around the lobby and they all peeked into the kitchen before sitting down. "I can't give you a tour of the guest rooms since they're full this week, but I can let you see the kitchen and my apartment if you'd like." They said they'd like that a lot. So, everyone got back up and followed me into the kitchen and through the door into our apartment.

Iggy was reading on the loveseat in the sitting room and said, "Good evening, ladies. Come to solve all of your advertising problems?"

They laughed and followed me back to the lobby, a few of them lingering in the kitchen to admire the stainless-steel cupboards with the mesh sides. "Where did you find those cabinets?" asked Lomira.

"I found them at a specialty kitchen supplier in the States. I knew how humid it is in Anguilla and wanted to have air flow to prevent mold and mildew."

"Very smart, but most of them do not have doors. What about bugs and mice getting in your supplies?"

"I have a double cupboard with mesh doors so I can put baked goods in there to cool and I store my ingredients in this row of small garbage cans that I keep carefully closed when I'm not using what's inside." The women murmured and nodded. "Shall we get started?" Everyone found a seat at the tables, and most of them pulled out a notebook and pen. I passed notepads and pencils to those that hadn't thought to bring them, and we got started brainstorming.

The discussion was lively and varied. Some women had tried advertising in the tourist brochures with limited success and others had printed their own brochures but found them too expensive to keep reprinting or changing with the times. Anne had spoken with her friend at the Anguilla Tourism Board about ways we could band together to advertise all our hotels to benefit us all instead of just one or two. Most of them had spent some time thinking about what made their place unique so we could emphasize the advantages of each place without putting down the others.

"My hotel is on a beach where the sunrise is visible. Early risers like to get up and greet the day with a mug of coffee," one woman said.

"Aren't we all on a beach?" I asked.

Heads shook.

The woman sitting with her arms crossed said, "Not all of us are lucky enough to have the island's best beach at her doorstep. I am in a neighborhood. I do not know what an American can do to help my business."

There were a few indrawn breaths and clicked tongues.

"Stop listening to Mrs. Whiting, Eloise, and use your common sense," another innkeeper said. "We are all trying to improve our businesses together. Eight minds are bound to be better than one." She turned back to the group. "My bed-and-breakfast is near to The Old Valley, where people can walk to the museum and visit the craft market. There are quite a few restaurants and cafes within walking distance, too, so my guests are often people who are interested in the island's history."

"Rose Inn is in the middle of Island Harbour," Terese Whiting said. "We are near to the beach, and we have a full-service restaurant, not just breakfast."

Anne spoke up. "All of my rooms have bathrooms and kitchenettes. People who are staying for an extended time appreciate the convenience of being able to prepare simple meals."

Another woman said, "A lot of my guests are hikers. They stay with me because I am near the Katouche Valley where there are trails and a small piece of rainforest. I have bicycles for them to rent. Many of them pedal all over the island to the other trails."

"I am near Shoal Bay and many of my guests are windsurfers and the beach volleyball crowd," said a fifth woman.

Lomira was last. "Mine is the Ferryboat Inn in Blowing Point. I have trouble attracting return guests. I also have a full-service restaurant, but my beach is beside the ferry dock. Not very easy to relax when those noisy boats come in and kick up a wake. The diesel stink keeps people away too. I do not know what I can do. Maybe you all have some ideas."

"I'm sure someone will have an idea to help you." I thought for a minute. "What about aiming your advertising toward business travelers? Say something like 'Get off the ferry and be right at home.'"

Lomira looked thoughtful. "That might work. Thanks."

I looked around the table at the women. "I'm impressed at the variety of accommodations and amenities we have in this small group. What do you say to inviting Anne's friend from the Tourism Board to our next meeting? She might help us draft advertising that will highlight each of our places, help us reach the kinds of people we need."

Everyone nodded their agreement with the plan, and we sat back, smiling at each other. Even Eloise was wearing a small smile. I realized I was the only American in the group, but we had worked together to reach our common goals without me putting my foot in my mouth.

I went into the kitchen for the plates of sandwiches and pitchers of beverages. Anne and Terese came along to help carry. Another of the women whose name I hadn't caught passed out plates and napkins and yet another gave everyone a glass. We sat around the table munching on sandwiches and cookies, sipping tea or lemonade, and keeping the discussion going.

One woman joked, "What? No alcohol? Are you teetotal, Rose?"

"No, although I'm not much of a drinker."

Iggy came out into the lobby. "Is there anything left for a starving husband?" He reached into the middle of the table for a couple of sandwiches, which he put on a paper plate. "It has been a long time since supper."

The women laughed at his remark, teasing him about always being hungry like some teenager.

"I worked hard all day," he said. "Have pity on a poor working man."

"Oh, yes Ignatius," Anne said. "We all know how hard you work. You are the one Solomon man who never rests."

"I will not tell our brother Johnno you said that. He would not appreciate the humor."

Soon the sandwich plates were empty except for a few crumbs and the pitchers of drinks were nearly empty. It was a productive two hours, and I felt more welcome and more a part of the island community than I ever had before. I stood at the door, shaking hands, and thanking each woman for coming and taking part.

Terese said, "Next time we should meet at Rose Inn. Mama makes the best johnny cakes on the island and I am sure I can convince her to make some for us."

"That's a wonderful idea, Terese," I said. "I love johnny cakes and can never make them so they're edible."

She winked at me. "There is a trick to making them. Maybe when you have been here a little longer, you can persuade Mama to teach you how."

"I look forward to the opportunity."

It only took Iggy and me a few minutes to rearrange the tables and chairs in the lobby, back into position for the morning breakfast service.

"How did it go, Rose?"

I exhaled a big breath. "It went well. No one made me feel like an outsider, and they all seemed to appreciate my ideas. For the first time, I felt like a part of the island community."

"That is good. I was happy to hear laughter instead of arguing."

"And you got to come out and grab a snack before all the goodies were gone."

"You know I love pimento cheese, and I am coming to enjoy olive and nut spread. Anne's ginger cookies were very good too. Will you be meeting again?"

I nodded. "Yes, we're going to Rose Inn next, and Anne will invite her friend from the Tourism Board to advise us on how to best spend our advertising money."

Iggy pushed the last chair into place at the table and draped his arm over my shoulder. "I am glad your meeting went well and that you are feeling more comfortable with the other businesswomen."

"Me too. I was really nervous about it. What if they'd decided not to come? What if they weren't willing to work with me but cut me out of the group?"

"But that did not happen. You were worrying about nothing."

CHAPTER 47

Rose

The sun had barely peeked over the horizon when the snorkelers gathered. Iggy and I walked down the beach toward the crowd at the pier. He carried his old duffle with his new snorkeling gear in it. "Are you sure you do not mind me going today?" he said, looking down at me at his side. "It is Saturday, and you have a lot that needs doing today. I could help with the laundry or the cleaning if you would like."

I squeezed his hand. "No, I don't mind. Geneva and I can handle the chores just fine. I'm glad you're going off snorkeling with the guys. You'll have fun. I promise."

As we joined the group, Dimitri said, "The rumbling of the engines and the diesel fumes makes me feel like I am running away from home, George."

George nodded his agreement.

I imagined they were both looking forward to spending a day without having to look over their shoulders to make sure their wives weren't around. Several months into their membership in the club, they had ceased to worry about tales being carried back to Susan and Irina. Enough of the men in the group were members just to escape the scrutiny of their wives' eagle eyes, that the unofficial motto of the club seemed to be "what happens at snorkeling, stays at snorkeling."

Davis and Ezra, Franz's dreadlocked first mate, helped stow all the gear on deck and put the coolers filled with drinks and food under the awning near the controls. Dimitri had used yards of duct tape to secure the lid on a big Styrofoam cooler and bungees to close the Coleman cooler's lid, so nothing got lost or jiggled out on the crossing. By 8 a.m. everyone was onboard, all the gear was stowed, and the lines were untied from the pier.

***

I stood waving on the sand and watched the fast ferry pull away from the pier in the center of Road Bay. I had been tempted to go along with Iggy on the day trip to Dog Island, but at the last minute I had decided against it. It was Saturday, my most recent guests were all leaving that morning, which meant Geneva and I would spend the day cleaning bedrooms, doing laundry, cleaning bathrooms, and getting ready to welcome a new complement of guests.

This week it was the six-person yoga group that had stayed at Seaview last year coming back again. That meant that the week would be filled with vegetarian breakfasts, the aroma of incense, and the low hum of chanting that accompanied their afternoon meditations in the garden. Even though I had only four rooms, the yoga group didn't mind doubling up. The weather report was cooperating too. I'd hate to think how disappointing a yoga retreat on a rainy Caribbean island would be. Not the publicity I needed.

With a steady stream of guests filling all the rooms most weeks, my bank balance was slowly growing. Even with having to pay Geneva, I was staying in the black and gaining. Nothing had broken lately, well, nothing Iggy couldn't fix, and I had paid my Henry's Hardware account in full, so I didn't have that monthly bill anymore. I was feeling pretty confident that things were going my way.

The business had settled down to about half repeat visitors and half new guests, but it swung mostly toward the repeats in September and October, the off season. I still had a good number of writers visiting. Janet Fielding had been back twice, each time for a month, since Seaview had opened and that trio of writing women from Milwaukee had been back again, too. My little writers' library of paperbacks and journals written or worked on at the bed-and-breakfast was growing nicely.

I finished my mug of coffee as the last bag of gear and cooler was lifted off the pier and loaded onto the fast ferry. I promised myself that the next time the snorkel group planned a day trip, I'd go along. As long as it wasn't on a Saturday.

Geneva and I worked side by side after the guests had checked out. Once the first load of sheets was in the washer, I went to pick up the mail from the post office box. I laid the stack of mail on the kitchen island with one official-looking envelope on the top. As I carried the last basket of towels out to the washer, I glanced down and stopped. I set the basket down and picked up the letter. The return address was the Anguilla Lands and Surveys Department. I wondered who they were and what they were mailing me about. I slit the envelope open and pulled out a single sheet of paper. It was a property tax bill. I hadn't thought of needing to pay property taxes, but it made sense that I would have to.

"Oh my god," I said.

"What is it?" Geneva came out of the back room, where she was organizing the clean linens.

I looked at the total and gulped. It was a big number. A little smaller than my bank balance. I checked the due date, and it was six weeks away. Good. That would give time for more deposits and payments for stays to be posted to my account so that I'd have enough to pay my taxes and still buy groceries and pay Geneva.

"It's my property tax bill. I wasn't expecting it. I don't remember paying one last year."

"You must have, Mrs. Rose. The Lands and Survey Department does not miss a chance to collect money. Do not panic."

"I'm not panicking. I'm just surprised and relieved that I have enough in my account to cover it with a little extra." I probably shouldn't have said that to my employee, but I just blurted it out.

She reached over my shoulder and touched the paper. "Did

you see you can pay it in two installments? That way, you will not empty your account all at once."

"No, I didn't see that. Maybe I am panicking a little. That's good news, and it takes a load off my mind. Thank you."

I thanked my lucky stars for happy repeat guests who spread the word about Seaview to their friends.

All afternoon I thought about the property tax man coming to Seaview and insisting that I pay the entire bill at once, saying, "Now a real Anguillan can take over. Things will be as they should be."

I shook my head to drive out those thoughts. Iggy would be home around sunset, and he and I would work out a plan to pay the taxes.

CHAPTER 48

George and Dimitri

The silky morning air caressed George's face as he stood out on the bow of *Maggie's Salvation*. The just risen sun glittered on the ripples and flying fish leaped from the water and sailed away from the speeding boat. Dimitri, Iggy, and the others sat on the benches on the deck; a few were below staying out of the wind until the sun climbed higher and warmed the air. Iggy fiddled with the strap of his duffle bag, looking a little sorry he had agreed to go. George was always happier out in the wind and spray, happy when he could see all around, which he assumed resulted from all those years of looking at everyone and everything with suspicion.

He glanced at Ezra, who was steering the boat into the rising sun, his dreadlocks flowing out from under his cap and flapping in the breeze. The tall Rasta man stood barefoot on the deck with his long fingers gentle on the wheel, and his lips moving either in prayer or song. George liked Ezra; he was always cheerful and always willing to lend a hand when work needed to be done.

Franz had laughed, saying that Ezra was a good worker as long as you kept your eyes on him. Only one eye and Ezra would lean on the shovel more than he was digging with it, Franz said, but George had found Ezra to be a willing worker quick to finish a job.

The boat had just rounded the southernmost point of the island when a large flock of flamingos flew over on their way to the salt pond, where they would spend their day stalking in the pale pink water seining out the shrimp that gave them their characteristic color. He was always amazed to see that their wings were mostly white and black, neither color visible when they were walking. It intrigued him that such enormous birds could propel their massive bodies with such slow flapping. The sound of their honks and the heavy beat of their wings made him wish he could lift his arms and fly off with them for a night.

Iggy stood up and pointed toward the shore. "George, there is my house in West End Village. We should go snorkeling there again soon."

"We'll plan on it. Maybe invite the whole crowd."

Iggy nodded. "That would be good."

"Mistah George," Ezra said.

George looked at him and Ezra raised a crooked finger to point at a small gray bump on the horizon. George frowned and shrugged his shoulders.

Ezra shook his head and said, "It's de island, Dog Island, where we headed, mon."

Feeling foolish for not realizing that he could see the island so soon floating there just over the horizon, he nodded and waved his thanks to the relaxed figure at the wheel. The cluster of men sitting under the awning had also heard, and a few dragged out their binoculars to get a closer look. They watched the small gray bump grow as they approached, the gray turning into a cluster of dark green cacti thrusting their arms into the sky above pale-yellow ground.

Dog Island looked to be a few acres, barely keeping itself above sea level. When they got closer, Ezra slowed the boat and turned to motor around the shore to the Marine Park mooring where they had permission to tie up.

The squawk from the radio when Ezra called Davis to let him know they had arrived safely reminded George of all the hours he had spent huddled around a radio receiver, hoping to understand what was being said with no need to turn it too loud.

Looking over the side as they slowly motored along,

George was grateful that he had retired to such a beautiful place. The water was nearly crystal clear, and he saw the patches of coral reef with all the colors of fish darting around it. As he watched the day unfold, he resented being called back to work. When would they leave him alone, so he got to be fully retired?

Finally, Ezra cut the engine, and the boat glided toward the mooring. Gomez, the deckhand, lifted the long boat hook and snagged the mooring line, hauling it aboard and looping it around a cleat on deck. Gomez nodded to George and walked away without a word.

George leaned on the rail and watched the excited movements of the group. They spat into their masks, swished them in the ocean, and slid on their fins while standing at the opening in the railing. One by one, they slipped over the side to explore the reefs of Dog Island.

"George," Dimitri called, "what are you doing standing there? Get over here and let's go." The Russian looked like a black stork in his close-fitted neoprene suit. Iggy stood next to him, squirting defogger in his mask before putting it on.

George understood how the sight of her usually dignified husband in his getup would offend Irina. Thanking Ezra for the ride as he passed, he walked back to don his snorkeling gear and slip into the quiet world of the reef. Iggy tagged along with Dimitri and George, sticking close to George, the more experienced snorkeler.

By the time most of the men had been in the water for an hour, Ezra and Gomez had ferried the grill, coolers, and food over to Dog Island in the dinghy, setting them up in the shade of a grove of scrubby trees. Most of the trees on the island were the divi divi trees that pointed the way of the prevailing wind, but a few other varieties grew on the shore, making just enough shade to keep a man from frying his brains.

In small groups, the men waded ashore shaking seawater from themselves like old dogs after a swim. Nothing tasted better than a beer after a long snorkel in saltwater and the aroma of grilling meat lured them to stand around the barbecue talking about the fish they had seen that morning. Iggy was surprised that the men treated him like one of the group, asking what he'd seen and how he was enjoying his newfound interest.

A few of the men had brought along beach chairs, but most of them stretched out on their towels in the shade and dozed before heading back into the water to explore the rest of the reef along the leeward shore.

The sun was getting low in the sky as Ezra and Gomez hauled all the coolers and the grill back to the boat while George and Dimitri rounded up the snorkelers for the trip back to Anguilla. Before leaving the shore for the last time, George insisted on walking up the beach to ensure nothing was left behind. He was swimming back to the boat when Ezra turned the key, and nothing happened.

Ezra went from leaning most of his weight on one hip to standing up and bending over the key. He turned it again, his head cocked as if the sound of the key would tell him something. Gomez stood at the bow with the mooring line unhooked from the cleat held in his hand, ready to release it as the boat moved away. Ezra shook his head, then stepped around the men and leaned over the stern to check that nothing was wrapped around the propeller. Gomez hooked the line back around the cleat and joined him. The two of them conferred at the stern before Ezra went back to the wheel and turned the key again. By then, the men realized that there was something wrong, and all conversation had stopped. One or two of them had their own boats and offered suggestions, but Ezra and Gomez seemed to be in their own little world, Ezra at the key and Gomez at the stern. Gomez pushed himself up and went below. Once out of sight of the passengers, they heard him calling the boat names and then, when it still hadn't started, cooing at it as if to a stubborn child. He poked his head out of the hatch and said, "Call Franz, she won't budge."

Ezra picked up the radio mic and called. Nothing. He twiddled knobs and called again. No response. Now it was getting dark quickly like it does in the tropics and things weren't looking so good for getting home. Dave, whose dad had been a mechanic, offered to help, but Ezra politely refused his offer. "Mistah Franz, he does not like people messing with his machinery." Dave frowned, but sat back down. Iggy offered to check the radio's wiring, but he was turned down too.

Both Ezra and Gomez went below, and the men could hear clanking and swearing coming from the stern, and the smell of gasoline rose on the breeze. George leaned over the stern and saw the greasy rainbows on the water that meant leaking gas. Could they have run out? Ezra stomped back onto deck and turned the key. For a moment, the engine rumbled to life, then it backfired, and all was silent again.

"Ja rules," the Rasta said, shaking his head, which several of the men decided was a polite way of saying shit. Ezra tried again to raise someone on the radio, but that too seemed to be possessed by demons and remained silent. By that time, the passengers had pulled on shirts as the sun was nearly down and the breeze was cooling them.

The moment that the sun sank below the horizon, George got a feeling of inevitability. They weren't going home that night.

Ezra came up to George as he stood colossus-like on the bow, glaring at the horizon. "Mistah George?"

"Yes, Ezra, what is it?"

The young Rasta shuffled his feet and kept his eyes down. "Mistah George, the boat she no go no matter what me and Gomez try. The radio is mashed too. I am thinking we having to stay here on Dog Island for the night. Someone will wonder where we got to, and they'll come out in the morning."

George nodded in agreement. "I think you're right, son. We're going to have to sleep out here."

The snorkeling group had broken up into a few clusters of men, some silent, some talking among themselves.

Dimitri came up and said, "So, what did Ezra have to say?"

George raised his voice, so it carried to all the men. "As you've probably guessed, the boat's motor can't be fixed, and the radio is either shorted out or just plain broken. Looks like we'll be spending the night here."

"Here? On this boat?" one man said.

"If anyone's interested, they can sleep on Dog Island, but remember, you'll be mostly wet when you get there. The only way to get to the island is to wade from the dinghy."

Mike said, "I saw some driftwood on the windward side to make a fire with. I'd like to go ashore for the night. I've got a few things in my bag."

A voice came out of the darkness. "You got any hootch in there, Mikey?"

Everyone laughed, and Mike shook his head. "Sorry, Dave, no hootch, but I've got some power bars and energy drink powder. Never leave home without it."

Rod and Don, who had been sitting on the coolers, were on their knees sorting through the remains of their lunch. "There's plenty of buns and salad stuff, only one hot dog apiece, though," Rod said.

George said, "Anything to drink left?"

Don shook his head. "Not unless you want to drink melted ice."

Ezra stepped out of the cabin hatch where he had been listening. "We keeps a case of bottled water in the hold for selling to the ferry passengers. Maybe two might be down there."

"Everyone should get one bottle of water," George said.

Ezra ducked down below decks and handed up a case that Iggy passed out to the others. Mike and a couple other men went over to the island to make a fire, thinking it'd be warm and would serve as a signal fire. Those left on the boat laid out their towels and shared the life jackets for use as pillows. It was beautiful under the clear sky.

The stars looked close enough to touch as George lay on his back with his hands under his head.

"Do you think our wives will be worried?" Dimitri's voice came out of the darkness.

George laughed. "I think first they will be angry that we're not back when we said we would be. Then they will call the other wives to make sure that you and I aren't the only ones missing. Finally, as the night grows later, I think they will be worried that we've had an accident." He sat up and looked at the fire blazing on the beach closest to Anguilla. "I wonder if there's anyone doing a night dive that will see that. Or maybe a fisherman will see it. Can you see Dog Island from your house, Iggy?"

Iggy shook his head. "No, George, even with my house on that little bluff, Dog Island is too far away for me to see. Sorry."

"Well, I was hoping one of your neighbors would see Mike's fire and let someone know we're out here."

Dimitri grunted. "I think I won't mind staying here for the night. It's peaceful, and no one is goading me to do my job."

George said, "I wish I had never opened that envelope."

One by one, the surrounding voices quieted as the men drifted off. The breeze dropped so their beach towels were adequate cover, if a little short. A few times in the night George awoke to see Ezra turn the key, which produced only silence, as did his attempts to contact anyone by radio. Surely, he mused, Franz must know that they weren't back on Anguilla. Surely, he would send a boat out to find them.

CHAPTER 49

Rose

I rapped lightly on Susan's door. It opened almost immediately.

Susan said, "Did you forget your key?" Her smile faltered when she saw it was me.

"Hi. The snorkelers aren't back, and I could use some company."

Susan swung the door open wide and ushered me into the living room. "How did you know that I'd need knitting support?"

"I need it myself. Have you heard anything?"

Susan shook her head. "No. I tried calling Franz and Davis, but they must be out for the evening. I left messages. I guess we'll just have to wait until morning."

"Too bad we can't call the Coast Guard. They'd send out a search boat."

"The Coast Guard? Anguilla has a Coast Guard?"

I pulled out the sock that I was knitting. "Unfortunately, no, the Coast Guard is an arm of the US Armed Forces that patrols the coast. They're the search and rescue team in the Great Lakes and all around the coastlines. Too bad we're in the Caribbean and not the Gulf of Mexico. I'd bet we could mobilize them then. It'd be a relief so see their big gray boat come into the bay towing Franz's fast ferry, which had run out of gas or something simple like that."

Susan confirmed the rumors that had been flying around the island, that George and Dimitri had been spies on opposite sides of the Cold War and that Billie Holland-Smythe engineered a very public meeting between the two men at her king's birthday celebration.

I kept my eyes on my sock knitting and let Susan talk. It was almost like I wasn't there.

Susan talked about all the years when George was away, and she didn't know where he was. She talked about George's cover job in the British Fisheries Department and how all of their relatives kept after him for a discount on expensive fish, so he had developed a network of fishmongers over the years to perpetuate the lie. I kept quiet.

"I don't know what I'll do if George doesn't come back," Susan said, tears in her voice. "All those years when he was in harm's way, I never worried as much as I'm worrying now. Why, after all these years of being retired, do they have to start things up again? I thought our countries were friends, or at least not blatant enemies anymore. Why couldn't they just leave well enough alone?"

"This is Iggy's first group snorkeling trip and I'm afraid he'll decide it's too much trouble or too dangerous and give up. You'd think if the radio worked, they'd have put out a distress call. Iggy's an electrician. If the radio didn't work, he'd be able to fix it. At least it's not cold and rainy."

By then it was after midnight, too late since I had to be up early to make breakfast, so I took my leave and drove home across the darkened island, wishing that my headlights were brighter. It was darker on the island than it had been at home. Of course, there weren't streetlights strung along all the roads on the island like there had been on the city streets of home. Sometimes I missed living in the States, missed my old hometown with its twenty-four-hour grocery stores and the ease of finding what I wanted with a stop at a single supermarket. By now I was used to having to make three stops to do my weekly marketing and never finding everything on my list.

Of course, if I hadn't bought Seaview to refurbish, I would never have met Iggy, and he made my life so much richer. Not only his warm, loving personality, but it was lovely to have a live-in handyman. Jim had been a wonderful man, but he was no handyman. He could change light bulbs but faced with a broken switch or a clogged drain, he had to call a professional. And he didn't know a thing about cars except for where to put the gas in and how to put air in the tires. I, with my carpenter and mechanic grandfathers, knew a lot more about how to fix things and how to keep cars running than Jim ever did. Thoughts of Jim carried me through the dark night, down the hill into Sandy Ground, and up the road to my parking space next to Seaview and my new husband and life.

I went into the apartment, brushed my teeth, put on a nightshirt, and slipped into bed. I kept thinking about that boat full of men lost in the night. It was hard to sleep. My alarm would ring too early in the morning, and I was glad that I had made an egg bake to slide into the oven before making coffee.

That night, my dreams were of shipwrecks and drowning men.

CHAPTER 50

George and Dimitri

"Ezra!"

The shout woke George, and he was relieved to hear a boat motor. He sat up to see Franz and Davis coasting toward them out of the pre-dawn darkness. "Thank god," he said and turned to see heads popped up all over the deck like garden eels. Everyone scrambled to their feet, hands scrubbing stubble and attempting to comb their hair flat.

"I am glad to see you, Franz," Ezra said. "The boat she won't go, and the radio is mashed."

Davis grabbed the line Gomez tossed him and pulled the boats close enough for him to jump across to the snorkelers' boat. He went down to the engine compartment. They heard him swearing at the uncooperative machine. Then there was a grumble from the engine, and it roared to life.

"Hooray!" they all shouted. Davis's face appeared in the hatchway. "You were out of gas. All you had to do was switch to the second tank."

Ezra's head hung so low that his dreadlocks fell below his shoulders. "I sorry, Mr. Davis, Mr. Franz," he said, "Me and Gomez forget."

George looked around at the stunned faces of the other men in his group. "No harm done, Ezra," George said. "Now we have an adventure to tell our wives. If they're still speaking to us."

Dawn light sparkled on the light chop as the boats slowly motored to the pier. The snorkelers talked in low voices about their night on the island and what their wives would say.

"Do you think they will be at the pier?" Dimitri asked. No one had to ask who "they" were. Every man was certain that his wife would be the angriest when they got to shore.

"Susan will have called the Coast Guard, I'm sure of that," George said.

Dimitri nodded. "I am wondering why they didn't find us first."

George shook his head. "Maybe they called Franz, who said he would come to find us and would call if he needed help."

"Sorry to disappoint you, but there is no Coast Guard in Anguilla," Iggy said. "She cannot have called them out."

Dimitri shook his head and covered his face with his hands. "Irina will have decided that you sabotaged the boat to interrogate me in peace."

George snorted. "And Susan will think the same. We must confess, Dimitri. We have to tell them the truth." He rubbed the back of his neck to work out a crick. "I'm tired of sneaking around like I'm having an affair. I'm retired, you're retired. Let's write reports on each other saying that we are harmless and blameless, that we refuse to be drawn back into their paranoia."

"Our wives or our handlers?" Dimitri asked.

George looked him in the eyes and said, "Both. I'm too old for this foolishness."

"Me too."

Silence had fallen over the other men as the two retired spies talked. Without realizing it, their voices had risen to be heard over the engine noise, so everyone became part of the secret.

George and Dimitri looked around at the wide eyes of the other expats and, for the first time in their long careers, realized that they had blown their cover.

Dimitri gave a long sigh. "Now I know I am too old. I would never have been so careless."

George looked at each man in turn. "Sorry, chaps, you'll need to excuse a couple of old duffers and keep our secret a while longer until we straighten out with our wives."

Mike looked back at them and said, "If you're still alive."

An uneasy laugh rumbled across the deck.

George nodded. "If we're still alive."

Even at a slow speed, the ride back to the pier seemed too short. Before they knew it, Ezra had throttled back, and the boat was coasting in to the pier, bumping against the tires. Gomez jumped onto the pier with a mooring line and walked the boat in. He secured the bow and then caught the stern line that Ezra tossed him.

***

The men eyed the group standing silently, staring back at them. Wives, girlfriends, and other expats stood there looking tired. Some were jubilant, others angry, but all of them looked like they had barely slept. A few of the men waved at their wives and got a small wave back, but it was obvious that there would be hell to pay when they got home. Each man gathered up his bag of gear, then touched his hat before lining up to step onto dry land. Wives stepped forward to corral husbands. They exchanged small hugs. Iggy was one of the last to step onto the sand from the pier. Rose reached out and engulfed him in a hug. Dimitri got off second to last, right in front of George, and their wives came forward to embrace them. The men stood with their backs to each other so that the women faced each other. They hissed like old cats and George had enough.

"Stop," he said, "just stop." Everyone on the pier stopped

moving. He looked at Susan. "Dimitri and I are friends, have been for months." Susan's eyes widened, and he heard Irina's indrawn breath. "Yes, m'dear, friends." He wrapped an arm around her and pressed his lips to her temple. "Dimitri is the only one, besides you, who understands what my life has been like. Neither of us had workmates. We've been alone all these years, and it's time to retire. Time to put our careers behind us once and for all."

Dimitri stirred behind him. "Da, Irina, stop. George and I agreed to finish this last job, tell the truth, that we are both too old and too tired to keep on, and settle down to be friends."

"But, Dimi," Irina said, "what will happen to your pension?"

George turned to her and said, "We talked about that. We'll write our reports with enough information to satisfy our handlers, but nothing that will lead to further letters from headquarters. We both need to be freed of this."

Irina nodded and looked at Dimitri with tears in her eyes. "You agreed to this? You think it will work?"

He put his arms around her. "It will work. Haven't I always taken care of you?"

Each man picked up his gear and steered his wife toward their cars. The rest of the group exhaled a breath none of them realized they had been holding and started for their own cars.

They left Billie Holland-Smythe standing alone in the sunlight. She looked deflated, but it wouldn't be for long. There had to be another secret she could uncover and exploit for her own amusement. It was only a matter of time.

***

"What is going on?" Iggy put his arm around my shoulders as we walked up the beach to Seaview.

I leaned into him. "That was the Iron Curtain coming down. From what I could overhear, George and Dimitri confessed their friendship to their wives and asked them to stop fighting."

"Do you think it will change how the women treat each other?"

I turned to look at him. "I think Susan will slowly change, but I seriously doubt that Irina will. She has too much anger and disdain toward the Clemments and, to be honest, all of us. I can't imagine the two couples ever being social friends. Oh, George and Dimitri will keep birdwatching and snorkeling together. They'll keep up their breakfasts at Rose Inn and be friendly at cookouts and parties, but not the wives."

I picked up my empty coffee mug off the porch railing and started into Seaview. "Time to make breakfast."

THE END

If you enjoyed Spies Don't Retire, please go to Amazon.com and leave a review. Reviews help others decide to read my books. Thanks! I truly appreciate it.

Visit my website: barbara-writes.com
for more info about my books and me.
Sign up for my monthly newsletter!

Follow me on Facebook:
https://www.facebook.com/barbara.malcolm.writes/

BOOKS IN THIS SERIES

The Seaview Series

Widow Rose Lambert buys a ramshackle hotel on a Caribbean beach. Follow her story as she refurbishes it with the help of local craftsmen, welcomes her first guests, and works to become part of the island community.

The Seaview

She knew it would be hard work, but what she didn't plan on was the electrically charged subcontractor and the way he made her feel.

Despite her son's vehement objections, Rose buys the ramshackle Caribbean beachfront bed and breakfast. She's confident that she can oversee the work in time for the start of tourist season. That is until the Health Inspector locks them out of the building.

Desperate to get the crew back to work she pleads with the plumber to get the key and finish at least one bathroom. The plumber has his own agenda. Rose's confidence is nearly destroyed by this major setback.

Can Rose and her crew finish the job before the first guest arrives?

The Seaview is the first book of The Seaview Series. If you like engaging islanders, breathtaking scenery above and below water, and a little romance this book is for you. Pick up a copy today!

Open For Business

It's opening day, and Rose eagerly awaits her first guest. Juggling excitement and nerves, she's determined to keep her new bed & breakfast afloat despite bad weather and a lecherous plumber.

Now that Seaview is refurbished and reopened Rose's dream seems to be coming true, but the arrival of Hurricane Alphonso might end her dream before it can really begin. Her first guests are in residence and one of them acts like the hurricane with its wind, rain, and power outages is a personal affront.

Her attempts to fit into the island community are thwarted by nasty rumors spread by a local woman who resents Rose's romance with Ignatius "Iggy" Solomon. And a lecherous plumber just won't take "No!" for an answer.

In Open For Business, the second book of The Seaview Series escape to the Caribbean island of Anguilla. Enjoy Seaview with its changing cast of guests and the ever-faithful Iggy for delectable homemade breakfasts, beachside dancing, and rum punch as you dive into a tropical women's fiction story. Grab your copy today!

ABOUT THE AUTHOR

Barbara Angermeier Malcolm

 Barbara is an avid traveler and former retail SCUBA sales professional.

She has journeyed to countless islands with her family on diving vacations, collecting inspiration and stories along the way. A passionate storyteller, Barbara has been crafting tales for years.

When she's not writing, you'll find her sketching, painting with watercolors, knitting, cooking, or doting on her grandchildren. She is an active member of the Green Bay writing community and a proud member of the Green Bay Area Writers Guild and Wisconsin Writers Association.

BOOKS BY THIS AUTHOR

Horizon

Gail Logan, a widow in her mid-fifties, has lived her life by what other people think. That has to change.

Signing up for a watercolor class and thrifting a new wardrobe with a young classmate makes a good start. Replanting her regimented flower garden is another idea, but at the garden center, Abel Baker dismisses her plan and tells her what to buy. Gail doesn't appreciate his interference.

Widower Abel turns up in Gail's path again and again, but she buried one bossy man, and she's not interested in another. Should she give Abel a chance?

Her sons and her best friend feel threatened by all of Gail's changes. Should she go back to her dull existence or keep moving forward?

Immerse yourself in Gail's journey for a fresh perspective on life in Horizon. Enjoy her adventures learning to paint with watercolor, making new friends, and changing her life to please herself in this mature love after loss women's fiction story. Get your copy today!

Better Than Mom's

Better Than Mom's is a neighborhood diner in a small city

in Wisconsin where good food and interesting people come together.

Meet Brady, the warm-hearted owner who takes pride in making homemade food for his customers, Fay, the sassy morning waitress who cares for people more than she lets on, Naomi, the welfare mom who cooks like an angel and needs a job, Steve, who sits in the back booth and won't let anyone see what he's writing, and Officer Bates, who comes to investigate a crime but ends up sweeping Fay off her feet.

Stop in at Better Than Mom's for a bowl of homemade soup, a lighter-than-air biscuit, and a visit with people who could be your neighbors. Get your copy today!

Island Dreams

Ella Thomas and Dan Martinson leave their families and friends behind and move to the island of Bonaire in the Caribbean to pursue their dream of owning a dive shop

Dan finds a job as a diving instructor immediately, but Ella can't get a work permit and is reduced to cleaning vacation rental homes on the side for cash. His days are filled with the excitement and beauty of the coral reefs and her days are filled with cleaning up other people's messes.

They are dedicated to saving as much money as they can so that when a dive shop becomes available, they can jump on it, but an unexpected opportunity threatens to drive a wedge between them.

Follow the ups and downs of life with Ella and Dan as they chase their Island Dreams.

ACKNOWLEDGEMENT

I want to thank my critique partners, Connie Anderson and Lisa Lickel, for helping me shape this manuscript into its final form.

Thanks also to the women of the Women's Writing Retreat at The Clearing Folk School in Ellison Bay, Wisconsin, led by Judy Bridges and Sharon Nesbit-Davis, for all their insightful comments and encouragement through the years.

www.ingramcontent.com/pod-product-compliance
Lightning Source LLC
Chambersburg PA
CBHW070921260626
47162CB00007B/2749